Dear Mystery Reader:

With pacing like a well-executed fast break, John Feinstein's bestselling nonfiction firmly established his page-turning credentials as an athletic writer. (One of his books spent 30 weeks on the *New York Times* list!) His writing in *A Good Walk Spoiled* and *A Season on the Brink* was so knowledgeable and just so darn exciting it made all the armchair jocks reading them feel as if they were mixing with the best of 'em—either walking the links or making that perfect swish on the basketball court. Feinstein's graceful and incisive style also makes his readers feel they're receiving the inside scoop.

Well, storytellers know that fiction can go places nonfiction cannot, sometimes telling even greater truths. Now I'm not exactly saying that college basketball scouts are resorting to murder to recruit the latest hoop shooting wunderkind, but...well, in *Winter Games*, somehow it doesn't seem so farfetched. It's an intriguing mystery, and you just might be a little shocked by some of the goings-on described.

After all, it's only a game, right? Read on.

Yours in crime,

Dana Edwin Isaacson

Dana Edwin Isaacson
Senior Editor
St. Martin's DEAD LETTER Paperback Mysteries

Other titles from St. Martin's
Dead Letter Mysteries

GETTING OUT OF HAND

"Hey, Scott, what the hell are you doing?" Kelleher poked his head into the car and shook Harrison's arm. Then he saw the blood. Suddenly terrified, he reached across the seat and pulled Scott's shoulder up so he could see what had happened to him. As Scott's head came up from the seat, Kelleher screamed. There was a bullet hole in Scott Harrison's head, with blood gushing from it. Even as he screamed, Kelleher shook Harrison, hoping for some sign of life.

Kelleher let go of the body, which slumped back onto the passenger seat. That was when Kelleher noticed the phone. He heard someone screaming. It was him.

WINTER GAMES

JOHN FEINSTEIN

St. Martin's Paperbacks

The characters and events in this book are fictitious. Any similarity to real persons, living or dead, is coincidental and not intended by the author.

Published by arrangement with Little, Brown & Company.

WINTER GAMES

Copyright © 1995 by John Feinstein.

Library of Congress Catalog Card Number: 95-4837

ISBN: 0-312-96149-9

Printed in the United States of America

Little, Brown & Company hardcover edition published in 1995
St. Martin's Paperbacks edition/March 1997

St. Martin's Paperbacks are published by St. Martin's Press, 175 Fifth Avenue, New York, NY 10010.

10 9 8 7 6 5 4 3 2

This is for Bill Brill and Bob DeStefano . . .
Excellent teachers, better friends

WINTER GAMES

ONE

HOMECOMING

THE BILLBOARD had never failed him. Every time Bobby Kelleher saw the big red letters spelling out "Claudio's," he started to smile, no matter how bleak his mood. Today, of course, the words "Closed for the Season" were stripped across the board, but that didn't bother Kelleher.

Not now, anyway. All he knew was that he was almost home. For as long as he could remember, the Claudio's sign had been the first thing he saw when he pulled off the last exit of the Long Island Expressway. Exit 73 was many miles east of any bottlenecks, and the end of the expressway marked the beginning of the back roads that would take him to Shelter Island.

Kelleher hadn't gone to school on Shelter Island. He had never been listed as an official resident, and he didn't own property there. His dad had bought the house there when he was two, and he had spent every summer of his boyhood there. When Kelleher thought about growing up, he thought of Shelter Island: his first dance, his first date, his first clumsy attempts at sex. He thought about father-son softball games and eating pizza at Nettie's. He still hadn't found pizza anywhere in the world that tasted as good. He remembered Mr. Wroble teaching him how to swim, and Wednesday morning golf lessons, when he spent a lot more time checking out the girls than his golf swing.

He remembered quaking in his boots the first time he used his fake ID at the Chequit, and celebrating his eighteenth birthday there three years later, when Frenchie the bartender bought him his first legal drink. He remembered the beach parties and the keg parties, and he remembered his father grilling steaks on Saturday night while Bobby helped his mother shuck the corn.

All the memories came flooding back, sometimes all at once, every time he wheeled his car past the Claudio's sign. He knew he was exactly twenty-four miles from the ferry — twenty-four miles he had once driven in eighteen minutes to catch the last boat on a Friday night. He was older now, too smart to gun the car to ninety the way he had back then. But as the road widened briefly to four lanes, the old urge came back, and he could feel himself letting up on the accelerator to avoid temptation.

It was almost five o'clock; the winter sun was beginning to fade on what had been a remarkably pretty February afternoon. Kelleher figured he would get to the ferry just before sunset, exactly as planned. On a day like this, there were few sights more spectacular than Shelter Island seen from the North ferry just before dusk.

As he reached the end of the eleven-mile stretch of four-lane highway that had been built when he was a teenager, Kelleher slowed the car from seventy to a more reasonable sixty, and then down to fifty when he fell behind the inevitable creeper who insisted on driving the speed limit. Five miles from the ferry, and Kelleher had to remind himself to be patient. The road had too many curves in it to try to pass, so he had to bide his time until he made the turn at Chapel Drive to cross over to Route 25.

From there, it was less than two miles to the ferry: past the

7–Eleven on the right, where Kelleher would stop if it were after dark and he knew everything on Shelter Island would be closed when he got there, then past Greenport High School on the left. Finally, a block beyond the arrow that said "Shelter Island Ferry," he would turn right on Fourth Street. If you followed the arrow and turned on Fifth Street, you hit an extra stop sign.

Kelleher's first-night routine was always the same. He would stop at Fedi's for food, lingering at the meat counter to talk sports while Doug cut a steak for him. From there he would drive home, going the long way past Looey's Beach, to make certain everything looked the same. He would speed up and down the hills on Nostrand Parkway, just as his father had done — much to his mother's dismay — when he was a kid. Once he reached Silver Beach, he would slow down to enjoy looking at the familiar old houses. This time of year, they would all be empty.

Kelleher's parents had kept their house open year round. It had been one of the first ones built on Silver Beach that had heat, and the family came out on weekends almost all winter. Even now, at thirty-one, when Kelleher thought about the holidays, he thought of Shelter Island, even though he hadn't spent one there since college.

The house wasn't very big, but it was comfortable, and it had a breathtaking view of Peconic Bay. His dad had paid $22,000 for it in 1965, the best investment he had ever made. Since his parents were in Florida now, they only used the house during the summer.

It had been years since he had been to the island in February. As much as he loved the place, there was no denying its bleakness during the dead of winter. What's more, for his entire adult life, wintertime had been his busiest time, and even when he had the urge to visit for a few days, there was never any chance.

Now, Kelleher had nothing but time. He was unemployed. Six days earlier, he had submitted his formal resignation to J. Wynton Watkins, executive editor of the *Washington Herald*. Kelleher had quit before Watkins had gotten around to firing him. His newsroom sources had told him that Watkins was planning to assign him to a new beat when the Maryland state legislature adjourned in April: night police.

Night police was the newspaper version of Siberia. It was where you started or ended in the business. If you were a kid, learning the ropes, you went to night police. If you were someone the paper wanted to dump but couldn't because of union rules, you landed back on night police. Being sent to night police when you had been at the paper six years was like being sent back to the minors. Kelleher had decided to quit the *Herald* before it quit him.

His departure was full of bitter irony. He had left Washington on February 22, exactly one year after the assassination of Maryland Governor Barney Paulsen. Paulsen's murder had been the story of Kelleher's career. Revealing the conspiracy behind Paulsen's death and tackling a gunman to save the life of Meredith Gordy, Paulsen's successor, had made Kelleher a hero.

Kelleher knew he had been anything but heroic. Only freakish luck had kept him alive and put him into the hero's role. His partner and best friend, Maureen McGuire, had been killed saving him. His best source and close friend, Alan Sims, had also been killed. He had violated every code of journalistic ethics by sleeping with another source, using the weak rationale that he was in love. In the end, Andrea Kyler had gone home to Kansas to pull her life together, and Kelleher had been left alone in Annapolis to play the role of false hero.

Kelleher had fervently hoped he would get out of Annapolis when assignments for the following year's national elections were handed out in the fall. All he'd wanted was a presidential campaign to cover — any campaign, no matter how obscure the candidate. He would cover Harold Stassen if they wanted. Anything to get away.

The assignment never came. When Metro Editor Tom Anthony called him in late October to tell him he was going back to Annapolis for one more session, Kelleher knew he couldn't deal with it. Once, Annapolis had seemed like heaven to him: the perfect town, the best assignment. Now it was haunted by the ghosts of his friends and all that had happened. He sent his résumé to papers around the country and put the word out locally that he might be available. People in the business knew his name because of the Paulsen story; he was certain to find a job.

He was right. The *Washington Post* and *Baltimore Sun* made him offers — to cover the Maryland State House. One of the tabloid TV shows offered him a job as an investigative reporter, doing stories on subjects like people who had seen Jesus and Elvis singing together.

Forced to stay in his old job, Kelleher tried to throw himself into it. There was no way. Every time he walked into the *Herald*'s office and saw the young reporter sent to replace McGuire, he thought about Maureen. Every time he went up to the second floor of the State House, he thought about Alan Sims and Andrea Kyler, who was a thousand miles and several worlds away in Kansas. The stories that had once excited him bored him. Sitting in Fran O'Brien's, the hangout for the political crowd, he felt like an old man who had outlived all his friends. Sadly, there was a lot of truth in that.

Ostensibly he was working on several stories. He would take sources to lunch or to dinner, ask questions, and take notes. But he knew, deep down, he was never going to write anything. Having time to write a long profile of Big Jim Immel, the legendary House Ways and Means chairman, would once have seemed like a dream come true. Kelleher knew a thousand anecdotes about how Big Jim made things work. Once, he would have demanded five thousand words for the piece and screamed if they had cut a single phrase. Now he couldn't think of a second paragraph.

Early one Monday morning, he was in the office preparing to drive to Annapolis for the start of another week when Jane Kryton, the Maryland editor, came by and suggested they get some coffee. Kelleher knew what was coming: Bobby, when are we going to see some copy? Bobby, what about the Immel profile? Bobby, the session's half over.

He could have handled that.

Seven words in, Kelleher knew Kryton wasn't making a plea for copy. "Watkins called us in the other morning," she began, sending a chill straight down Kelleher's spine. "He said he's had it with you, that you've been a completely unproductive whiner since the night Maureen died."

Kelleher felt his face flush; for a split second, he felt dizzy. "No doubt I should have just forgotten the whole thing in a couple of days."

Kryton held up a hand. "Tom and I both talked about all the trauma you've had to deal with. Watkins told us he thought a year was plenty long enough."

Kelleher was beginning to get the picture. "So I've blown deadline on trauma recovery, huh? What does he want from me, a thank-you for sending me back to Annapolis, where I can see Maureen every time I turn a corner or hear Alan whenever I walk up the State House steps?"

Kelleher and Kryton had worked together for six years. He had never seen her so pale. "We went through all of that, Bobby. Tom begged him to be more patient, to reconsider the change of scenery we've all pushed him to give you."

"And?"

"And Watkins said, 'I'm going to give him a change of scenery: night police.' "

Kelleher didn't even try to respond. It was as if his entire system had shut down. He didn't feel any anger or pain or sadness. He couldn't even think of a wiseass comeback. All he felt was empty and dazed, as if his life had gone off the road somewhere into a ditch, with no way to get back on track. He had always figured his twenties would be a warmup act for his thirties; that he would do the local reporter thing until it was his time to move up to the national staff to cover big-time politics; that he would settle down with a family in a big suburban house and go to Florida for a month every winter. Now he was so far away from all that, he wasn't even sure it had ever really been the plan in the first place.

He stood up, his legs wobbly. "I'll go write my letter of resignation."

"You don't have to do that. Tom and I will keep fighting for you. This may blow over in a couple of months."

"Jane, to tell you the truth, I don't care if it blows over or not. I'm done here. I should have figured that out months ago. Fuck Wyn Watkins."

He spent his last night as a *Herald* reporter making the Monday-night rounds in Annapolis. He visited all the old haunts, made sure to say goodbye to a few people he still felt close to, then spent most of the next day in bed in his room at the Annapolis Marriott, waiting for the hangover to pass. He finally got up and showered just before dinnertime, packed his bags, and went to the bureau to pick up some tapes and notebooks he had left there. He took one last walk around State Circle and ended up standing at the bottom of the State House steps, staring up at the dome one last time.

"Thirty-three steps," he murmured to himself, remembering all the times he had counted them as he sprinted up, late for session. He began to choke up and stopped himself. Enough tears for the past, he told himself. It was time to deal with the future.

The next morning, he handed his letter of resignation to Wyn Watkins, who looked at it as if it were a note reminding him where he was having lunch. "Goodbye, Kelleher," he said, barely looking up.

Kelleher had expected nothing different. "Not exactly goodbye, Mr. Watkins. You'll still need my address to forward the thirty-one weeks of vacation pay the paper owes me."

Leaving Watkins sitting there, the letter still in his hand, Kelleher walked out of the office and out of the building without saying any goodbyes. He had left Tom Anthony and Jane Kryton notes. Kryton called him at home that afternoon to tell him Watkins had gone ballistic when he found out the paper did, in fact, owe Kelleher thirty-one weeks of vacation pay.

It was almost enough to make Kelleher smile. He flew to Florida that night, because he thought he should tell his parents what had happened face to face. He knew his dad would be disappointed. His mom would be worried. "What do you do now?" his father had asked.

"Go to Shelter Island. They have to pay me for all the vacation time, plus sick leave and severance. That's about nine months. I imagine I can get myself straightened out by then."

"Won't you be lonely?" his mother wondered. "There's almost no one out there now."

"Which is exactly what I need, Mom."

He flew back to Washington that Monday night, loaded his car up, and made the drive to Shelter Island the next morning.

Now, as he pulled off the ferry, he felt safe again — protected, somehow, by the water surrounding the island. Shelter Island had no movie theater, not a single traffic light, no 7–Eleven. Not even a McDonald's.

To the people who lived there, Kelleher was still the kid who had cleaned clubs and golf carts at Gardiner's Bay Country Club. Some of the older people still asked him every spring how things were at school. Kelleher had been out of college for ten years. He always smiled and said, "Great," figuring they might still tip him.

He found comfort in that. He knew that most people out here were vaguely familiar with what he did. Many of them, no doubt, would recall something about his connection with the Paulsen murder story. They might wonder why he was here at this time of year, but if he said, "Oh, I'm just taking some time off," that would be all the answer they'd need — or want.

At Fedi's, he picked up a steak big enough to feed three people. Then he stopped at Carol's, to get newspapers. Carol was just closing the front door when he pulled up. If she noticed he hadn't been on Shelter Island for eight months, she didn't show it. She was standing in the doorway, key in the lock, when he pulled up.

"What do you need, Bobby?" she asked.

"*Newsday* and the *Reporter.*"

"Out of *Newsday.* You got fifty cents for the *Reporter?* The register's already locked."

Fishing in his pockets, Kelleher found a dime.

Carol shrugged. "Drop it off when you get a chance." Stepping past her into the darkened store, he grabbed the newspaper off the counter and stepped back outside.

"Thanks, Carol. I can't go through my first night back without the *Reporter.*"

Kelleher jumped back in his car. The sun was down and the temperature was dropping quickly; he would need to get the heat up in a hurry once he got home. But he had everything he needed now: the huge steak, coals, garlic, Coke, pretzels, canned corn, orange juice, coffee, milk, sugar, and cereal.

And the *Reporter*. The first newspaper Kelleher remembered reading was the *Reporter*. Then, it had been a twelve-page paper during the summer months, published, edited, and written by the same man. The gossip column was called "Overheard in an Osprey's Nest," and the author went by the name "Ima Byrd." Kelleher was fifteen before he got the joke.

Now, the *Reporter* was all grown up. Even during the winter it was a twenty-four-page weekly. During the summer, it came out three days a week, chock-full of ads, many of them from off-islanders trying to lure Shelter Island residents across the ferry to their restaurants, shops, or movie theaters.

The *Reporter* had been sold twice in recent years and was now part of a conglomerate of East End newspapers. It was a big moneymaker, especially in summer, when it employed six or seven part-time writers. And Ms. Byrd still had her column.

In many ways, the *Reporter* was typical of what was going on in the news business. The small papers and the giant ones made all the money. The mid-sized papers, especially afternoon papers, struggled — and in many cases failed — to survive. That was a bit frightening to someone who had just walked away from one of the giants. It wasn't as if the world were full of openings for unemployed reporters.

Kelleher pushed those thoughts aside as his parents' house loomed on the right. It had been gray when he was a kid. Now it was white. The three pine trees that once stood in the front yard were gone, removed by his dad so Bobby and his friends could have open space to play ball.

The house was freezing. Kelleher dropped his groceries on the kitchen counter and sprinted into the utility room to turn on the heat, breathing a sigh of relief when he heard the old oil burner kick over. He flipped on the hot water heater and heard it start to hum. Thirty minutes and he could take a shower.

Kelleher unloaded the car and began to unpack. By the time

he was finished, he was sweating profusely. Pulling off his coat, he turned the heat down from 80 to 70. He pulled the indoor barbeque from the fireplace and walked to the edge of the yard to dump the ashes on the beach. He paused to look out at the water. The moon was almost full. He was shivering, partly from the cold, partly from the knowledge that he was completely alone. For as far as he could see, not a single light was on in any house.

He walked inside, poured the fresh coals, put the garlic in the steak, and went upstairs to take his shower. He had just settled in under the soothing hot water when the phone rang.

"Damn." No doubt it was his mother, calling to make sure he had arrived safe and sound. Soaking wet, he raced to the phone, reaching it on the fourth ring.

"Everything's fine, Mom — the drive went okay, and the heat and hot water are working."

"You mean your mother hasn't called yet?"

Kelleher cracked up. It was Bob DeStefano, someone who knew Kelleher's first-night routine cold. Bob had been the golf pro at Gardiner's Bay for thirty-five years. He had taught Kelleher to play golf when he was young and then employed him for seven years during high school and college. They had stayed close. Bob DeStefano was always Kelleher's first call when he got to Shelter Island.

This time, though, he hadn't called Bob to tell him he was coming out. He hadn't told anyone except his parents.

"How the hell did you know I was here?"

"Ran into Carol at the drugstore. She said she opened up so you could get a *Reporter*, and then you stiffed her for the fifty cents."

Kelleher laughed. There were no secrets on Shelter Island. "You know she didn't reopen."

"But you did stiff her."

"She wouldn't take my dime."

"I would have taken the dime and figured I was doing pretty well."

They both laughed.

"What are you doing here in the middle of the legislative session?" DeStefano continued, his tone implying that he already knew the answer.

"Long story. I'll tell you all about it tomorrow."

"Why not tonight?"

Kelleher loved Anne DeStefano's cooking. But he had big plans for that steak downstairs, and he really didn't feel like putting on any clothes that weren't pajamas for the rest of the night. The house was toasty warm. The world was very cold. "I already bought my dinner. How about tomorrow?"

"I'm not inviting you to dinner. That steak needs to be eaten. But when you're done, meet me at the basketball game."

"Basketball game?"

"Haven't you heard about our basketball team?"

Kelleher did remember something about Shelter Island actually having a decent team this year. Because it had a tiny year-round population — a tiny, virtually all-white year-round population — the high school's basketball team usually ranged from merely bad to pathetic. In one three-year span, Kelleher remembered, they hadn't won a single game.

"What are they, five and ten?"

"Close. Try seventeen and one."

That *was* a surprise. The eastern end of Long Island wasn't exactly a mecca for high school basketball players. The only top-notch players Kelleher could remember were the Wood brothers, Howard and Kenny, who had come out of East Hampton. Howard had started on very good teams at Tennessee, and Kenny had been a star at Richmond. Even so, for

Shelter Island to be 17–1 was remarkable, no matter how soft the competition.

"What'd they do, go out and recruit a couple of black kids?"

DeStefano laughed. "Not exactly. I'm surprised you haven't heard about Rytis Buzelis."

Since he had been recruited by quite a few schools coming out of high school and had played in — or, more accurately, *not* played in — the Atlantic Coast Conference, Kelleher did know a number of people in basketball. He occasionally took advantage of that background to do freelance magazine pieces on basketball. A lot of basketball people remembered his name, since he'd been on some highly ranked teams at Virginia, which helped him with access. The fact that he had averaged 0.9 points per game during his career didn't seem to matter all that much.

But Kelleher hadn't heard a word about anyone named Rytis Buzelis. His current problems no doubt had had something to do with that, but it was also pretty likely that Buzelis — no matter how different-sounding the name might be — wasn't quite as big a star nationally as he was on Shelter Island.

"How does a kid named Rytis Buzelis end up on Shelter Island?"

"You ask all the right questions. It's simple. He got shot."

"Excuse me?"

"I'll tell you about it at the game. Why don't you meet me in the front lobby at ten to eight."

Kelleher glanced at the clock next to his bed. It was only 6:30. He could finish his shower, grill his steak, and still make it to the gym. But he hesitated. The clean sheets on the bed would feel so good. However, his interest was piqued. Employed or not, he still had a reporter's heart and head.

"Okay," he agreed finally. "The lobby at 7:50."

"Give yourself a couple extra minutes for traffic."

"Yeah, sure. Traffic on Shelter Island in February."

"I'm serious. The place will be packed. People are coming from all over to see this kid. Coaches. Reporters. *Newsday* was here last week."

If *Newsday* had sent someone all the way out here, that meant Buzelis was pretty good. Coaches showing up didn't surprise Kelleher. Most of the top players these days formally committed to college during the early signing period in November. If Buzelis was any good, there might even be a few Division 1 schools looking at him as a backup.

The thought that he might encounter something resembling traffic on Shelter Island made him giggle as he stepped back into the shower. Who knows, he thought, this might be fun.

He took a deep breath as the water warmed him. For what felt like the first time in almost a year, he relaxed a little. One hour on Shelter Island, and already life was getting better.

TWO

THE KID

KELLEHER DIDN'T HAVE TIME to read the *Reporter* before he left the house, but he did glance at it long enough to see a picture of Rytis Buzelis dunking. It was almost eight o'clock by the time he walked into the lobby of the gym. DeStefano hadn't been kidding about the traffic. Kelleher had to park three blocks from the school.

"What is this, the last scene of *Field of Dreams*?" he asked as he and DeStefano exchanged their annual welcome-home hug.

"I told you people are coming. This kid's no ghost though — he's real."

Kelleher decided he would be the judge of that. Even before he had gotten into journalism, he had been a skeptic by nature. He was also an expert on the difficulties of making the leap from the high school playing level to the college level. He had averaged twenty-six points and nine assists a game as a high school senior and had been recruited by more than a hundred schools. His dad had urged him to go to an Ivy League school, in part because of the education he would get, but also because he thought that was his son's playing level. Being a seventeen-year-old who knew far more about everything than his father, Kelleher rejected his counsel. He knew he was good enough to play in the ACC and, once he caught a glimpse of the Virginia campus, he was hooked. He knew he would have to back up Jeff Jones at point guard for a couple of years, but after that, he figured he would be The Man. What he didn't count on was Virginia's recruiting Othell Wilson. Or Ricky Stokes. Or Rick Carlisle. Or his first ACC game as a freshman, when Duke's Tommy Amaker cleanly stripped him three straight times trying to get the ball across midcourt. His coach, Terry Holland, had to call time just to get him out of the game. It was a humiliation Kelleher never forgot and, in a sense, never completely recovered from. He still had occasional nightmares about Tommy Amaker.

Kelleher was pretty certain that Rytis Buzelis was the same kind of high school player he had been: good enough to star at this level, but probably not good enough to make the quantum leap into the big time college game. Still, it would be interesting to see if there were any Division 1 recruiters in the building. Given Shelter Island's location — an hour's drive and a ferry ride from anything resembling a major airport — a recruiter would have to be serious to make the trek here.

DeStefano waved toward the people pushing their way into the gym. "We better hustle if we want to get a seat." Kelleher shook his head in wonder and coughed up the three dollars they were asking at the door.

The starting lineups were being introduced as they walked in. Almost every seat in the place was taken. Carefully, Kelleher and DeStefano picked their way through the bleachers.

Three rows up, Kelleher almost stepped on Rick Pitino's hand. He stopped short, mouth open, and was about to point him out to DeStefano when he spotted Mike Krzyzewski sitting ten seats down from Pitino. Roy Williams was next to him. Just behind them were Jim Calhoun and Lon Kruger. Further down the row, Kelleher saw Gary Williams and John Calipari. He stood frozen, his foot still perilously close to Pitino's hand. The head coaches of Kentucky, Duke, Kansas, Connecticut, Florida, Maryland, and Massachusetts were sitting practically on top of one another.

They were all here, in the Shelter Island High School gym on a cold winter night at a crucial time in their seasons to see Rytis Buzelis play. Amazing. No, not amazing. Impossible.

Only it was possible. Kelleher shook his head, thinking he would close his eyes, reopen them, and find that the guy he thought was Pitino was really the coach from SUNY-Binghamton and the Krzyzewski he was seeing was really the coach from Illinois–Chicago Circle. On the contrary. They were all still there. He pulled himself together, followed De-Stefano up to the top row, and stared around the gym.

"This isn't happening."

"I told you all the coaches were checking this kid out."

"You said coaches, not icons. Do you realize who's in this building? Christ, the only guy missing is John Wooden, and he's probably outside getting popcorn."

DeStefano laughed, enjoying the stunned look on Kelleher's face. He sat down. Kelleher continued standing, looking for more familiar faces. There were plenty: Joey Meyer from De-Paul, Brian Mahoney from St. John's, Dave Odom from Wake Forest, and on and on. Kelleher also recognized at least a dozen assistant coaches. One of them was Tom Perrin from Virginia, an old friend. He waved to get Perrin's attention, but the game had started and, like everyone else, Perrin had eyes only for Rytis Buzelis.

"I can't believe I never heard of this kid," Kelleher said, talking as much to himself as DeStefano. "I know I've been distracted, but if he's this good, I would have heard of him from the summer camps or something."

DeStefano shook his head. "Never went to a summer camp. Didn't even play as a junior. His parents moved here last year, and he had to sit out because he transferred. The family's Lithuanian. They emigrated to New York about two years ago. Apparently Rytis wandered into the middle of some kind of gang fight and got shot in the shoulder. His father decided that was it, he was getting the family out of the city before one of his children got killed. They had close friends in Greenport, and they came over here one day for a visit. The father decided that Shelter Island was about as safe and quiet a place as he was going to find.

"They moved here last winter. The father's a carpenter, does work all over the East End now. No one had heard of Rytis, because he was only six-one two years ago. He's grown five inches in the last year. No one had any idea who he was until this season started."

"Last of the great sleepers, huh?" Kelleher smiled. Recruiting had become so sophisticated in recent years that it seemed there was no such thing as a sleeper anymore — a kid who came out of nowhere to become a star. There weren't any nowheres left — except maybe Shelter Island.

Once the game started, it was easy to pick Buzelis out of the crowd. He was wiry, with the kind of build that would allow him to put on muscle without losing quickness. It took about thirty seconds for Kelleher to understand why most of the men listed in *Who's Who in Coaching* had made the trip to Shelter Island.

Even against the meager opposition provided by East Hampton, it was easy to see how special the kid was. He had hands like Julius Erving's, so huge they made the basketball look like a baseball. He couldn't be stopped going to the basket; in fact, the only time he didn't go past the entire East Hampton team was when he passed to a wide-open teammate for a layup. Occasionally he would pull up and shoot a three-pointer, just to make sure everyone knew he could hit it. He made four in the first quarter and had twenty-one points. Shelter Island led, 31–14. Buzelis's passes had set up eight of the ten Shelter Island points he hadn't scored.

At halftime, it was 58–29. Buzelis, looking a bit bored, scored only fourteen in the second quarter. That gave him thirty-three for the half.

"What's he averaging a game?" Kelleher asked DeStefano.

"Forty-seven. But he almost never has to play the fourth quarter."

An hour earlier, Kelleher had wondered when, or if, he would ever get the old urge to be a reporter again. Now, for the first time in months, his reporter's soul was stirring. This was a great story. But who could he write it for? Maybe the *New York Times*. Unlikely — he didn't know anyone there. He knew lots of people at the *Washington Post*, and he would love to see the look on Wyn Watkins's face if Kelleher's byline showed up in the *Post* right after he had quit the *Herald*.

That was for later. Now he had to find out more. At halftime, he picked his way down to the floor and found Tom Perrin.

"Why aren't you off playing politics?" Perrin asked as they shook hands. "I thought you only came out here in the summer."

"You really remembered that my folks had a place here?"

Perrin grinned. He looked more like a professor than a coach, with short-cropped brown hair, glasses, and a button-down shirt and dark tie. "Actually, when we first heard about this kid, I almost called you to see what you knew about him or the family. But then I figured you probably hadn't seen him, since he didn't play last year. Guess I was wrong."

"You weren't wrong. An hour ago, I'd never heard of him. But Jesus, he's just un — "

Kelleher broke off in mid-sentence. Someone had lifted him off the ground in a bear hug from behind and was screaming in his ear: "Kelleher, you don't know a goddamn thing about basketball! You couldn't play, you can't write, and you wouldn't know a player if you fell on top of him!"

"Put me down, asshole," Kelleher retorted, struggling and laughing all at once. Perrin had a huge grin on his face. Kelleher's assailant finally let go, and Kelleher turned to face him.

"As I live and breathe, the great Scott Harrison on Shelter Island. *Never* did I think I would see this day. I mean, Rick Pitino and Mike Krzyzewski, maybe. Roy Williams, sure. But Scott Harrison? *The* Scott Harrison? God's gift to coaching, hoops, and women — if he does say so himself?"

"Don't make me hurt you, Kelleher," Harrison warned, trying to look menacing.

Harrison's ability to hurt Kelleher was not in doubt. He was six feet four and, even at thirty-three, looked like he weighed the same 215 as when he had played at Georgia Tech. He had come to Virginia as a graduate assistant during Kelleher's junior year, and they had become friends. Both had had big dreams, even though neither had become the player he had thought he would. By then, most of Kelleher's attention was focused on the student newspaper. He knew that was where his future was. Harrison knew he wanted to coach, and he had talked Terry Holland into hiring him as a graduate assistant. Back then, Virginia had Ralph Sampson, a top-ten team, and lots of games on television. Harrison knew a young coach at Virginia would get noticed quickly by other programs.

Even though he had never become a great player, Harrison had star quality. He had blond hair, blue eyes, and an athlete's build. His personality lit up any room he walked into. Women seemed to fall at his feet wherever he went, but he was one of those rare guys whom men liked almost as much as women did. Even if you wanted to hate Harrison because of the way women reacted to him, you couldn't. He was smart, funny, and a loyal friend.

He had spent three years at Virginia, then two years as the part-time assistant at Wake Forest. He had gotten his first full-time job as a recruiter at Nebraska. Three years later, he became Jim Valvano's top assistant at North Carolina State. It had looked like the perfect springboard to a head coaching job before Valvano ran into trouble and was forced to resign. With Valvano's blessing, Harrison had applied for the job, but when it became apparent that the school wanted all of Valvano's people gone, he had hooked on with Bobby Taylor at Minnesota State.

Kelleher remembered reading about that move and wondering why Harrison would go there. Taylor had succeeded the immensely popular Bennie Sharpless. Sharpless had won 521 games in twenty-one years and had probably broken every rule in the NCAA recruiting manual. In a famous magazine piece several years back, a reporter had sat in the MSU players' parking lot and recorded the cars the players were driving: four BMWs, three Mercedes, two Lexuses, and a Chevy Blazer. Clearly, the guy in the Blazer needed a new agent.

Sharpless had been forced to quit when the NCAA threatened to shut down the Minnesota State program completely. Taylor, who was as squeaky clean as anyone in the business, had come out of retirement to take the job. The alumni and boosters screamed bloody murder when Taylor was hired, and now, in his third year, they were still screaming. Sharpless had been in the NCAA Tournament for fourteen of the last seventeen years, missing only the years when the team was on probation. Taylor had produced back-to-back 18–10 records, good enough for the National Invitation Tournament, better known as the NIT — Not Invited (to the NCAA's) Tournament. Kelleher didn't know their current record, but he knew it wasn't much better than the first two years. It wasn't like Scott to hook on with a loser.

"Where the hell is Taylor?" he demanded, giving Harrison a shove. "I'm going to tell him he's got an assistant running around threatening reporters."

"And if there was a *real* reporter around, he'd probably be concerned," Harrison replied. "But there isn't, and he's not here anyway. I realize you don't recognize the existence of basketball outside the ACC, but we do have a game tomorrow at Indiana. Which, if you pick up a newspaper, you will find is ranked number one in the country right now. Several places higher, I might note, than your beloved Cavaliers."

"Who are still quite a few notches higher than the once-mighty Purple Tide," Perrin put in, jumping to the defense of Kelleher's — and his — Cavaliers.

Kelleher heard a strange sound at that moment. It was him: laughing.

No doubt a psychiatrist could have a field day analyzing why men, especially men involved in sports, felt the need to show affection through put-downs, dirty jokes, and a never-ending exchange of profanities. But that was the way it was. It had been that way since Kelleher had been in high school, and it was that way now. You just didn't walk up to someone in the jock world, throw your arms around him, and say, "Gee, it's really great to see you."

"What *are* you doing here, Bobby?" Harrison asked, finally

turning serious. "I remember you telling me you never came out here in the winter."

"Long story," Kelleher said, addressing both Harrison and Perrin. "I needed a break. It's been a tough year. For me, this is the best place in the world to get away."

"I can certainly see why," Perrin remarked. "There's nothing out here."

"Except Rytis Buzelis," Kelleher added.

"Which is clearly more than enough for the likes of us," Harrison put in, sweeping a hand around the gym at the assembled coaches.

"Either of you guys got a shot at him?" Kelleher asked.

"Among present company, only us," Harrison said.

Kelleher looked at Perrin, hoping he would respond to Harrison's bluster. "They're in it," Perrin said almost apologetically. "But we still think he may want an ACC school. The parents don't want the Big East, because they don't want him anywhere near a big city. We're in it, so's Duke, and so's Carolina. But it's still wide, wide open. He hasn't even announced where he's going to take his official visits. That's why the whole world is here."

"Is JJ the only ACC head coach *not* here?" Kelleher asked.

Jeff Jones, Kelleher's ex-teammate, was now the coach at Virginia. Perrin shook his head. "Dean isn't here because Carolina's playing Notre Dame tonight. I told JJ he should be here, because I'd be outranked by all the big stars. But we have Duke at home tomorrow, and he didn't think he could get away."

Kelleher pointed at Krzyzewski, who was signing autographs. "That doesn't seem to bother him."

Perrin laughed. "He's eighteen and two, has won two national titles and been to a hundred Final Fours. We're fourteen and six and trying to make sure we get into the tournament."

Kelleher couldn't argue with that logic. Since the Duke-Virginia game was in Charlottesville, Virginia had a legitimate shot to win. In fact, before his life had changed so dramatically a week ago, he had planned to drive down to see the game.

"So, what's the deal," he asked, turning to Perrin. "Have we got any kind of shot at this kid?"

"We?" Harrison repeated, in a voice loud enough to turn heads. "I thought you were a reporter now, Bobby, unbiased in every way."

"Any reporter who tells you he is unbiased is a liar," Kelleher said, nonetheless embarrassed by his slip.

"Which brings us back to your original question," Perrin reminded him. "On a level playing field, I think we're one of four or five schools with a legitimate chance to get the kid. Scott's certainly in it, Duke, Carolina, maybe Kansas, and us."

"What do you mean by level playing field?"

"You know what he means, Bobby," Harrison said. "Come on, you're a big boy — look around the gym. Do you see coaches from every school that's been on probation the last ten years?"

Sure enough, it seemed like every school that had a bandit reputation was in the place. "Okay, so the cheaters are here. The five schools Tom named aren't cheaters."

"And until a couple of weeks ago, those looked like the schools that were in contention. Now, it isn't so clear. If you turn slowly and look up in the corner of the stands, you'll see exactly what Tom's talking about."

Kelleher turned his head in the direction in which Harrison had nodded and saw three men standing in a corner of the bleachers. Two wore the coach's recruiting uniform — jacket and tie. The third wore a running suit. "No clue. Give me a hint."

Harrison and Perrin both laughed. "He's been covering politics too long," Perrin joked.

"That's for sure," Harrison agreed. Kelleher turned to take a closer look. "You need to get back with the real people, Bobby." The guy in the sweatsuit was looking at him. Kelleher knew he had seen him somewhere before.

"Hey," Harrison said. "Don't stare at the guy. The last thing you want to do is call attention to yourself." His tone had changed completely. It was urgent, almost fearful.

"What the hell's the big deal, Scott — some guy in a running suit and two coaches, so big deal . . ."

"The guy in the running suit is Miles Akley. Believe me, he is a big deal. And not someone for you or any of us to be messing with."

Kelleher knew the name. But where from? It came back to him. "Brickley Shoes. The pied piper of basketball. Maybe the biggest scumbag in the history of the game."

Harrison nodded. "You're a little slow, but that's right. The other two guys are Bill Eller and Tom Shivley, Murray's assistants."

Now it began to fit. Fred Murray, longtime coach at the University of Louisiana, was one of the few men in the game who might be smarmier than Bennie Sharpless. The difference was that Louisiana hadn't run him off the way Minnesota State had finally run Sharpless off. He was far too powerful, a legendary figure in the South, even though everyone in the game knew he had been buying players for years. Everyone also knew that Miles Akley was his chief bagman, delivering many of those players to him, wooing the kids first with free shoes and clothes and equipment, becoming their pal, then promising them that if they went and played for Coach Murray, a lucrative Brickley contract would surely await them when they turned pro.

Aided by Akley and his shoes, Murray had actually wrested control of his state from Dale Brown at Louisiana State and had been to two Final Fours. Murray was one of the game's great charmers: handsome, superbly dressed, always available to the media. You couldn't turn on a U.L. game without hearing the TV drones go absolutely rapturous over the genius of Fred Murray.

To Kelleher, Murray's genius was in keeping his public persona so shiny when it was apparent to anyone who followed basketball that he was a fake, a prop for Brickley — and, if truth be told, that he could have won a couple of national championships by now with the talent he had been delivered had he been able to coach even a little bit. Kelleher remembered something that Bill Foster, the recently retired Northwestern coach had once said about Murray: "He's living proof that crime *does* pay."

That comment was probably better applied to Akley, who was in charge of Brickley's "board of coaches" — a euphemism for coaches on the Brickley payroll. In return for large sums of money — Kelleher remembered reading that Murray made $350,000 a year from Brickley — coaches wore Brickley clothes and shoes, as did their teams. They did clinics for Brickley and spoke at corporate outings — a gimmick started and perfected by Nike in the seventies and eighties. Brickley had hired Akley to put together a stable of coaches comparable in power and visibility to the Nike crowd.

Murray was Brickley's centerpiece, the same way Georgetown coach John Thompson had been Nike's main man. That meant it was vital to Akley and Brickley that Murray continue to have great players, in order to keep his team in the national spotlight. Since the NCAA categorically refused to pass rules controlling the access that the sneaker hucksters had to athletes, Akley could do things that no coach or alumnus could possibly do: give players all sorts of freebies, get them into games and concerts, have them over to his house whenever he wanted to, and fly them free of charge to the summer basketball camp that Brickley sponsored.

Dozens of basketball players around the country would tell you that Miles Akley was their very best friend. If you asked them why that was so, they would say something like, "Well, he gets me lots of stuff." In return, they were often willing to take his advice on where to attend college.

At the back end of their college careers, the best players would find Akley waiting for them one more time. Since Brickley was now into representing athletes in addition to clothing them, a great player could be a Brickley man from cradle to grave.

Kelleher shuddered a little thinking about Akley and Murray invading his safe haven. This was where he came to escape the reality of people like them. And yet, if he turned around, he would be looking right at Miles Akley and two of Murray's henchmen.

The buzzer to start the second half jarred him. "You have time for a beer afterwards?" Harrison asked.

"There's a place to get a beer?" Perrin wondered. "I thought everything shut down here in the winter." ·

"Almost everything," Kelleher said. "Where are you guys staying?"

"Back at the airport in Islip," Perrin said. "I have a seven o'clock flight to D.C. in the morning."

"My flight to Chicago is 7:15," Harrison added.

"Last ferry's 11:30," Kelleher said. "I'll take you guys to the Dory."

"The what?" they chorused.

"You'll see."

He glanced over his shoulder at Akley one more time, then made his way back up to DeStefano.

"Who were those guys?" DeStefano asked.

"Couple of old friends. Tom Perrin, the guy with the glasses, is an assistant at Virginia. The big blond guy is Scott Harrison. He was at Virginia when I was there. He's at Minnesota State now."

"Isn't that the place where they're trying to run the coach out of town?"

"Something like that. I didn't get a chance to ask Scott about it. Maybe after the game."

"You really do know all these guys, don't you?"

"Not exactly. But I did play in the ACC."

"Yeah, I know. First guy in league history to go four years without needing a postgame shower."

Kelleher winced. The line was his — a frustrated crack to a reporter at the end of his senior year — and had provided him with his one moment of college glory, turning up in *Sports Illustrated*'s, "They Said It."

Buzelis was brilliant again in the second half, but it didn't feel the same to Kelleher. The joy of watching him play had been replaced by uneasiness. Every couple of minutes he stole a glance at Akley and his Louisiana henchmen. Kelleher knew just how dirty the recruiting game could get, and this was starting to look like a gloves-off deal.

The reporter in him was wound up, trying to figure out all the possible scenarios connected to the story, but the Shelter Islander in him was horrified by what he was seeing. What he really should do, he thought, was go home, crawl under the covers, and pretend he had never heard of Rytis Buzelis. But he knew he wasn't going to do that — he had never been that smart.

Buzelis came out of the game with six minutes left and Shelter Island leading, 92–55. He had scored 51 points in twenty-six minutes. The final was 105–84. By the end, the gym was almost empty. Most of the off-island crowd had left as soon as Buzelis came out, no doubt to catch the ferry and get home. The coaches were all still there, though, lurking, waiting, eyeing each other. The end of the game for the players meant the beginning of the game for the coaches.

"Ready to go?" DeStefano asked when the final buzzer sounded.

"Absolutely not," Kelleher said. "Just sit here a couple minutes and you'll see the real game."

"What the — "

"Just watch."

As soon as the two teams had shaken hands and disappeared into their locker rooms, the coaches began maneuvering, ever so slowly, for position.

"This is what they all came for," Kelleher explained. "According to NCAA rules, these guys aren't even allowed to say hello to Buzelis or any member of his family. But that won't stop them from making sure the kid and his parents know they're here — that they've made the long journey because they all care so very much about Rytis." Kelleher peered around, then pointed triumphantly at a tall, handsome-looking couple standing near the corner of the bleachers, surrounded by a number of fans.

"The parents?"

"You got it," DeStefano nodded, as a young boy walked up and handed a piece of paper to Mr. Buzelis. The kid turned and pointed in the direction of Mike Krzyzewski, who waved at the Buzelises, indicating they should read the note. Just then, Rick Pitino walked by, calling Jim Boeheim's name as if he were looking for the Syracuse coach. As he did, he bumped smack into Mr. Buzelis.

"Oh, Mr. Buzelis, excuse me," Pitino said, barely breaking stride. "Rytis played great. Can't talk, you know — rules.

Please tell him I said nice job, and I'll give you folks a call soon."

"Now there," Kelleher explained, "were two classic examples of famous coaches not breaking the rules. Krzyzewski never made contact with the parents, other than a wave. That's allowed. And Pitino pulled a textbook 'bump,' literally bumping into the parents by accident, then being courteous but nothing more. What that would be called in an NCAA courtroom is 'unavoidable contact.'"

"Isn't it all kind of silly?" DeStefano asked. "So what if they want to say hello to the kid and his family after a game?"

Kelleher shook his head, the wise old sage. "If it was that simple, you'd be right. But how many coaches are in this gym? Fifty, sixty? Before the no-bump rule, when Rytis walked out of the locker room, it would take him at least another hour to get out of here — every coach would be lined up to make sure he saw them and to pay homage. This way, they can nod or wave or pass notes, but they can't keep him here half the night having his ring and his rear end kissed."

Several coaches lingered around the locker room door, wanting to make sure Rytis saw them when he came out to greet his parents. Others, including Perrin and Harrison, had surrounded Joe Dierker, the coach. Kelleher's only memories of Dierker were bad ones: he was a notorious non-tipper at the golf club.

"Look at Joe with all those guys," Kelleher said. "He must think he's died and gone to egomaniac's heaven."

"Rytis has made him a star," DeStefano said. "This is his fifteen minutes."

Kelleher stretched his arms. It was time to end Dierker's fifteen minutes, at least for tonight, and drag Harrison and Perrin away. "You want to come get a beer with us?" he asked DeStefano.

"No thanks. I'm up at six."

"In the winter? Come on, there's not that much to do, and —"

Kelleher stopped. The locker room door had just opened, and Buzelis had come out, causing the coaches who had been talking to Dierker to dump him in order to jostle for position. All they could do was wave, smile, mouth words. The kid had to feel like a beauty pageant contestant on the runway. How he responded to them would be analyzed and discussed at length the next morning in basketball offices around the country.

"When I waved, he didn't exactly smile, but he definitely nodded as if he was happy to see me . . ."

"He swiveled his head around to make sure I knew he saw me. Very encouraging. . . ."

"He didn't even make eye contact. We're dead . . ."

This kind of teenage hieroglyphics analysis made young coaches old coaches. But they all did it.

It wasn't the sight of Buzelis or the scrambling coaches that had caused Kelleher to break off his sentence. He had seen the postgame mating dance enough times in his life that it didn't mean that much to him. He had even done the runway number himself a few times. What froze him was the sight of Miles Akley practically arm in arm with Buzelis. Akley was talking, the kid was laughing. Since Akley wasn't a coach, he didn't have to play any of the silly coaching games — no rules governed sneaker salesmen. He was, in a very significant sense, above the law.

If Akley was concerned about any of the coaches being upset with him, it didn't show. When he and Buzelis reached the kid's parents, Akley enveloped the mother in a hug and shook hands warmly with the father. He then gave the kid a high five and walked back across the floor to where Murray's two assistants waited for him. A huge smirk was written all across his face.

"Jesus, I think I'm going to be sick," Kelleher said.

"Too much steak?"

"I wish. I'll call you tomorrow."

Kelleher went to find Perrin and Harrison. They were standing under one of the baskets, watching the Buzelises make their exit.

"Now do you believe me about Akley?" Harrison asked. "Did you see that routine?"

"Every bit of it. Why doesn't someone scream bloody murder to the NCAA?"

They both laughed. "I can see we're going to have to reacquaint you with the realities of coaching." Harrison was looking over Kelleher's head at something — or someone. Kelleher turned to look. The Buzelises were gone. Mike Krzyzewski was talking to a woman in blue jeans.

"Tom, is that the local reporter talking to K?" Harrison asked.

"Yeah. I think her name is Tammy something. She called me the other day."

"If she's the one I'm thinking of, she's a hell of a lot better looking than your run-of-the-mill Bobby Kelleher."

"Married men don't notice," Perrin reminded him.

"You know, it's been a while since I've said hello to Krzyzewski," Harrison mused. "Why don't you guys give me a minute."

"Come on, Scott," Kelleher admonished. "We've got seventy-two minutes to get a beer and get you to the ferry. You can hit on this poor kid some other night."

"Okay, okay." Harrison started for the exit with them. He bounded a few strides ahead, then stopped when he reached Krzyzewski. Kelleher heard him say, "Coach, Scott Harrison, Minnesota State. My boss asked me to say hi if I saw you."

"Oh yes, right, Scott," Krzyzewski said, shaking hands. "Please give Bobby my best." He turned to the reporter. "Do you know Tamara . . . ?"

"Mearns," the woman said, shaking hands with Harrison. "From the *Shelter Island Reporter*. Nice to meet you, coach."

Kelleher and Perrin had continued walking, not wanting to be drawn into the conversation. But Kelleher did hear Harrison's reply.

"Oh yes, that's right. It's nice to put a face with the byline. I've enjoyed reading you whenever I've been out here."

"Jesus," Kelleher muttered. "Does he use lines like that in recruiting?"

Perrin smiled. "I don't know, but I suspect he may do better there than with Rytis Buzelis."

Kelleher nodded. This might be one of the very few times in Harrison's life, when, given a choice between a teenage boy and a good-looking woman, he would, if forced to choose, prefer to spend time with the kid and strike out with the woman.

Kelleher had figured that the Dory would be empty, but, as had been the case all night, he was completely mistaken. The place was packed. It seemed as if Rytis Buzelis had changed winters on Shelter Island radically. Everyone wanted to spend a few minutes talking about what they had just seen before heading home.

During the summer, the Dory was one of Kelleher's favorite places. The back porch overlooked a quiet pond that was a hangout for most of the ducks in the area. Often, the ducks would crowd around the porch waiting for food and quacking up a storm. Now the porch was shut tight.

Kelleher and the two coaches found a table near the back door, where Kelleher launched into a lengthy description of what the porch was like when the weather was warm.

"No offense, Bobby, but from what I've seen, this place

appears under the definition of 'godforsaken' in the dictionary," Harrison said.

Perrin was more sympathetic. "Well, we've only seen it in the dark."

"Lucky for us."

"Hey," Kelleher retorted. "Stick around for sunrise, and I guarantee you'll feel different."

"Come Friday, I might just do that," Harrison said. He had walked away from his "bump" of Krzyzewski and Tamara Mearns with a big grin on his face. He admitted he had made a date for dinner with Tamara for Friday, before Shelter Island's game against Mattituck. Kelleher hadn't even gotten a very good look at her, but he had to admit his old friend still had the magic touch when it came to women.

"I'm sure Coach Taylor will be thrilled to know he's spending MSU's recruiting budget so you can bang some girl reporter," Kelleher needled him. "From what I've heard, you damn well better get this kid — or someone else — if you still want to be working next year."

Kelleher had hit a nerve. "What have you heard?" Harrison asked, not even a hint of the smile left.

He hadn't heard a thing beyond the general TV and newspaper gossip that always swirled around coaches who were struggling, so he bluffed.

"All I hear," he said with a shrug, as if it were no big deal to him, "is that people are saying Taylor's gone if you guys don't make the tournament or at least sign a stud. And from what I can see, this guy's the only stud left."

Harrison shot a look at Perrin, who looked away, as if embarrassed for his colleague. "How can you have heard that?" Harrison demanded as a waitress put the beers on the table. "I'm not even sure our athletic director knows that yet."

Little bells were going off in Kelleher's head. What had he stumbled on here? If it *were* true, how could the AD not know? The answer came to him a split second later.

"It's the president who's pressuring you guys?"

Harrison nodded. "The guy's a wimp. The boosters are all over him to get Bobby out of there and hire Bennie Sharpless, Jr., because young Bennie's been coaching junior college for ten years and the old man is telling them that he'll bring in all the JUCO talent in the world if they hire him."

"Wouldn't hiring young Bennie be a backdoor way of putting his father in control again?"

"Of course. That's exactly what the boosters want. But if we win twenty, or if we can say we've recruited the best player in the country, they can't fire us."

"What are you guys now?" Perrin asked.

"Same as you — fourteen and six. Which isn't bad. But at MSU, they want thirty and three every year. That's why the building is half empty every night, even though we've got a pretty good team."

"Pretty good doesn't cut it there," Kelleher agreed. "They're used to seeing future pros all the time."

"What do you mean, future?" Harrison asked. "Most of Bennie's guys took pay cuts when they left MSU for the NBA."

Kelleher knew that was true. "So getting this kid is do or die for you guys?"

Harrison shrugged, waving at the waitress as he did. "Can we get another round?"

The waitress was Holly Gains, whom Kelleher remembered as having been quite pretty once. Now she had her blond hair teased and curled and was wearing enough makeup to sink the North Ferry. She gave Harrison a come-hither look and retreated to the bar to order three more beers.

"You could probably have that tonight," Kelleher said to Harrison, gesturing at Gains.

"If it ever gets that bad, Bobby, don't ask a single question, just get a gun and shoot me." He didn't even laugh when he said it — a strong indication that he was really brooding. "To answer your question," he continued. "Do or die? I don't know. But it's too damn close for comfort to watch Miles Akley walk away with him."

"If the kid or his family are willing to be bought, there's not much any of us can do," Perrin said.

"Which is exactly the point." Harrison slammed an open palm on the table. "Come on, Tom, doesn't it piss you off that a slimy SOB like Akley can wield the power he does? We have to do that stupid ritual dance and he can waltz in and out with the family, slip them shoes, clothes, who knows what else, and no one says a goddamn word? There are nine zillion rules governing us and alumni and not a single rule for a guy who has more interest in whether Louisiana gets this kid than anyone alive, with the possible exception of Fred Murray. How the hell can that be right or fair?"

He was as upset as Kelleher had ever seen him. "So what's the answer?" Kelleher asked.

"There is no answer," Harrison said. "That's why coaching sucks."

"What if you went on the record?" Kelleher asked.

Both coaches laughed. "Bobby, I swear, you are such an innocent," Harrison said. "First of all, who cares what some peon assistant coach thinks? If I said something or if Tom did, all that would do is make life tougher for our bosses."

"Why?"

"Because Akley and Brickley wield a lot of power. Kids like to wear their stuff and go to their camp, and they like having Akley and his people kiss their butts. Hell, they look up to Miles

Akley. You rip him publicly, they look down on you. There are only two kinds of coaches these days: those who have a Brickley contract and those who wish they did." He looked at Perrin. "Tom, if Brickley came in and offered JJ double what he's getting right now, would he take it?"

"I would think so."

"And even if they didn't offer double, he might sign with them because of all the power and influence they have. It'd be foolish for him to turn them down. No one is going to take on Brickley, Bobby. I'll bet even Mike Krzyzewski wouldn't take them on."

Kelleher grimaced. "That's hard to believe."

"Why is it hard to believe? It doesn't matter who you're talking about — Krzyzewski, Dean Smith, Bob Knight, any of the icons. They all know the same things we know, but they don't have any more proof than we do. I can sit here all night and tell you I know Akley is up to no good with Buzelis, but I'll never prove it in this lifetime."

"The old Digger Phelps theory?"

"You mean that you can't prove cash? It goes beyond that. Akley can go ahead and give a kid almost anything, and you still can't prove he's done anything wrong. He's got to go way over the line to get caught."

Perrin stood up and looked at his watch. "Well, if there's a kid he might go too far with, it's this one. He's that good, and Louisiana needs a great player just about as badly as you do, Scott. And we both need to get to the ferry." He threw twenty dollars on the table.

"I'll get the next one," Kelleher offered. "I guess you guys will be back Friday?"

"Unless JJ calls me off because of Akley," Perrin said. "And I wouldn't count on it. With a European kid, a lot can happen."

Harrison nodded. "We're in this until the bitter end — and

it may get awfully bitter." His voice dropped. "Do me a favor Bobby — don't go blabbing that stuff about the trouble we're in. I don't know where you heard it, but if it got out, it certainly wouldn't help things."

Kelleher put a hand up and nodded.

They walked out into what had become a very cold night. "You'll be here for a while?" Harrison asked.

"Oh yeah." Kelleher hadn't really thought about how long he'd stay on Shelter Island. Now he knew he'd be here at least a couple of weeks. He wanted to know more about Rytis Buzelis and his family. A lot more.

THREE

TAMARA MEARNS

T HE MESSAGE LIGHT was on when Kelleher walked back into the house at a few minutes before midnight. It was his mother. "I guess the fact that you have a message on announcing that you're there means you're there," she said, logical as ever. "Call us in the morning."

Kelleher laughed and started to walk away. There was a second message. "Mr. Kelleher, this is Tamara Mearns, from the *Shelter Island Reporter*. Would you call me in the morning? My number at the office is 749-1481."

Why would Tamara Mearns be calling him? In fact, how would she know who he was or that he was here unless Harrison had said something? And why would Scott do that? He walked into the bedroom and picked up the *Reporter* from where he had left it lying on the bed. Inside was a story headlined "For Buzelis, They All Ride the Ferry." The byline on the story was Tamara Mearns.

Kelleher stretched out on the bed and read the story. The writing was clean and clear. Nothing flashy. What jumped off the page was the reporting. "Okay Tamara," he said aloud as he finished. "I'll be happy to call you in the morning."

He glanced at the clock as he finally climbed under the covers. Midnight. He was exhausted. Sleep would come easily. It had been a long time since that happened.

Even though he slept soundly, Kelleher was up by seven. For him, that was ultra-early. At home, if he didn't have someplace to be, he was almost never out of bed before nine. Shelter Island was different. Something about the air — or maybe it was all those years working at the golf club, when he had to be at the pro shop by six-thirty or deal with an unhappy Bob DeStefano. Whatever it was, he rarely slept past seven in this bed.

He jumped up, feeling refreshed, showered, and headed straight for Gardiner's Bay Country Club. It was much too cold to play golf, and the clubhouse was technically closed for the winter. But the coffee gang would be there.

Twelve months a year they showed up for morning coffee, an hour after sunup. When the weather was warm, they went out and played golf after their coffee. This time of year, they would move into the main dining room, build a fire, and play cards until lunchtime. The dining room had a panoramic view of Gardiner's Bay — on a clear day you could see all the way to Fisher's Island, about halfway across Long Island Sound.

The youngest member of the coffee gang was DeStefano, and he was fifty-four. The rest were retirees, men Kelleher had known for as long as he could remember. There weren't very many things Kelleher enjoyed more than sitting around drinking early morning coffee with this group — even if he disagreed with them on almost everything.

"What the hell is that sticker on your car?" he remembered Frank Hallock asking when he was still in high school and learning to drive.

"You mean the one that says, 'Impeach the Cox-Sacker?' "

"Yeah, that one. What are you, anti-Nixon? This whole thing's a media concoction, you know."

Frank Hallock still believed Watergate was a media concoction. He would walk in this morning and lecture Kelleher about everything that that crazy liberal Bill Clinton was doing wrong. Newt Gingrich and Rush Limbaugh were no doubt his current heroes.

Charlie Dominy would be there too, and so would George Hillsdon and Jim Gibbs and Ken Lewis, unless this was Ken's day to be in the city. No one on Shelter Island ever called New York anything except "the city." They would ask him why he was home, he would tell them he needed some time off, and then they would ask him what the hell was wrong with the Knicks.

DeStefano was sitting on the porch alone, waiting for the rest of the group, when Kelleher pulled up. He tossed fifty cents into the kitty, poured himself a cup of coffee, and sat down.

"So what happened?" DeStefano asked. "You quit or get fired?"

Kelleher smiled. He should have known that Bob would know. But how?

"You don't take vacations unless there's absolutely nothing going on," DeStefano observed. "That isn't your way. And you don't show up here in February unless you're looking to get away from something."

Kelleher told him what had happened, just finishing the story as the others began walking in. A heated argument on who was more selfish — athletes or owners — ensued. By the time Kelleher left, it was almost nine o'clock, and the sun had pushed the temperature above freezing.

He stopped at Carol's for the papers, adding the fifty cents he owed her, then swung by the drugstore for some cough medicine. His throat was a little scratchy after an hour and a half of arguing.

Coming out of the drugstore he decided to stop in at the *Reporter* office a few doors down. Rather than call Tamara Mearns, he could drop in to see her. He was curious, he admitted to himself, to get a better look at her, since he really hadn't had the chance the night before.

The front door was open. He walked in to find the place empty — except for Tamara Mearns. She was sitting at a small desk near the back of the room, talking on the phone and taking notes. Kelleher lingered near the counter marked "Classifieds — deadline Tuesday 4 p.m."

Ten minutes later, as he was about to leave, she hung up the phone and looked up. "Sorry, the classifieds deadline was yesterday."

"Not a problem," Kelleher said, walking back to her desk. "I'm Bobby Kelleher."

"Oh, yes." She stood and shook hands. "You didn't need to come down — a call would have been fine."

Her tone was crisp, cool. Too cool, Kelleher thought, for a reporter. Making people feel at ease was part of the job. That didn't seem to be Tamara Mearns's style. She was about five-six, with shoulder-length dirty-blond hair and almond-shaped brown eyes. She wore a blue sweater, jeans, and sneakers. Kelleher guessed she had once been an athlete. She was slender, someone who worked at staying in shape. Kelleher decided right away that her eyes were her best feature.

"Actually, I was going to call you," he said. "But I was in the drugstore picking up some cough medicine and thought I'd drop by. I haven't been in here since they remodeled a couple of years ago."

"You've been on Shelter Island for a few years?"

"A few. Since I was two."

If she thought that was clever, she didn't show it. "Oh, you stay with your parents."

"In their house." He felt put down by her tone. "They live in Florida now, so I take care of the place most of the year."

"Sounds like a pretty fair deal to me."

She *was* implying he was some kind of rich kid living in mommy and daddy's house. He started to defend himself, then decided not to bother. "You called me." He tried to sound as cool as she did. "What can I do for you?"

"To tell you the truth, I was looking for some background on this recruiting business. I'm not a sportswriter, so I'm coming to all of this cold. I understand you were a sportswriter — "

"Actually, I'm a political reporter," he interrupted, fed up with her imperious tone. Why is it, he wondered, that people who know nothing about sports always feel compelled to brag about their ignorance? "Who gave you the idea I was a sportswriter?"

"Coach Harrison, from Minnesota State. I thought he said you covered him when he played in college."

Kelleher laughed. "I don't doubt Scott said something like that. I am a reporter — he did get that part right — but I covered politics at the Washington *Herald*. The Maryland State House. I quit last week."

She arched an eyebrow. "To come back to Shelter Island? In February?"

"To get away from the *Herald*. It's a very long, very boring story. But I have written some sports, and I was once a recruited athlete, so I'll be glad to help you out if I can."

She looked at him suspiciously. "Recruited athlete?"

"Basketball player." He made it sound casual. "I wasn't a Rytis Buzelis, but I did get recruited by quite a few schools."

"And you ended up playing somewhere?"

"Virginia. That's where I know your friend Scott Harrison from. He was a graduate assistant coach there my junior and senior years."

"Virginia?" she asked, genuine surprise in her voice. "As in the University of Virginia?"

"As in Yooveeay." He thought briefly about not saying anything about his career, but figured full disclosure was a better idea. "I never played much down there."

"Benchwarmer?"

"On very good teams," he said more defensively than he needed to.

She almost smiled. "Well, if you were recruited by Virginia, I imagine a lot of smaller schools thought you were really hot stuff."

She was a fast learner. "I guess you could say that. My dad still hasn't forgiven me for not going to Yale. Back then, I could have played quite a lot there."

"So what do you mean, 'my' friend Scott Harrison?" she said, clearly having heard enough about his playing career.

Kelleher shrugged. "You are having dinner with him, aren't you? Come on, don't feel bad. I know what a good-looking guy Scott is."

"Oh you do, do you?" She folded her arms and shook her head. "What is it with you men? I agree to go to dinner with a source and you're all yucking it up, no doubt, about how your pal is going to bang the girl reporter. Believe me, Mr. Kelleher, I've had dozens of men a lot more attractive than your buddy Scott hit on me in my lifetime. Just because he scored with some of your jock-bimbos back when you boys were at Yooveeay doesn't mean every single woman he meets goes ga-ga and falls over dead at the sight of him."

She was really angry. Kelleher felt guilty. He should have

kept his big mouth shut. But her attitude had really annoyed the hell out of him. "I'm sorry," he said. "You're a hundred percent right. There's a double standard in our business for women reporters, especially in sports where we all have a macho-jock complex."

"Gee, thanks for noticing."

"Hey, I said I was sorry."

"Apology accepted. Thanks for coming by. I suspect I can handle this story without an ex-jock maven like you." She gave him a look that was as dismissive as her tone. Kelleher started to snap back, but he had already been rude once. No sense putting his foot in his mouth again.

"Well, good luck with it," he said. "I'll look forward to reading you the next couple weeks."

"No work on the horizon?"

"Not searching the horizon yet."

"Well, a job is a job, isn't it?" she said, indifferently, smiling coldly. "And as a matter of fact, I have to get back to it." She returned to her desk. He stared at her for a second, then walked out of the office, feeling annoyed and put down.

He stood on the sidewalk, trying to decide what to do next. Tamara Mearns had stirred his competitive juices. Maybe she thought the Buzelis story was hers to work on alone. Not anymore. For now, he would concentrate on getting the story himself. Once he had it, finding someone to publish it wouldn't be a problem.

"Okay, Ms. Mearns," he said aloud, "we'll find out who the real reporter is. Right here, right now."

The question was, where to begin. The answer was easy: with the Buzelis family. Kelleher walked across the street to the post office. He needed to tell Sue Mills not to forward his mail for the next few weeks, and she would have a phone book. There didn't figure to be too many Buzelises in the Shelter Island directory.

The book said that Arturas I. Buzelis lived at 46 Burns Avenue. Kelleher knew almost exactly where that was — right down the street from Klenawicus Airport, the tiny strip where private planes occasionally landed.

After chatting with Sue Mills for a few minutes, Kelleher headed toward Burns Avenue. Passing the airport, it occurred to him that he had no idea what he planned to say once he got to the Buzelis house. In all likelihood no one would be home, and he would have to come back or call another time.

A maroon Pontiac was sitting in the small driveway when he pulled up to the white, two-story frame house. Kelleher parked on the street and walked up the cobbled steps to the front door. There was no bell, so he knocked. About sixty seconds went by. He was about to knock again when the door opened.

It was Mrs. Buzelis. Kelleher remembered from the previous evening that both parents were quite tall, but he hadn't really paid much attention. Now, he noticed. Rytis Buzelis's mother was about six feet tall. She had blond hair tied back behind her head, and piercing blue eyes. Kelleher guessed she was in her early forties. He remembered Scott Harrison telling him that as a coach, you knew you were getting old when the mothers of the kids you were recruiting started to look good. Kelleher suddenly knew what he meant.

"May I help you?"

Her English was clear, accented, a bit clipped, but at least as easy to understand as some of the southerners Kelleher had gone to college with. Realizing he had been staring, he stumbled through an introduction.

"Oh yes, thank you, uh, Mrs. Buzelis, hi, I'm, um, I'm Bobby Kelleher."

He put out a hand, proud that he had remembered his own name.

She shook hands, peering at him, he thought, a bit suspiciously. "Why yes, Mr. Keller, yes. You are well?"

Kelleher smiled at the formality of her English and the mispronunciation of his name. "Yes, thank you. I'm sorry to bother you at home like this, but I wondered if you had a minute or two to talk?"

Now she really looked confused. "Mr. Keller, I do not wish to be rude, and maybe I have made a mistake, because sometimes my husband and I do not understand everything. But this is not against the rules?"

Rules? After a moment, he understood: she thought he was a coach. "Mrs. Buzelis, I'm sorry, I didn't introduce myself properly. I'm not a coach, I'm a newspaper reporter."

Her confused look was replaced by a smile. "Oh, please come in. You would like some coffee?"

If he had another cup of coffee, he would spend the afternoon in the bathroom. "I would love coffee."

"Please then," she said, holding her arm out to point him to the living room. "I will leave you for only a moment."

She walked down a short hallway. The living room was small but immaculate, with two chairs, a couch, and a love seat. On the mantel were a number of pictures. Kelleher checked his shoes to make sure there wasn't any mud on them before setting foot on the Buzelis's red-and-white carpet. Once the shoes had passed inspection, he quickly crossed the room to the mantel.

The pictures of Rytis in his basketball uniform were predictable. The family pictures were what caught Kelleher's eye. Apparently Rytis had two sisters. One had darker hair and, like Mr. Buzelis, broad shoulders. She had a warm smile and pretty, dark eyes. It was the other sister who caused Kelleher to murmur, "My God!" The second Buzelis sister had long blond hair, what appeared to be a perfect figure — at least as far as Kelleher could tell from the picture — and blue eyes so piercing that Kelleher looked away, convinced she was staring at him.

He was still trying to regain his composure when Mrs. Buzelis came into the room carrying a tray with coffee and cookies. "You have seen the pictures of my family, then?" she asked, a broad smile on her face.

"Oh yes, absolutely." He wondered why he couldn't get his mouth to work properly. He pointed at the picture. "Those are your daughters?"

She nodded. "Vida is the oldest. She is my smart one. She was the first to come here after Gorbachev began perestroika. She came to study economics. Nikki is my beauty, as you can see. She is now a model."

"In New York?"

"Yes. She and Vida share an apartment in Greenwich Village, which pleases me, since Nikki is, you would say, a little wild." She pronounced Greenwich the way it was spelled.

"Vida works in New York too?"

"On Wall Street. She is an analyst."

"I guess her English is quite good?"

"All my children speak very good English," she declared proudly. "When they were little, some of our basketball players brought back English books and tapes from their travels. My husband knew some of them, so he was able to get some tapes. They studied even then."

"Rytis grew up as a basketball fan?"

"All Lithuanian boys grow up loving basketball. It is not so different than here. The two biggest heroes in our country are Marchulonis and Sabonis. You know them?"

Anyone who had followed basketball for more than fifteen

minutes knew Sarunis Marchulonis and Arvidas Sabonis. They were the key players on the Soviet team that beat the Americans in the 1988 Olympics in Seoul. Sabonis was now in Spain, making millions. Marchulonis, who Kelleher remembered speaking almost perfect English in television interviews during the Olympics, was now in Seattle, playing for the Supersonics in the NBA.

"Of course. So Rytis was inspired by them?"

"A little bit. But really, he was not so good a player when we were still in Vilnius. When we first came here two years ago, he was not nearly so tall as now."

"That was when you were in New York?"

"Yes. Actually, we didn't stay there very long. Too big, too dirty, too dangerous in the streets for a teenage boy. Arturas said there must be other places. We had friends in Greenport, so we came out last summer. We took the ferry one day to come here. It was so beautiful, Arturas said this is where we should live."

"He has no trouble finding work on the island?"

"Sometimes he goes off. But there is always work for a good carpenter."

"I guess Rytis never had a chance to play in New York, where he would have been seen by all the college coaches?"

Nadia Buzelis put her coffee cup down and laughed. "It could have been worse?"

Kelleher laughed too. "Getting a little tired of the attention?"

She held up the coffee pot to ask if he wanted more. He held out his cup. As long as she was comfortable sitting and chatting, he didn't want to break the mood.

She poured herself a second cup.

"At first, you know, it was fun. We didn't let Rytis play when we were in New York. Studies came first, and he was spending afternoons taking extra English classes. But we knew he was playing in the gym at school all the time. The coach came to us and said please to let him play. By then he had grown to two meters."

Kelleher did some quick math in his head, remembering his metric lessons in high school. Two meters was about six feet six.

"We told the coach that if Rytis did well in school, he could play the next year. He did well, so when we came here, we gave him permission to play. We thought it would be a nice way for him to meet new schoolmates. But this, we never could have dreamed."

It suddenly occurred to Kelleher that he had a pretty good interview going here and that his notebook was sitting on the front seat of his car. Silently cursing himself for not being better prepared, he wondered if he should run to the car for it. That probably wasn't a good idea. Nadia Buzelis was comfortable right now, sitting in her living room, sipping coffee, telling a polite young man how she felt about the sudden changes in her life. If he stopped her train of thought and came back with a notebook in hand, he would change the chemistry completely. Better to rely on his memory, as he had in the past.

She was staring at him. "Mr. Keller?"

"Sorry," he said, roused from his musings. "I was just trying to picture what it must be like for you with all these people suddenly wanting to be your best friend."

She laughed, nodding her head. "Oh yes. I have told Arturas that perhaps we should make tapes of all the wonderful things these men have told us." She pointed to a rose-filled vase on the corner table. "Those are from this morning. Every day, it seems, there are more."

"Those roses come from Miles Akley by any chance?" He tried to sound casual.

Her look answered the question before she did. "How could you know?"

He shrugged. "I've known Miles for years. He can be very charming when he wants something."

"And you think he wants my son?"

"Don't you?"

"But for whom?"

"Who do you think?"

"You first." She was smiling, her blue eyes hinting that this was fun.

He leaned back. "Oh, I don't know. Maybe, just for argument's sake, let's say the University of Louisiana."

The blue eyes narrowed. "You also know then Coach Murray?"

"Not as well as I know Miles."

He wasn't lying. He had been in the same gym with Akley. The closest he had ever come to Murray was seeing him on TV.

"Do you think they are both honest and good men?"

"Do you?"

She stood up. "Mr. Keller, I think you are a very smart young man. I think maybe you know many things. Perhaps sometime you can come back and talk with my husband."

He stood up too, understanding that the game was over and his time was up. "I'd like that. Maybe I could call this evening."

She stopped at a small table in the foyer, wrote something on a piece of paper, and handed it to him. "This is our number. We had to change it twice already this month because the coaches call so often. Now, reporters too. But you call. I would like you to talk to Arturas."

"Well, I'd like to talk to him. And maybe Rytis too."

Her smile was less enthusiastic than it had been. "I would

like that. But you must speak with Arturas first. He is not very trustful of American reporters."

"Maybe Rytis should go to Georgetown."

"What?"

"Nothing. Sorry. Just a joke." He smiled. "Maybe you could tell Arturas I'm a good guy."

For the first time, she didn't return his smile. "I must be careful. Arturas is very deep with all this."

The comment screamed for a follow-up question, but the look on her face told him it was time to get going. He put out his hand. "Thank you so much for the time and the coffee. I hope we talk again soon."

As they shook, she put her left hand on top of his hand. "You call," she said softly. "Please."

"Tonight. Promise."

He walked out the door into a light rain, feeling both exhilarated and disturbed. He seemed to have made a friend in Nadia Buzelis. But it was clear that his new friend was troubled. The mention of Miles Akley's name had changed the mood quickly.

There was more to this story than just the tale of a Lithuanian kid who could play. Kelleher had plenty of work to do. Of course, at some point he would have to figure out just whom he was doing the work for.

FOUR

INVESTIGATIVE REPORTER

KELLEHER KEPT HIS PROMISE to Nadia Buzelis and called the house that night. His phone conversation with Arturas Buzelis did not go well, to put it mildly.

"How dare you invade my family's privacy by coming to my home!" Arturas Buzelis roared before Kelleher had even finished introducing myself. "Do you always go around banging on people's doors and barging into their homes? Or do you only do that to foreign people who deserve no respect because you are a great American reporter?"

Kelleher was so stunned that he sat and listened for several seconds without even trying to respond. "Mr. Buzelis, I'm sorry," he said finally. "Your phone number is unlisted, so I thought I would take a chance and see if someone was home. Your wife was very gracious and — "

"She will not ever be so gracious again!" There was so much venom in his voice that Kelleher wondered for a moment if Buzelis had hurt his wife. "If you come here again, you will be sorry, I promise you!"

He slammed down the phone, leaving Kelleher staring at the receiver. In all his years as a reporter, he had never heard so much anger in someone's voice, and he had dealt with a lot of people who had plenty more reason to be angry with him than Arturas Buzelis.

All day Thursday he worked the telephone, calling everyone he knew in college basketball and a number of people he didn't, trying to find out what they knew about Akley and Murray and what they had heard about the recruitment of Buzelis.

Most of it he already knew: Akley was a sleaze with a license to cheat, courtesy of the NCAA and a thick wallet. No one wanted to do battle with him. Murray needed a new star, and Akley was pulling out all the stops to deliver Buzelis. Most of the coaches he talked to agreed — as long as he wasn't quoting them — that the kid was bound to end up at Louisiana.

"When John Thompson *had* to have Alonzo Mourning back in the eighties and Sonny Vaccaro was his guy at Nike, Sonny delivered," Davis Andrade, who had once been a Wake Forest assistant but was now working in the NBA, told him. "This is the same deal. Miles will land the kid for Murray."

The mention of Thompson's name reminded Kelleher of his crack about Georgetown. With the demise of the KGB, Georgetown basketball as run by Thompson was probably the most secret organization on the face of the earth. Thompson was so obsessed with secrecy that when he was on the road, he didn't even tell his own athletic director what hotel he was staying in. Judging by Arturas Buzelis's reaction to his visit, Kelleher thought, Thompson would probably be the perfect coach for his son. But Nike wasn't in the recruiting business the way it had been when Vaccaro was there.

It was Doug Doughty, Kelleher's old friend at the *Washington Herald*, who finally said something Kelleher hadn't heard a dozen times or more. "You know, someone told me a while ago that Brickley really wanted to make a move in the international market. All the shoe companies are doing it, but it's tougher for Brickley, because they haven't got any big tennis players or golfers. They've got to find a way to do it through basketball."

Bells went off in Kelleher's head. Of course! This wasn't just about getting a player for Fred Murray. This was about landing a player who could be Brickley's Michael Jordan, European style. That raised the stakes considerably. "If Brickley sees this kid as their bridge into Europe, then we're talking millions of dollars here."

"Wrong. You're talking millions and millions and millions. How much do you think Jordan was worth to Nike?"

"A hundred million?"

"You're low. Way low. Now let's assume this kid isn't Jordan, because no one is Jordan. But if he's even Scottie Pippen or Sean Kemp and he's Lithuanian, hell, you're talking a virtually untapped market. You've heard all the stories about what people over there will do to get their hands on a pair of American sneakers. They've replaced blue jeans as the thing to have."

Kelleher was trying to keep himself under control. Doughty had covered basketball for twenty years and was not given to hyperbole. It was one hell of a leap from talking about a high school kid on Shelter Island to a worldwide, multi-multimillion dollar business deal.

"You're my hero, Doug. Do me a favor and don't talk about this to anyone — at least for a little while."

Doughty sighed. "Since I haven't got time to work it myself, I'd rather you get it than someone else. But when you accept the Pulitzer, remember to thank me."

"Spell the name again?"

Kelleher's heart was pounding when he hung up the phone. Sure, it was just a hunch. But his gut told him that Doughty had

hit on something important. Maybe that was why Arturas
Buzelis had jumped down his throat. He could still hear Nadia's
voice: "Arturas is very deep with this."

Maureen McGuire had always had a theory that the best
stories raise more questions than answers at the beginning.
"Simple answers mean a simple story," she had always said.
"The ones that are hard are the ones worth chasing."

This one was getting harder by the minute.

Kelleher picked up a *Shelter Island Reporter* Friday morning to
see what Tamara Mearns had to say about Buzelis. She had
written in great detail about Tuesday's game and mentioned all
the big-name coaches who had been there. There was no mention, however, of Akley or the Louisiana assistants. "Clueless,"
Kelleher said to himself, tossing the paper aside as he sat in
front of the fire he had built in the living room.

He had told Scott Harrison he would meet him at the gym
at six and was killing time until it was late enough to leave.
Harrison had called from Minnesota the night before to be-
moan a double overtime loss to Indiana. Kelleher was tempted
to run Doughty's theory by him but decided to wait. His friend
sounded uptight.

"The wolves are baying at the front door," Harrison said.
"Bobby won't say it, but if we don't get this kid . . ."

"You don't think the deal is done for Louisiana?"

"As a matter of fact, I don't. At least, not if the mother has
anything to say about it."

The comment fascinated Kelleher. He knew that Harrison
was famous for working the mothers of recruits. With his All-
American good looks and charm, Harrison could usually win
over women of any age, race, size, or shape. He wondered if
Harrison had met Nikki Buzelis.

Kelleher was so hopped up that he left for the gym at 5:30.

It was starting to snow, and he wondered for a moment if Harrison's plane would make it. Then he thought about Tom Perrin, who he knew had to fly a prop plane from Washington. At least Harrison's plane was a jet.

Since it was almost two hours before game time, the parking lot behind the gym was empty when Kelleher arrived. He pulled in next to a white Cadillac with a Z as the first letter on the license plate. Kelleher had rented enough cars to know that all rental cars in New York had Z as the first letter of their plates.

It was still only 5:40 when he walked into the empty lobby. He found a bench, sat down, and stretched his legs out on it. He hadn't been there more than a minute when he heard footsteps on the stairs that led up from the basement. He put his feet down on the floor so he didn't look too much like some drifter who had wandered in from the cold. Why he worried about what a couple of strangers thought, he didn't know.

The two men who appeared at the top of the steps weren't strangers. One was Joe Dierker, the suddenly famous Shelter Island coach. The other was Miles Akley. Now Kelleher knew whom the Cadillac belonged to. When Dierker and Akley saw him, Dierker started whispering in Akley's ear. Akley nodded, patted Dierker on the back, and walked directly across the lobby to Kelleher. Dierker turned and disappeared down the steps.

Kelleher stood up as Akley approached. Akley was a big man — about six-four, Kelleher guessed — with broad, sloping shoulders and curly black hair. He was smiling as he approached, but on his face it came off more like a sneer.

"Bobby Kelleher?" he asked, hand extended. "Miles Akley."

"Nice to meet you," Kelleher said, grudgingly accepting the proffered hand.

"Meet me?" Akley said. "I understood we were old friends."

Damn! Nadia Buzelis had mentioned — no doubt to her husband — Kelleher's claim that he had known Akley for years. He didn't like starting a new relationship, especially an adversarial one, on the defensive.

"Where did you hear that?" he asked, feigning innocence — at least for starters.

"According to Arturas Buzelis, you barged into his house the other day, claiming to his wife that you had known me for years."

Kelleher smiled. At least he wasn't the only one exaggerating. "If knocking on someone's door and being invited in for coffee is barging in, then I guess that would be an accurate description. And what I said to Mrs. Buzelis was that I had known *about* you for years."

Akley folded his arms. "Oh really. What is it that you've known?"

Kelleher shrugged, trying to act bored. "Mr. Brickley Shoes, Fred Murray's pal, kingmaker of college coaches."

"Very flattering. Mr. Buzelis had the impression, somehow, that you thought I might be trying to sway his son in the direction of the University of Louisiana."

"Gee, I wonder why anyone would think that? I'm sure you've been spending all this time on Shelter Island just because it's such a pleasant place to be in February."

Akley laughed. "I'm here for the same reason I'm anywhere. I have a lot of friends in the coaching business who I need to see during the season. I like to see the great young players. Rytis wasn't in our camp last summer, so I hadn't seen him."

Now Kelleher was ready to go on offense. "So you need to see him ten times? You need to be escorting him from the locker room to his car? You need to be hanging around his parents constantly? You need to send Nadia Buzelis roses?"

"I like to help kids," Akley countered. "If I can help this kid — "

"Why don't you go help some kid who can't dunk or shoot threes?" Kelleher demanded, his voice rising. Akley's patronizing, phony demeanor made him angrier and angrier. "Why don't you go help some kid who doesn't have half the world at his doorstep offering him heaven and earth? Jesus, Akley, who do you think you're talking to, some TV geek who's going to buy your BS?"

The sneer disappeared from Akley's face. He took a step closer to Kelleher and stood directly over him, his face right in Kelleher's. "Now you listen to me, hotshot," he snarled, his voice low and menacing. "I don't know who you are and I don't care. But this isn't any of your business on any level. The Buzelises trust me, because they know I'd never do anything to hurt Rytis or hurt them, so don't come in here spewing all your self-righteous reporter crap and think anyone's going to listen.

"I know you went to Virginia and I know Scott Harrison is your pal, so don't give me any bull about just wanting what's right. In fact, as a Virginia alum, you could be turned in for an illegal contact with Mrs. Buzelis the other day."

Kelleher was tempted to shove Akley to get him out of his face, but he didn't think that was a good idea. Instead, he stepped back to clear some room for himself.

"That's bullshit, Akley, and you know it. I went in there strictly as a reporter. In fact, I never mentioned *any* school while I was in the house, or any coach."

"Fine. But take my advice and stay away. This means nothing to you."

"You threatening me, Akley?"

The sneer returned. "You think you know all about me, Kelleher? Fine, check me out. Ask anyone if I ever make threats."

He turned and walked back across the still-empty lobby. Kelleher was tempted to shout something at him, but resisted. There wasn't much doubt about what had just happened. Akley had threatened him. Kelleher was shaking, partly from the confrontation, partly from adrenaline. Rytis Buzelis was very, very important to Miles Akley, there was no doubt about that. Doug Doughty's theory about Brickley wanting him to be their bridge into Europe made even more sense now.

He had just reseated himself on the bench and pulled out a notebook to try and recreate as much of the conversation as possible when the door swung open and Scott Harrison and Tom Perrin walked in, along with Tommy Amaker. It was Amaker who had ruined his life as a Virginia freshman by stealing the ball from him three straight times. Now he was an assistant at Duke under Mike Krzyzewski.

"Bobby Kelleher, as I live and breathe," Harrison said, leading the contingent across the lobby. "Boy, you must be excited about seeing us if you're already here."

Kelleher stood up to greet them. Harrison had a huge grin on his face. Perrin, as always, was poker-faced. Amaker looked a little wobbly. "Bobby, do you know Tommy Amaker?" Perrin asked.

"Know him?" Kelleher said, laughing. "The man ruined my entire life. Of course I know him."

Amaker smiled. "I was just lucky that night. Every guard in the world has had a bad-luck night like that."

"I'll bet you never had a night like that."

Amaker smiled weakly. "Yeah, sure I did. Excuse me for a minute."

He walked in the direction of the men's room. "What's with him?" Kelleher asked.

"Rough flight," Perrin said. "That prop plane bounced around the entire way up from Washington. I wasn't feeling so good when we landed either."

"How about your flight?" Kelleher asked Harrison.

"I don't know. I slept the whole way."

"God, I hate people like you," Perrin said. "I've never slept a minute of my life on an airplane."

Harrison laughed. "So Bobby, you been keeping busy out here in this thriving metropolis?"

"Busy enough to get threatened by Miles Akley."

Both coaches' eyes opened wide. "What're you talking about?" Harrison asked.

"Let's go inside and I'll tell you."

Since no one was manning the doors yet, they walked into the gym without having to pay. A couple of the Maltituck players were warming up at one end, but the bleachers were deserted. Amaker joined them coming out of the bathroom, and the four of them made their way up to the top row. Kelleher told the coaches about his meeting with Nadia Buzelis and his confrontation with Akley.

When he finished the story, there was a long silence. "Sounds like Miles has the hooks in deep," Amaker remarked.

"Bye-bye Cavaliers," Perrin added. "He would have looked so nice in orange and blue."

Harrison slammed his hand against the bleacher. "Listen to me, Bobby, don't fuck with this guy. He's mean and he's ruthless, and if he thinks you're in his way, he'll hurt you."

Kelleher laughed. "Oh come on, Scott, what's he going to do, have me kneecapped? He's a sneaker salesman. He may try to intimidate people and act like a tough guy, but come on! I've dealt with killers. I'm not going to go running from some guy in a warm-up suit."

Harrison shook his head. "Bobby, this guy's capable of anything. Trust me."

Kelleher looked at the other two coaches. "He's mean as a snake, and he's ruthless too," Perrin affirmed. "But do *anything*? I'm not sure I'd go that far."

"He might go in for kneecapping," Amaker said. "And he'd probably hire someone a lot more efficient than the guy who went after Nancy Kerrigan."

Harrison sighed. "Look Bobby, I can't tell you how to lead your life, but I'm your friend and I'm telling you, this guy is very capable of hurting you if he thinks you're in the way."

He stood up and walked down the bleacher. "I wonder if they're selling hot dogs yet?" People were starting to trickle into the gym.

"Bring me one if they are," Perrin called after him.

Harrison looked back at the other two. "How about you guys?"

Kelleher shook his head. Amaker shook his vehemently. "Please don't even mention food."

As Harrison made his way down to the floor, Kelleher turned to Perrin. "Is he just trying to shake me up?"

"He's trying to shake you up. But it's because he really believes Akley's a bad guy. Which he is. The funny thing about it is, we both heard this week that Scott might be the one guy who had a real shot at the kid, other than Louisiana."

"Really?"

"The mother likes him. She say anything about that to you?"

No, she hadn't. But Scott had mentioned her on the phone. Maybe if Minnesota State had a shot at the kid, Scott knew more about Akley and his methods than the other coaches. He ran that idea past Perrin and Amaker.

"Possible," Perrin said. "But I'll tell you what — when we met Scott at the airport, he didn't seem shaken up about anything. In fact, he was in a great mood."

"Great enough to make me think he *was* way ahead of the rest of us," Amaker added.

That was different than the mood Kelleher had heard on the

phone. Kelleher needed to talk to Scott without any of his competitors, even friendly ones, around. He stood up. "You know, I think I could use a hot dog myself. You sure you guys don't want something?"

"A Coke," Perrin said. If he or Amaker thought Kelleher's sudden appetite was a transparent excuse to go find Harrison, they didn't give it away. The Shelter Island players had wandered onto the court to warm up. Both coaches were gazing longingly in the direction of Rytis Buzelis.

Kelleher walked down the bleachers and paused at the door to get his hand stamped — why pay the three bucks when he was in fact working? — and then out into the lobby to find Harrison. Although the concession stand had just opened, Harrison was nowhere in sight. Kelleher figured he had gone to the bathroom, so he bought two Cokes, one for Perrin, one for himself, and sat down to wait.

A few minutes later, he had finished his drink and was still waiting. He walked into the bathroom and found it empty. Feeling a little strange, he called Harrison's name, then peeked under the doors of the stalls to make sure no one was there.

Still holding Perrin's Coke, he walked back into the lobby. Scott might have gone downstairs to the locker room area, or he might have gone outside. It was unlikely Scott would try to get near anyone — even Dierker — before a game, but he decided to check downstairs anyway. When he got to the steps, a security guard stopped him. "I'm sorry sir, teams only downstairs."

"That's fine. But tell me one thing — how long have you been here?"

The guard looked at him for a second. "Since 6:30."

"Did a big blond guy show up here about fifteen minutes ago and try to talk his way past you?"

The guard shook his head. "I did see a tall blond guy go outside about fifteen minutes ago."

"Front door?"

The guard pointed behind him. "Side door."

"Thanks." Kelleher headed for the side door, which led to the baseball field. It had gotten very cold. Kelleher looked around and saw no one. He walked to the corner of the building and started to turn left, intending to circle around the back. There was a jungle gym for the elementary school kids that he remembered playing on years ago and, as he turned the corner, he could see two people sitting on a small play bench right next to it.

He stopped short, then saw that one of the people was Scott. He opened his mouth to call his name, then stopped. In the dim light from the back door of the school, Kelleher could see that the other person was a woman. He could also see that she and Scott were holding hands and talking in hushed tones, their faces very close.

Kelleher stepped back and peered around the corner. He wasn't close enough to make out any words, but the conversation appeared fairly intense. He stood there, rooted to the spot, as the conversation continued. After a couple more minutes, Kelleher felt himself shivering. Perrin's coke was starting to freeze to his hand, so he put it down.

Harrison stood up and so did the woman. She was almost as tall as Scott and had what looked like long blond hair. She gave him a melodramatic hug, causing Kelleher to wonder if there might be a camera crew hidden somewhere. Harrison pulled away, kissed her on the lips, then began walking toward Kelleher. The woman stood there for a second, then began walking in the direction of the back door.

Kelleher turned and sprinted back to the side door, wondering what he should do next. He walked back to the bathroom and was glad to find it uncrowded. He walked into one of the stalls, locked the door, and sat down. What had he just witnessed? More important, *who* had he just witnessed?

It had to be the younger Buzelis daughter. Even in the bad light, he could tell she was quite tall and quite blond. Kelleher added up what he knew: the word on the coaching grapevine was that Minnesota State and Louisiana were leading the race for Buzelis. He knew why Louisiana was in contention: Akley. But why MSU? Apparently, the answer was his old friend Scott. And just as apparently, the grapevine had picked the wrong Buzelis woman as the reason: it was Nikki, not Nadia, that Scott was working.

Kelleher unlocked the door and headed back into the lobby. He joined Harrison in line at the concession stand.

Harrison gave him a big smile. "Hey, Bobby, sorry I've been gone so long. I had to work the room a little."

"Yeah, looked like you were working hard out by the jungle gym."

Harrison's smile disappeared and his face reddened. "You following me?" It was an angry hiss.

"As a matter of fact, no." They were now at the front of the line. Kelleher ordered two drinks. "You want anything, Scott?"

"What? Oh, yeah." He turned to the teenage girl behind the counter. "Hot dog and a Coke."

Kelleher handed her a five-dollar bill. They walked away, Kelleher sipping his drink while Harrison bit into the hot dog. Kelleher heard the national anthem.

"Listen, Bobby, I don't know what you saw or think you saw, but don't go jumping to any conclusions."

"I haven't reached any conclusions, but I've got a lot of questions."

"Fine — after the game, I'll explain the whole thing."

Kelleher sighed. "You better come up with something

good — because you know as well as I do that what you were doing out there goes way beyond the definition of illegal contact with a family member."

Harrison looked at him quizzically. "How would you know who that was?"

"Saw her picture when I was at the house."

Harrison shook his head, finished the hot dog, and started into the gym. "You know something, Bobby, you really are becoming a pain in the ass."

The gym was packed; the teams were being introduced. The two men picked their way back to the top row, where Perrin and Amaker were holding on to two small spaces for dear life.

"Where the hell have you two been?" Perrin demanded as Kelleher handed him his drink.

"Girl-watching," Kelleher retorted. Perrin shot him a look that said, "What the hell is going on?"

Kelleher glanced across the court to see if he could spot the Buzelises. They were four rows up, behind the home team bench. A stunning young woman with long blond hair sat next to Nadia: Nikki. Next to her was another young woman with darker hair who appeared to be the older sister, Vida.

"I see the whole family's here tonight."

"Sure are," Perrin replied. "Hey Scott, you ever get a good look at the younger sister?"

"Not really." Harrison stared at the court as if fascinated by the way the teams were lining up for the tipoff.

"When she took off her coat, there was nearly a riot," Amaker said. "Isn't she a model?"

"Yeah," Kelleher said. "In New York."

Akley was up in the same corner of the bleachers as on Tuesday night. Only one Louisiana assistant was with him.

The first half was no different from the first game Kelleher had seen three nights earlier. Buzelis was a man among boys, swooping to the basket for dunks, making perfect passes to teammates whenever he was double- or triple-covered, and pulling up whenever he felt like it to shoot his feathery jump shot. He had thirty-three points by halftime; Shelter Island led, 51–29.

There was little conversation among the coaches during the half — just occasional gibes or comments about a play Buzelis had made. Harrison was clearly distracted — staring, or so it seemed to Kelleher, into the bleachers across the way rather than at the court.

As soon as the half was over, Harrison stood up. "I need to call Coach Taylor."

"Good luck," Amaker said. "There's only one phone in that lobby, and you'll never get to it."

"My cellular's in the car."

"I'll go with you," Kelleher volunteered. "I could use some air."

"What are you two, lovers?" Perrin joked.

"Please keep our secret." Kelleher turned to follow Harrison, who had started down the bleachers without responding to Kelleher's sudden urge for fresh air. Kelleher caught him as they reached the door. Harrison said nothing until they were in the lobby. Then he stopped.

"Look, Bobby, don't follow me around. I said I'd tell you everything when the game's over, and I will. I really am going outside to call my boss, I give you my word on that."

"Fine, then you don't care if I walk out there with you."·

"*Yes I do!*" He stopped himself, realizing he was raising his voice and turning heads. "Look, this is coach-to-coach-type talk, nothing you need to hear."

"It isn't coach-to-coach talk I'm interested in."

"I know that. Look over there by the steps — what do you see?"

Kelleher looked and saw the Buzelis family — all four of them, Nikki included.

"Nikki's standing right there. You see her walk out the door, you feel free to follow her, okay? Otherwise, let me go talk to my boss in peace, and I promise I'll fill you in on the whole thing after the game at the whatchamacallit."

"The Dory."

"Right. Be patient for an hour and you'll understand everything, okay?"

Kelleher hesitated. He looked over at Nikki Buzelis, who was sipping a drink and talking to several people, a wide smile on her face.

"Okay. But if she goes out the door, I'm going with her, and if she heads for you, you'll have to explain what's going on to her and to me."

"Deal." Harrison walked to the front door without so much as a glance toward Nikki Buzelis.

Trying to look casual, Kelleher went and stood by the door that Harrison had just exited, keeping an eye on Nikki. It wasn't difficult: she was taller than most of the people in the lobby, and her blond hair was like a lighthouse on a dark sea.

Five minutes went by, then ten. The crowd started back inside. So did the Buzelises. It occurred to Kelleher that Nikki might wait until everyone was seated, then slip out, so he walked back inside and stood in a corner where he could keep an eye on the family. Nikki Buzelis sat down next to her mother and, as the third quarter began, turned her attention to the game.

There was still no sign of Harrison. Kelleher decided to wait a few more minutes before returning to his seat. The quarter was almost over when, out of the corner of his eye,

Kelleher saw Miles Akley coming back into the gym. Where had Akley been? If Harrison returned in the next few minutes, he was going to have a whole new set of questions to answer.

Kelleher looked up at Amaker and Perrin. By now, they probably *were* convinced that he and Harrison were lovers. A buzzer sounded; Kelleher realized the third quarter was over. Shelter Island had stretched the lead to 80–44. He hadn't even noticed.

Still no Harrison. Nikki Buzelis hadn't moved. Akley was back in the bleachers with his pal from Louisiana. Kelleher decided to go look for Harrison. He walked back through the lobby, turned right, and headed toward the main parking lot. This side of the school was unlit; it was pitch-dark.

He walked around the parking lot for a while, calling Harrison's name. Then he heard the hum of a car engine from the far corner of the lot. Maybe Scott was sitting in his car talking on his cellular; that made more sense. But for forty-five minutes? Kelleher started toward the humming engine and was suddenly struck by how alone he was. The wind rustled in the trees and, for a second, he thought he heard a voice.

He stopped. "Scott?"

He kept walking toward the sound of the engine, his heart pounding wildly. A few feet away, he noticed the door on the driver's side open just the slightest bit. "Scott?" he said more urgently, desperately wanting to hear his friend's voice.

He reached the door and gingerly pulled it open, causing the inside light to come on. Someone was stretched across the driver's seat, his head on the passenger side. "Scott? What're you doing out here, napping?" He was still not even certain it was Scott. He saw blond hair and Minnesota State purple on the arm of the sweat suit. Thank goodness — at least he hadn't stumbled on a couple of kids trying to make out.

"Hey Scott, what the hell are you doing?" He poked his

head into the car and shook Harrison's arm. Then he saw the blood. Suddenly terrified, he reached across the seat and pulled Scott's shoulder up so he could see what had happened to him. As Scott's head came up from the seat, Kelleher screamed. There was a bullet-hole in Scott Harrison's head, with blood gushing from it. Even as he screamed, Kelleher shook Harrison, hoping for some sign of life. There was nothing.

Kelleher let go of the body, which slumped back onto the passenger seat. That was when Kelleher noticed the phone. He heard someone screaming. It was him.

FIVE

MURDER ON SHELTER ISLAND

DURING THE WINTER, Shelter Island had a six-man police force. Ronnie Johnson, whom Kelleher had played pickup basketball with as a teenager, was the first person to arrive. He had been in front of the school on Rte. 114, setting up flares to guide people out of the darkened parking lot, when he heard Kelleher screaming.

Kelleher was sitting slumped by the car, staring at the blood on his hands, when Johnson got to him. He shone a flashlight in his face for a moment before recognizing him.

"Bobby, what the hell happened?"

Kelleher, trembling with cold and terror, got one word out: "Inside." He glanced toward the open car door.

Johnson shifted his flashlight. "My God!" He pulled a walkie-talkie off his belt and began yelling into it.

When he finished, Johnson knelt beside Kelleher. "Are you hurt? An ambulance is on the way for both of you."

"Don't need one." Kelleher was surprised he could find his voice at all. "It's not my blood. He's got a bullet in his head."

"Where's the gun?"

"No idea. I just found him and started screaming."

"Okay, Bobby, don't move — help's on the way."

George Ferrer, the longtime chief of police, arrived about the same time the ambulance did. As soon as he looked at the scene, he turned to Johnson and said, "We'll need Suffolk County over here ASAP."

One of the ambulance attendants, someone Kelleher recognized but couldn't put a name to, was standing by Ferrer. "The guy in the car is dead," he said. "Someone shot him in the head."

Ferrer sighed. "A murder on Shelter Island. Who'd ever believe that? Okay Tom, be careful getting him out. If you see a gun, don't touch it."

He turned to Johnson. "Take Bobby over to the station and clean him up."

He and Johnson helped Kelleher to his feet. "Bobby, you know this guy?" Ferrer asked.

"Scott Harrison." Kelleher was still having trouble catching his breath. He paused. "He's an assistant coach at Minnesota State University. *Was* an assistant. I've known him since I was in college."

Kelleher could hear sirens as more members of the Shelter Island volunteer fire department arrived, responding to the call that had gone out. They were going to be needed, Kelleher thought, for crowd control. The game would be over any minute.

"Chief, can you do me a favor?" Kelleher asked as he got into the front seat of Johnson's car.

"What's that?"

"Two coaches inside came here with Scott tonight — Tom Perrin and Tommy Amaker. They're on the top row of bleachers across from the benches. White guy with glasses, and a young-looking black guy. Ask them to come over to the station."

The drive to the police station took all of thirty seconds, since Town Hall, which housed the police force, was no more than three hundred yards from the front door of the school. Johnson pointed Kelleher to a bathroom so he could clean himself up, then went to make some coffee.

"Don't go wandering off on me now, Bobby," he warned as Kelleher went into the bathroom.

It was either that comment or the hot water he splashed on his face to try and rid himself of the shakes that made Kelleher realize the cops thought of him as a suspect. That was only natural. Often as not in murder cases the person who calls 911 is the murderer. At least when the victim and the murderer knew one another.

Kelleher pulled his face out of the sink and looked at himself in the mirror. He was a mess. No wonder. He had not had a great few hours. For the second time in a little more than a year, he had seen up close what bullets could do to a human being. This made three friends murdered in twelve months. He hadn't been nearly as close to Scott Harrison as he had to Maureen McGuire and Alan Sims, but still . . .

All of this over a basketball player? He couldn't wait to see Miles Akley again. He froze. Akley? What the hell was he thinking about?

He ran out of the bathroom yelling for Johnson. "There's someone else over at the game you've got to get over here!"

"Game's over, Bobby."

"He's probably still there, sniffing around the Buzelises. Guy named Miles Akley."

"The sneaker guy?"

Kelleher remembered that Johnson was a basketball fan.

"Yeah, exactly. He did this, Ronnie. I saw him walk back in the gym just before I went out and found Scott — "

"Whoa, Bobby, slow down. Save it for your statement. I'll see what I can do about finding Akley."

Johnson took him into a small conference room a few minutes later and gave him coffee. He turned on a tape recorder and asked Kelleher to tell him exactly what had happened. Kelleher thought for a second about asking for a lawyer. But no one had read him his rights, so this was strictly preliminary. He told Johnson only about the events from halftime on: Scott saying he was going to his car to call Bobby Taylor; Kelleher waiting for him in the lobby and then in the corner of the gym until the end of the third quarter; deciding to go look for him shortly after seeing Akley walk back into the gym. He left out the Nikki-Scott pregame meeting.

"Why would Akley have been talking to Harrison?" Johnson asked.

"I have no idea. That's what I was hoping to find out."

"And I imagine plenty of people could verify that you were in the lobby during halftime and standing in that corner of the gym during the third quarter?"

"I wasn't talking to anyone specific, but I would think, yeah, a lot of people would remember seeing me."

"You understand why that's important?"

"Sure I do, Ronnie. You find a guy with someone who has a bullet through his head, he has to be a suspect on some level."

Johnson nodded. "Okay, I just don't want you to think we're picking on you. Now listen to me. The Suffolk County detectives will be here soon, and they'll want you to tell the whole story again. Be patient."

"I'm not under arrest, am I?"

"Have you been in handcuffs? Have I read you your rights? No, you aren't under arrest. But you are going to have to answer a lot of questions."

Ferrer came in. "Those two coaches you asked for are here. You can see them for a few minutes, but then you have to talk to the Suffolk County guys. They just got to the ferry, so they should be here in fifteen or twenty minutes."

Amaker and Perrin came in looking shaken. "What in the world happened out there?" Perrin asked softly.

Kelleher told them. He considered filling them in on Nikki Buzelis's pregame meeting with Harrison but decided against it. He didn't need that all over the coaching grapevine — not at the moment.

"I waved to get your attention during the third quarter," Amaker said. "I couldn't figure out why you were standing down there."

"Good. Tell the cops that. The more people who verify that I was in the gym, the better off I am."

"They think you did it?" Perrin asked.

"No. But I'm automatically a suspect, since I was the one who found him."

"Someone needs to call Coach Taylor," Amaker suggested. "He shouldn't hear this on the news."

Perrin looked at his watch. "Do you want us to stay over?" he asked Kelleher.

Kelleher shook his head. "No. I'm fine. Go catch the last ferry. But Tommy's right, someone should call Taylor."

Once they were gone, two Suffolk County detectives came in. They introduced themselves as Detectives Nyquist and Tonelli. Nyquist was in his fifties, Tonelli in his thirties. They good-cop bad-copped Kelleher, which didn't surprise him. Nyquist kept demanding to know what had *really* happened between him and Scott Harrison, while Tonelli soothingly told him it would be better for him to tell the truth now, rather than later, if he had done it.

Kelleher had known enough cops in his day to understand they were just doing their job, so he tried to be patient. But as the night wore on, he began to get sick of the whole thing. "Why the hell aren't you guys questioning Miles Akley?" he asked as they started through the story for a fourth time. "I'm telling you, he's the one who did this."

"We're trying to find Akley," Tonelli said. "He wasn't at the gym when the Shelter Island guys went back looking for him at your request."

"Doesn't that interest you?" Kelleher asked. "The guy is here to woo the Buzelis family, and he doesn't even hang around after the game? What does that tell you?"

"Worry about yourself, Kelleher," Nyquist said. "We'll worry about Akley."

"Yeah, yeah," Kelleher replied. "Look, I told you guys, I'm a reporter. Don't you think I know a good cop–bad cop routine when I see it? I've done a few of them myself." The two detectives looked at one another and said nothing. "I didn't kill Scott. I wouldn't know how to shoot a gun on a bet and the guy was my friend. That's why I went to look for him. I was worried about him."

"But you admit, your fingerprints will be all over the car," Nyquist said.

"Of course. I touched the door, I touched the steering wheel and the seat. Have you found a weapon yet? If you have, I guaran-damn-tee you my prints aren't on *it*."

Ferrer walked in. "Can I see you gentlemen for a minute?"

The two detectives walked outside, leaving Kelleher alone. He glanced at his watch. It was almost two o'clock. A wave of exhaustion rolled over him; he wanted to go home and get some sleep. He wanted Miles Akley arrested, although part of him fantasized about chasing him down himself. He thought about Scott again. Dead. It was impossible. He remembered what Ferrer had said: "A murder on Shelter Island?"

The three cops came back into the room. Tonelli spoke to him. "Mr. Kelleher, Chief Ferrer says he's got a number of witnesses who remember seeing you in the lobby during half-time and several more who say they noticed you standing in the corner during the third quarter. So your story seems to hold up. In fact, there's a reporter — what's her name, George?"

"Tamara Mearns. She's our local person here."

"Yeah, well, anyway, she says she was getting up from her seat to go ask you why you were standing where you were when you turned and walked out at the end of the third quarter."

"And all of this means?"

"It means you're free to go. But I'm going to ask you to let Chief Ferrer know where you're going to be if you leave Shelter Island, at least until we have someone in custody."

"That's no problem."

"Do you need a ride home, Bobby?" Ferrer asked.

"Actually, my car's still at the gym."

"I'll take you to it."

Kelleher and Ferrer walked out, leaving the detectives behind. When they got to the tiny waiting area, it was deserted, except for one person sitting in a chair by the door: Tamara Mearns.

Ferrer smiled. "I'll say this for you, Tamara — you're persistent."

"Well, I've been trying to talk to him since the end of the third quarter." It was the first time Kelleher had seen her smile. Even in his state of exhaustion, he noticed that she had remarkable dimples.

"I was just going to give Bobby a ride to his car."

"How about if I do it?"

Ferrer turned to Kelleher. "Okay with you?"

Kelleher shrugged. "Fine with me." Ferrer gave him a pat on the back and returned to the conference room.

Kelleher looked at Mearns. "I guess I owe you that much."

"You don't owe me a thing. But I do think we should talk."

"Okay. Your car or mine?"

He wanted to get out of his clothes, which still had Scott Harrison's blood on them, so she dropped him at his car and then followed him to his house. Kelleher knew Mearns wanted to talk to him about the murder, and he was wired enough to ignore his exhaustion. He knew he wouldn't be able to sleep, so he might as well talk.

He showed Mearns where the coffee and coffeemaker were and then went to change. When the coffee was ready, they sat down in the living room. She took a sip and smiled, showing the dimples again.

"So, just how awful do you feel?"

He forced a laugh, half sad, half bitter. "On a scale of one to ten, ten being really awful, I'm about twelve. But that's down from fifteen a couple of hours ago."

She nodded. "Just how well did you know him?"

"Since college. He was a graduate assistant coach my last two years at Virginia. It wasn't like we kept in close touch, but we would talk a couple times a year, or I would run into him at a game someplace. We were friends, but not close friends."

"For someone who's a big media star, you haven't had a whole lot of luck keeping friends alive in the last year, have you?"

It brought him up short. "What are you talking about?"

She stood up and walked over to the fireplace, still holding the coffee mug. "After I acted like such a jerk in the office the other day, I called a friend of mine in Washington to see if you really had worked at the *Herald*. You can imagine how embarrassed I felt when she told me who you were and your role in the Paulsen story."

He was tempted to tell her the whole story so she would understand, but he resisted. "My role in the Paulsen story wasn't nearly as big a deal as a lot of people think it was."

She drained the coffee and sat down. "Anyway, I found out you were a big-time reporter and I treated you like some kind of unemployed hack. Even if you were an unemployed hack, I shouldn't have been rude to you the way I was. I was having one of those days, and I just didn't handle the situation — "

He put up a hand. "No apology necessary. I wasn't exactly Mr. Warmth. Tell me why you wanted to talk to me."

He wasn't rushing her, but he was starting to feel profoundly tired in spite of the coffee. She looked at her watch. "It's almost four, isn't it? If you're really tired — "

"No, no. I won't sleep anyway, no matter how tired I am."

"Okay then. I know you think Miles Akley did this. And from what I know about Akley and this whole situation, he's certainly the most logical suspect — "

"Whoa, just a minute there. What do you know about Akley?" Nothing she had written in the *Reporter* — at least since he had arrived — had indicated she had any idea who Akley was or what he might be up to.

She folded her arms. "Miles Akley. Brickley Shoes. Fred Murray's bagman for years. Murray needs a player; Akley delivers. Murray desperately needs Rytis Buzelis. Akley is bound and determined to see to it that he gets him. And if your theory about tonight is correct, he'll stop at nothing to get him."

Kelleher was surprised and impressed. Just as she had underestimated him, he had underestimated her. "Why hasn't any of this appeared in the *Reporter*?"

"I can't get anyone to go on the record. And I don't want to write it until I've got it nailed — if I can ever get it nailed."

"I know what you mean about getting people on the record. But now the stakes are different. Now Akley has to deal with the cops."

"You're convinced he did it?"

"Who else around here would be that ruthless? We aren't talking about a fight that escalated into a shootout. This was cold-blooded, calculated, bullet-through-the-head murder."

"And Akley wanted Harrison dead because — ?"

"My guess is, he decided Harrison was the one serious roadblock left between him and the kid."

"You think there's anything to that?"

He wasn't sure. Nor was he sure just how much information he wanted to share with her. He shrugged. "Doesn't really matter if I think so. Apparently Akley thought so."

She stood up and pointed at his coffee mug. "More?"

He shook his head. "I'll never sleep again if I drink another sip."

She disappeared into the kitchen and returned with a full mug. She sat down and looked him right in the eye.

"Look, Kelleher, I realize we barely know each other, and we didn't exactly start off on the right foot. But I think we both might benefit if we work together on this story, even though I'm still not sure exactly who you're working on it for."

"Me neither. It's one of those things like the firehouse dog who hears the alarm and starts barking. I can't help myself."

She smiled. "I understand. The point is, you know a lot of these basketball guys. I know the family and what's been going on, because I've been here. We could help each other."

"I'm not sure you need any help. You seem to have a pretty clear idea of what's going on."

She shook her head. "You're wrong — I do need help. I speak English. These coaches speak basketball. You speak their language. I don't."

"How well do you know the family? I had the impression they're wary of the media — especially the father."

"They are. But they weren't at the start of the season. Rytis is always polite to me, but again, there's the language barrier — basketball, that is. I can't talk to him the way some-one like you could. Arturas was a lot more open with me be-fore Akley became a regular at the games. Nadia — well, to tell you the truth, she'll tell me just about anything."

"And what does she tell you about Akley?"

She held up a hand. "Are we in this together?"

He sighed. He wasn't really sure what *this* was anymore. It certainly wasn't what it had been a few hours ago when Scott Harrison was alive. It now involved people who would kill to get what they wanted. That scared him, but it also made him want the story all the more. The woman sitting across from him reminded him in many ways of Maureen McGuire. She was smart and attractive and knew what had to be done to get a story. But Maureen was dead. The way he was losing friends, he was almost frightened to take on another partner.

"You know my last partner ended up dead. So did my best source. Tonight makes three friends in twelve months."

"You think you're a jinx?"

"I don't know about a jinx. But I do appear to be someone it can be dangerous to hang around with."

"I'll take my chances."

He forced a laugh. "I suspected you would. Maureen would have said the same thing."

"Your partner."

"Yeah." He didn't want to talk about Maureen. "Tell me about Nadia Buzelis."

She took a long sip of coffee. "She's scared. This whole thing has mushroomed so quickly. I talked to her tonight for just a minute, right after you found Harrison. She was almost hysterical. She said something about making Arturas call the whole thing off. I couldn't keep her talking to find out what she meant about 'the whole thing.' "

"So she knows what Akley's all about."

"I don't think she thought he was a murderer, but neither did I. She's fully aware of the fact that his job is to make sure Rytis ends up at Louisiana no matter what the cost."

"Where was Nikki Buzelis while all this was happening?"

"Didn't see her. Why?"

He told her about the meeting he had witnessed between Nikki Buzelis and Scott Harrison before the game. Her eyes went wide as he described the conversation and the intimacy between the two.

"I see why Akley would consider Harrison a serious threat. Nikki and Rytis are very close."

She had told him something he didn't know. "How close?"

"Talk on the phone all the time, according to Nadia. She came out to games basically because he wanted her to. Or at least that's what I thought."

He leaned back in his chair. "We need to talk to Rytis and Nikki. And to Nadia again."

"Nadia is no problem — although with all this going on, who knows what Arturas is going to be like? Rytis and Nikki are another story. I've never done anything more than shake Nikki's hand. Rytis, like I told you, is polite to me, but that's about it."

"Think he'd talk to me?"

"If you could get him alone someplace, maybe. You could talk to him player to player. He might relate to that."

"I wasn't anywhere close to being the kind of player he is."

She shook her head vehemently. "Doesn't matter. You *played*."

"Okay, but when?"

She drained her coffee mug, which reminded Kelleher that he desperately needed to go to the bathroom.

"I'll be right back." He walked into the bathroom, shut the door, and was breathing a deep sigh of relief when suddenly there was a pounding on the door.

"Kelleher, I've got it!"

"Hang on a minute!" he shouted back.

When he came out, she had a sheepish grin on her face. "Sorry about that, but it just hit me. The last few weeks Rytis has been going down to the gym on Saturday mornings to shoot by himself. He likes to work on moves and things, and he enjoys the privacy."

"No one goes with him? Not even the old man?"

"No. He sleeps in on Saturdays. Rytis usually gets to the gym by eight, shoots for an hour, and is home by the time Arturas wakes up. He has his own key to the back door — you know, by the baseball field?"

He knew it well. "Nadia told you about this?"

"Yes. The question is, after what happened, will he still show up?"

"Only one way to find out." He looked at his watch. It was just past 4:30.

"Why don't I pick you up here at eight? You're on my way to the school anyway."

"I thought you said I should try to talk to him alone."

"You should. But I'll drive you down there. I can be a lookout in case someone shows up."

It wasn't a bad idea. "Okay. Deal."

He stood up and stretched, feeling the exhaustion in every single pore of his body. "You'll be here at eight?"

"Sharp."

He walked her out to her car, shivering without a jacket. Standing in the driveway, she turned around and looked at the water. "This really is a beautiful spot, isn't it?" she asked softly.

There was a touch of moonlight on her face and a couple of snowflakes in her hair. She smiled at him, and he felt suddenly drawn to her. He knew it was a combination of exhaustion and shock and cold and loneliness and her dimples. He also knew the last thing in the world he needed right now was to be involved with someone — even assuming she had any interest in him.

"What are you thinking?" It roused him from his reverie.

"That you're right, this is a beautiful spot. I forget sometimes."

She put out her hand. "I'll see you in about three hours."

He accepted the hand, resisting the urge to pull her toward him, feeling like a fool for having the urge at all. "I'll be here. Drive carefully."

She smiled and got in the car. Walking back into the house, he started up the stairs. Then he stopped and went back down. For the first time in almost thirty years, he locked the doors before going to sleep.

The alarm woke him about a minute after he fell asleep, or so it seemed. He had tossed and turned for a while, fighting to get the sight of Scott Harrison slumped across the seat out of his head. He finally did what he always did when he couldn't sleep: replayed basketball games in his head. He dropped into a heavy, dreamless sleep that was interrupted by the buzzer. He blinked his eyes at the clock, which said 7:40.

After stumbling into a brief, desperately needed shower, he made fresh coffee and walked out the door carrying two mugs — he figured Mearns would be ready for more — just as she pulled up.

"Thanks," she said, accepting the coffee. "Had one, but I can always use more."

"You really are a newspaper guy, aren't you?" Kelleher remarked.

The snow had stopped, but the roads were slick. They were also empty. Shelter Island on a snowy winter morning looked like a ghost town. The road directly in front of the school was still blocked off by police guardrails, so they circled around back and pulled into the parking lot by the baseball field. A mini-van was the only car in the lot.

"Arturas's car," Mearns noted. "Rytis is here."

"Yeah, but maybe Arturas came with him."

"Doubt it. Like I said, he sleeps Saturdays. He lets Rytis drive the van on weekends, when he's not working."

Kelleher was beginning to have second thoughts about this idea. He didn't want to walk into the gym and find Arturas Buzelis there — or, worse, Akley or one of his henchmen. And if the kid was alone, what was he going to ask him? "Have you been bought by Miles Akley?" "You know anything about your sister having an affair with the late Scott Harrison?"

She read his mind. "Even if someone's in there, you'll see them before they see you. And you don't have to ask the tough questions first, you know."

He smiled. "I know. I've done this once or twice before."

She blushed. "Sorry. But you know what I mean."

"You're right. Okay. If anyone we know shows up, stall them or something."

"Yeah. Or something. Good luck."

He jumped out of the car and sprinted for the back door. He walked down the hall in the direction of the gym, and heard the thud-thud sound of a ball being dribbled. He slowed as he approached the door. He was wearing a running suit and sneakers, and he was convinced the squeaking sound of the shoes could be heard for miles. When he got to the door, he paused. He wondered if he would hear voices, but all he heard was the ball: thud-thud, pause, *swish;* thud-thud.

Slowly, he peeked around the open door. The only person in the gym was Rytis Buzelis. He was at the far end of the court, his back to Kelleher, shooting short jump shots from the foul-line extended. He was wearing the brand-new Brickley 999 sweat suit and Brickley Aeroplane sneakers. Total cost, by Kelleher's estimate: five hundred dollars.

Kelleher stood in the doorway for several seconds watching Buzelis work. He had seen a few players during his lifetime who looked so comfortable with the basketball that it appeared to be almost an extension of their hand. Jordan had it; Bird; Magic. Kelleher could think of two or three others.

This kid had it. It all looked so easy, so natural. Kelleher was transfixed for a moment, watching. Then he remembered why he was there. Slowly, he started walking up the court. Buzelis was so intent on what he was doing that Kelleher was almost at the top of the key before he noticed him.

He stopped dribbling and turned around, a quizzical look on his face.

"Hi, Rytis," Kelleher said, extending a hand. "I'm Bobby Kelleher."

If the name meant anything to the kid, it didn't register on his face. He took Kelleher's hand and nodded. "I am Rytis Buzelis."

He was extremely handsome, with the same blue eyes as his mother and sister, and a firm handshake. He released Kelleher's hand and looked at him as if to say, "So?"

"You look very comfortable with the basketball in your hands," Kelleher said, hoping to make small talk.

Buzelis shrugged. "I know I need to work to become better." He paused. "I do not mean to be rude, but have I seen you before?"

Kelleher shook his head. "No, I've just been back here for a couple of weeks. I grew up here — summers, at least — and I'm here on a vacation."

"Now?"

Kelleher laughed. No one could seem to grasp the idea that someone might come to Shelter Island voluntarily during the winter. "Yeah, well, I was looking for some peace and quiet. Instead, I found you."

Buzelis frowned. "You are a coach, then?"

He *was* just like his mother. "Worse. A reporter."

If Rytis thought that was funny, he stifled his laughter. "I am sorry, Mr. — "

"Call me Bobby."

"Okay. I am sorry, Bobby. I cannot talk to the press."

"Because of your dad?"

He smiled. "Because I cannot talk to the press."

Something in the smile hinted at playfulness. It wasn't as if he were turning his back to continue shooting. Spur of the moment, Kelleher took a long shot.

"You know, once upon a time, about a hundred years ago, I played. I wasn't very good, but I loved to practice by myself early in the morning, just like you. That's why I took a chance you'd be here."

Buzelis had walked to within a few feet of Kelleher. Up close, he was bigger than Kelleher had thought, with the kind of body that appeared to be sculpted from stone. Kelleher wondered if someone had put him on a weight program or if he came by his build naturally.

"Yes, so, you played. Where?"

"Virginia. Although it would be more accurate to say I *didn't* play. I was a benchwarmer on some very good teams."

"You are here then to recruit me for Virginia?" The hint of a smile had become a real one.

"No, I'll leave that to the coaches. My interest in you is as a reporter."

"And, as I said to you, my father prefers that I do not speak to reporters."

Kelleher put a hand up. "I understand, but I'm asking you to do me a favor this morning, because Scott Harrison was a friend of mine. In fact, I'm the one who found him last night. Don't you see why it would be important to me to find out who killed him?"

The kid's face clouded. "I am very, very sorry about Coach Harrison. He was a good person. But I do not see how I can help you with this. And even if I could, I would still have to speak to my father first."

Kelleher was now ready to take his gamble. "I'll tell you what, Rytis. How about I play you to five, right now. If you win, I'll go away and leave you alone. If I win, you talk to me for a few minutes — right here, right now — and your dad will never know we talked."

The kid was studying him, trying to decide if he was serious or seriously nuts. "You would play against me? One against one? I score five points and you go?"

"Yup."

He stifled a giggle and shrugged his shoulders. "If this is what you want, I will do that."

Kelleher reached into the back of his sweatpants and tossed aside the notebook he had brought. "Give me a minute to take a couple warmup shots. I haven't played in a while." Buzelis tossed him the ball. Kelleher dribbled to about ten feet and tossed a jumper that hit the back rim.

It had been only a little more than a week since he had played; all he needed was a few shots to warm up. Shooting had never been a problem for him. Getting his shot off had been the problem. The notion that he could beat this kid one on one, even in a game to five, was absurd, except for a couple of factors he was counting on: watching Buzelis play, he had noticed that his fundamentals, especially on defense, were awful. That wasn't surprising, given his inexperience as a player and the fact that Joe Dierker couldn't coach fish to swim. Buzelis would learn fundamentals when he got to college — if he chose the right one.

The other thing Kelleher had going for him was attitude. His whole game in high school and college had been built around toughness and smarts. For forty minutes a night in the ACC, that wasn't enough to make up for his lack of size and speed. But for a couple of minutes, playing a cocky kid, it might be enough. He had to get the ball first, though, to have any chance. If Buzelis got it, he would score at will, and the game would be over.

Kelleher tried a couple more shots, never going outside fifteen feet. The stroke came back quickly, and he felt adrenaline beginning to pump. Having played pickup ball twice a week, he was in decent shape. He walked to the foul line, holding the ball under his arm.

"First one to make one takes the ball out?" he asked.

Buzelis dropped a second ball he had picked up. "Please, go ahead." The words were polite, but the tone said, "Go ahead so I can whip you fast and get you out of here."

Kelleher smiled, bounced the ball twice, and looked at the rim. He had often wondered, sitting on the end of the bench in college, how he would have responded had he ever been asked to make a free throw to win a game. Now he had the chance to find out.

Kelleher took a deep breath and shot. The ball hit the front rim. Then it rolled up, over, and into the basket. Buzelis smiled, not the least bit concerned.

"Your ball." He flipped it back to Kelleher, who retreated beyond the top of the key.

Kelleher tossed the ball back to him, giving him the school-yard check. When you played half-court anywhere, you always let your opponent have the ball before you started to play.

Once he passed it back to you, he was ready to go. For a moment, Kelleher wondered if Buzelis had played enough schoolyard ball to know the unspoken rules.

One year in New York had been enough. "Straight up?" Rytis asked.

In some schoolyards, the defensive team could go straight up with the ball for a shot after rebounding a miss. In most places, the ball had to come back beyond the foul line after a change of possession. That gave the team switching from offense to defense a reasonable chance to set up. Kelleher didn't want Buzelis grabbing his first miss and dunking unmolested.

He shook his head. "Take it back."

Buzelis nodded and bounced the ball back to Kelleher. He was a good five feet from him and wasn't even bending down to get into anything resembling a defensive stance. As soon as Kelleher caught the return pass, he took one quick dribble to the top of the key and shot. *Swish.*

"One-zip," he remarked, backing up. Buzelis smiled as if to say, "Okay, so you *have* played before." This time, when Kelleher gave him his check, he walked up within two feet of him.

Kelleher took the ball and put his head down as if to dribble. Buzelis went down with him. Without dribbling, Kelleher pulled the ball over his head, went up quickly, and got his shot off before Buzelis could react. It rolled around the rim and dropped through.

"Two-zip."

Buzelis said nothing. This time, he handed the ball back to Kelleher and got right in his face after taking his check. No more quick jump shots. Kelleher faked the move he had just used and got Buzelis off his feet trying to block the shot. A player who knew fundamentals would never have gone for that kind of fake. Buzelis bought it completely. As he dribbled past the stunned Buzelis, Kelleher remembered something Bobby

Knight had once said: "Is there anything better in life than a really good shot-fake?" As he laid the ball off the glass, it occurred to him that a good shot-fake might not be the *best* thing in life, but it had just climbed considerably higher on his list.

"Three-zip," he noted, taking the ball as it came through the basket and flipping it back to Buzelis, who was standing flat-footed at the foul line.

"How long since you last played?" Buzelis asked, a noticeable bit of sarcasm in his voice.

"A week."

Buzelis set himself on the floor, clearly determined not to go for any more fakes. Kelleher went back to basics, going straight up as soon as he caught Buzelis's return pass. Buzelis was so quick that he almost got to the shot — but not quite. The shot just cleared his fingertips and slid through the net. Kelleher hadn't felt this kind of rush in years. Maybe he could make a comeback at thirty-one.

"Four-zip."

Buzelis was not a happy camper. He didn't say a word as he passed the ball back to Kelleher one more time. Kelleher head-bobbed as if to shoot right away. Buzelis lunged at him. Kelleher cut past him and thought he had an open layup. This time, though, Buzelis hadn't left his feet completely, and he recovered more quickly than Kelleher had anticipated. As Kelleher went up, Buzelis came up behind him, leaped over his head, and cleanly blocked the shot.

Kelleher wanted to call a foul, but he knew he hadn't been fouled. Buzelis grabbed the loose ball, took two dribbles back to the foul line, turned, took one giant step, and dunked before Kelleher had a chance to do something stupid, like getting in the way.

"Four-one," he announced, giving Kelleher a look that said, "Party's over."

Kelleher's vigor had evaporated. He picked the ball up off the floor and flipped it to Buzelis, who gave him a check, took two dribbles, and went right over him for a layup.

"Four-two." The smile was starting to come back.

Kelleher nodded, trying to catch his breath. Buzelis made the exact same move again, and Kelleher realized the game was going to be over in about thirty seconds.

"Four-three," Buzelis crowed. Kelleher bent over and took a deep breath before tossing the ball back. Buzelis took one dribble right at Kelleher as if to go over him again. Bravely, Kelleher tried to step under him to take a charge, even though he knew perfectly well that there was no such thing as taking a charge in the schoolyard. The kid was laughing as he swiveled to his right, wheeled past Kelleher, and dunked.

"Four-four. I need to win by two?"

"No. Five does it."

He was done — he knew that. He cursed himself for not taking the jump shot at 4–0. He bounce-passed the ball to Buzelis at the top of the key and stood five feet away, hoping he might somehow be lucky and strip him off the dribble as he went by. To his surprise, Buzelis caught the ball and, without dribbling, went straight up to shoot.

"Three-pointer," he announced gleefully, going up from just outside the three-point line. The cockiness had returned. Resigned, Kelleher turned to watch the ball come down. It hit the back rim, bounded high into the air — and missed. Kelleher heard a screech of pain from Buzelis and felt him bearing down to try to snatch the rebound. Instinctively, he stuck his butt out to clear space and clutched the ball just as Buzelis reached over him for it.

With one last chance, Kelleher dribbled quickly past the foul line and turned to see Buzelis charging at him. If he tried to drive, the kid would smother him. He stopped the dribble short and went up to shoot as Buzelis launched himself. Kelleher saw the shot clear his hands and then heard a thud as the huge youngster crashed into him.

"Foul!" he screamed as they both went down. He saw Buzelis jerk his head in the direction of the basket, all the while trying unsuccessfully to catch Kelleher. Kelleher cushioned his fall with his right hand and felt a stinging in his wrist. He cried out as he landed, Buzelis on top of him.

"What happened?" Kelleher demanded.

Buzelis was stretched out on the floor, face down. For a second, Kelleher thought he was hurt. He could see the headlines now: "Superstar Injured in Pickup Game with Reporter." Talk about getting too involved in a story.

"You okay?" Kelleher asked tentatively.

Buzelis raised his head and forced a smile. "Your shot went in. You have won, five–four."

Kelleher wondered if he were joking. No. The look on his face was not that of someone making a joke. The pain in his wrist began to subside, and he felt himself grinning foolishly. "I made that shot? No kidding."

Buzelis was sitting up. "No kidding," he echoed. "My friends call that kind of shot a 'pierre.' "

"A *prayer*, Rytis; they call it a prayer." Kelleher tried not to laugh, but failed. As good as the kid's English was, his hoops slang needed some work.

Buzelis was actually laughing. "Yes, that's right. A prayer. In any case, I doubt you could make it again in a hundred tries. But you did make it."

Kelleher stood up, rubbing the wrist, dusting himself off. "I guess my prayer was answered. So, we talk?"

Buzelis nodded. "My friends have another name for you that I cannot remember — for someone who says he is no good but really is very good."

"A hustler?" Kelleher snorted. "If only it were true, Rytis. I'm just old and experienced. You'll be both those things soon enough, believe me."

"I should have won five–zero," Buzelis said, shaking his head.

"Damn right." Kelleher retrieved his notebook. "You still have some things to learn about playing defense, but that'll come. You just need some coaching."

Rytis smiled. "You do not think much of Coach Dierker, then?"

"I almost never think of Coach Dierker," Kelleher replied with a grin.

Buzelis was laughing. "Bobby, I think maybe you do know your hoops." He sat down on the empty bleacher. "You know, even if you had not made that shot, I would have talked to you, because I think you must be pretty smart about basketball to play as you do."

"Well, thanks, Rytis. I promise this will be painless."

Buzelis shrugged. "What is it I can tell you? If I can help find who killed Coach Harrison, I would be very happy."

"So would I, Rytis. So would I."

Kelleher started out with easy questions, sticking to basketball and the story he already knew, about how the Buzelis family came to Shelter Island. Buzelis had been through this before and talked easily about his memories of Lithuania, even going so far as to show Kelleher the scar just below his shoulder where the bullet had hit him two winters earlier.

They talked about his growth spurt, his trying to fit in, first in New York and then on the Island, and, finally, his reaction to all the attention and pressure. Kelleher liked Rytis Buzelis. He was modest without being patronizing, confident without being cocky. Maybe he had lost some cockiness in their little game.

It was the kid who changed the subject from basketball to murder. "You are asking me all very easy questions. That is very polite of you. But you said you wanted to talk about Coach Harrison."

"I do. In reporting, they teach you to ask the easy questions first."

Buzelis smiled. "How did you become a reporter?"

"I wasn't good enough at basketball." Buzelis laughed. Kelleher decided this was a good time to weigh in. "Rytis, what do you know about Coach Harrison?"

The blue eyes clouded. "I liked him very much. So did my family — except, I guess, for my father."

"Why didn't your father like him?"

Buzelis looked at him as if sizing him up. "No more easy questions, eh? I am not sure, Bobby, how much I should or should not say to you."

Normally, with a stranger, you avoided tipping your hand about how much you might know about a story. People were more likely to tell you what was going on if they thought it was common knowledge. But sometimes you had to take a risk — let the person know that you knew a lot — so they would tell you more to prove they were still ahead of you. Playing dumb, Kelleher decided, wasn't going to get him very far with Rytis Buzelis.

"Look, Rytis, I know all about Miles Akley. I know how much he wants you to go to Louisiana, and I know he's become close to your father. When I talked to your mother, I had the impression that your father wants you to go to Louisiana, but she isn't so sure. And maybe your sisters aren't so sure, either."

He was climbing out on a limb with the last statement, but he took the chance.

"What do you know about my sisters?"

"Your mother told me that Vida works on Wall Street and

Nikki is a model. I saw Nikki for the first time last night. She's extremely beautiful."

He wondered if Rytis even knew about Nikki's relationship with Scott Harrison. He wasn't about to bring it up — not yet, at least.

Buzelis sighed. "You are right about Miles Akley and my father. But it is not as simple as you probably think. Miles wants me to go to Louisiana, yes, and my father wants me to go there too, but it is not because my father is a bad man."

Now it was time to play the innocent. Trashing the kid's father would accomplish nothing and might blow the rapport he had established. "I don't have any doubt about your dad being a good man. But shouldn't the most important question here be what's best for *you*?"

"No. That is not the most important question."

"How can it not be?"

"You do not understand."

"You're right. Help me out."

He smiled. "On this, I cannot. Look, I think I have paid my debt. It is time for me to go home."

"Hang on, two more minutes." He was groping. "Your mom liked Scott. You liked Scott. What about your sisters, did they know him?"

Buzelis stiffened. "Yes, they did." His voice was soft now. Kelleher waited, not wanting to push too hard. "Nikki . . . liked him very much. But please — you must not write about that. Mother and father did not know anything. Only Vida and I . . ."

Kelleher leaned forward and put his hand on Buzelis's shoulder. "Rytis, this is really important. Is there any way that Miles Akley knew?"

Buzelis stared at him. "I know what you are thinking."

"And?"

"I do not know."

"Rytis, I think it's very important that I talk to Nikki. Sooner or later the police — "

He stopped, hearing footsteps in the hallway. He swiveled around on the bleacher seat just in time to see Arturas Buzelis and Miles Akley come racing into the gym.

"Rytis!" the elder Buzelis screamed at his son, who stood up at rigid attention at the sound of his father's voice. "What are you doing? Get over here right now!"

Rytis Buzelis jumped off the bleacher and took two quick steps to his father's side. Kelleher sat frozen, having no idea what might happen next. For one second he thought of making a run for it, but that was silly. After all, he wasn't doing anything wrong.

Arturas Buzelis spoke sharply to his son in Lithuanian for about thirty seconds. When he was finished, Rytis sprinted for the door. Then Buzelis and Akley moved in on Kelleher. He snapped his notebook shut and shoved it into his back pocket.

"How dare you!" Arturas Buzelis screamed. "Have I not warned you about speaking to my family before? Do you not have any respect for a family's privacy? I told you the rules!"

"The rules change when people get killed, Mr. Buzelis," Kelleher said, making certain to keep his voice calm and quiet. "I never got a chance to ask Rytis any questions, but if I had, I would have wanted to know about how you and Mr. Akley here felt about Scott Harrison."

He wanted to leave the impression that he really hadn't had a chance to glean any information from Rytis.

"I told you, Arturas," Akley said. "He was the one who tried to give the police the idea that I was involved. Isn't that right, Kelleher? You show up with the dead body, but you start screaming I'm the one who did it."

"*You* were the one who disappeared from the gym during the

third quarter, Akley. And you're the one who might have lost his star recruit because of Scott. Not me."

Akley walked over and, as he had done the night before, put his face right up against Kelleher's. "I'm getting really tired of your shit, you know that?"

"Did you bring your gun, Akley? Why don't you just put a bullet through my head, too?"

Akley grabbed Kelleher's arms and pushed him backward, so that both of them fell off the bleacher onto the gym floor. Kelleher turned his head to cushion the blow of hitting the floor and somehow managed to roll over on top of Akley. Before he could move, Arturas Buzelis grabbed his arms from behind and pulled him up. Kelleher struggled for a moment to free himself, but Buzelis was bigger and stronger than he was.

Akley got to his feet and came at Kelleher, who cringed, expecting to be hit. "I ought to just beat the crap out of you," Akley snarled. "But that would give you an excuse to run back to the police or something."

"It takes a real tough guy to beat someone up while his arms are being held," Kelleher retorted. "Make this one on one, and then we'll see what happens."

"Let him go, Arturas," Akley ordered, his face beet red.

"No, Miles — we are not here for a stupid fight. Say what you have to say and let's go."

Akley looked at Buzelis, then at Kelleher, and nodded. He stuck a finger in Kelleher's face. "Now look — I'll say this once, and that's gonna be it. I don't kill people. I wouldn't even kill a little scumbag like you. I have no idea what happened to Scott Harrison last night, or why it happened. I *liked* Scott Harrison."

He leaned forward and put his face even closer to Kelleher's. "But I'll tell you one thing. You go around accusing me of murder, and I promise — I mean *promise* — you'll be sorry. I'll hit you with libel and slander suits that will make your head spin!"

Kelleher felt an almost overwhelming urge to shove Akley out of his face. Instead, he stared back at him and said, "Truth's an absolute defense, you smarmy piece of shit. Anyway, you don't have to convince me you didn't kill Scott, you have to convince the cops. And don't threaten me. I don't know who the fuck you think you are or who you think you're dealing with, but I'll do or say whatever the hell I want." Buzelis had relaxed his grip. Kelleher pulled free and turned to face them. "I'll prove you're guilty, Akley. I promise you that!"

Before Akley could respond, Buzelis pulled him away. He pointed a finger at Kelleher. "I will not tell you this again. You stay away from my family. If you come near them again, I will call the police."

Kelleher had a lot of answers to that comment, but there was no sense continuing a pissing match that had already gone on too long.

"Whatever you do, Mr. Buzelis, I just hope it's what's best for your son."

Now it was Buzelis in his face, pointing a finger. "I will do what must be done. And whatever that is, it is none of your affair."

He turned and walked out of the gym, Akley a couple of steps behind. Kelleher didn't move for a minute after they left. Then he sat down and took a deep breath. He checked his back pocket to make sure his notebook was still there.

This story was getting curiouser by the minute. He wondered if the cops had talked to Miles Akley yet, and if so, what he had said to them. Finding that out would be easy. What really needed to be done wouldn't be as easy: locating Nikki Buzelis and getting her to talk about Scott Harrison.

He took a deep breath and started for the door. The two basketballs were still on the floor. He picked one up, dribbled to the foul line, and shot a jumper. It swished.

"Nice shot."

Tamara Mearns was standing in the doorway.

"You know, as a lookout, you're a little late," he remarked.

She smiled sheepishly. "I blew it. After you'd been in here a few minutes, I figured you had gotten him to talk and it would be a little while. I swung over to Carol's for coffee. When I came back, Akley's Cadillac was in the parking lot."

"You didn't come running to my rescue."

"I thought about calling the cops. Then I figured that was crazy — they wouldn't do anything stupid."

"Why not? They may have done something really stupid last night."

"Miles maybe, not Arturas. He's not that kind of man."

"Easy for you to say."

"Look, Kelleher, if you'll shut up a minute, I'll tell you the rest, and then you'll tell me I'm a genius."

"I wouldn't bet the ranch."

"I had just gotten out of the car to come look for you when Rytis came running out. He looked terrified."

"He was."

"Anyway, he sees me and comes running over."

"And?"

"He asked me if I had something to write on. I gave him my notebook. He wrote a phone number on the back and said, 'You must give this to Bobby. Tell him he must speak to Nikki.' Then he got in the car and drove off. I parked across the street and waited until I saw them come out."

"You have Nikki's phone number?"

She held out her notebook.

"You're a genius." On the back cover, Rytis had scrawled, "Nikki-Vida: 212-555-2346."

"Let's get out of here," Kelleher said. "You have to take me to get something to eat, and then we have to get going."

"Where?"

"You to the cops, to find out what they've done about Miles Akley. My guess is, you've got at least one guy over there who'll tell you anything."

"Such confidence. And where will you be?"

He held up the notebook. "The city. This is not the kind of conversation you have on the phone. I'm going to find Nikki Buzelis."

SIX

NIKKI

KELLEHER AND MEARNS went straight from the school to the drugstore to get breakfast and talk strategy. The Long Island edition of *Newsday* had put Scott Harrison's murder on the front page: "Terror in Paradise," was the headline. The picture was of a smiling Scott Harrison; the caption read, "Brilliant young assistant coach gunned down."

Kelleher forced himself to read the story, on the chance that the cops had told *Newsday* something he didn't know. He was relieved that his name didn't appear. The story didn't mention suspects, but it did say, "There is speculation, according to police sources, that the grisly murder is somehow tied to the bitter recruiting battle swirling around the phenom Rytis Buzelis, a Lithuanian immigrant who is averaging 47 points a game for Shelter Island High School."

After they finished breakfast, Mearns went to call the cops. There was no need, she and Kelleher had decided, to let anyone know they were working together — not yet. She was pretty certain Billy Hollister, another of Kelleher's old ballplaying friends, would talk to her on the phone. Hollister was the only unmarried member of the police force. Mearns admitted he had been hitting on her most of the winter.

"Not in a bad way. He's just asked me to dinner a couple of times, and I've told him I can't go out with people I'm covering. That was just an excuse, since there are never any real crime stories out here."

"Until now."

"Exactly."

Kelleher was drinking yet another cup of coffee when Mearns came back to the table. She sat down, opened her notebook, and began reading her notes. "Billy says Akley stayed at the Chequit overnight. They called Arturas at seven o'clock this morning to find out where Akley might be, and he told them. They asked Akley to come in, which he did — with Arturas. Arturas waited while the Suffolk guys questioned Akley. Akley told them he did leave his seat early in the third quarter — to go to the bathroom, because the lines were too long at halftime. He claimed he was back in his seat midway through the quarter, and Arturas backed him up on it."

"He's lying. They're both lying. When I left at the start of the fourth quarter, he had just gotten back."

"Billy says they're going to ask some other people if they remember him coming back in. The problem is, with the game going on, people may say they didn't see him, but so what? They were watching the game."

Kelleher let out a deep breath. "All well and good, and I understand where the cops are coming from. But Akley is lying to them, and Buzelis is covering up for him."

"Fine. How do you prove it?"

"At least three other people were sitting with Arturas: Nadia, Vida, and Nikki. I'll go looking for the sisters. You try to make contact with Nadia."

Mearns dropped him off at the house so he could shower and change out of his sweaty running suit. He called George Ferrer to let him know he was leaving the island for a few hours.

"That's fine, Bobby, but if you decide to stay overnight someplace, be sure and call me. The last thing I need is the Suffolk cops calling and asking where you are and me not knowing."

"I understand, George."

"By the way, where *are* you going?"

"The city, to see a friend. I just need a change of scenery."

"Bobby."

"Yes, George?"

"Don't try to be a hero on this. Let the police do their work."

Ferrer was not the first cop who had given him this advice. He knew it was meant in a friendly way. He also knew that any reporter who listened to advice like that would never in his life break a story.

"I understand, George."

Mearns called just as he was stepping out of the shower. She had gotten the answering machine at the Buzelis house and had not left a message. "No sense taking a chance that Arturas might hear it," she said. "I think my best shot is tomorrow. Nadia usually comes to church without Arturas on Sunday morning."

"You go to church?"

"You have a problem with that?"

"No, of course not."

"It just surprises you, because reporters are supposed to be more skeptical than that?"

"Sort of."

"Skeptics need a streak of idealism, Kelleher. Just as idealists need a streak of skepticism."

He didn't answer that one. Over the years he had learned that there were good reasons smart people didn't argue about politics or religion. If going to church meant that Mearns could talk to Nadia alone, he was all for it.

"I'll call you when I know something," he said. Then he hung up and made one more phone call before leaving — to his old friend Larry Siddons. They had met years ago, while Siddons was working at the *Roanoke Times and World News*, covering Virginia basketball. When Kelleher first started with the *Cavalier Daily*, Siddons had seen some of his stuff and encouraged him to keep at it. Now Siddons was the number-two man on the Associated Press's national sports desk. Kelleher needed to get into the AP office, and he thought he could use some advice from an experienced hand. Siddons lived in New Jersey, but he immediately volunteered to drive into the city to meet him.

"You working on Scott Harrison?"

"Oh yeah."

"It all sounds very strange."

"It's stranger than you know."

They agreed to meet at John's, the famous Greenwich Village pizzeria that had opened two uptown restaurants. Siddons said he could be at the one on West 65th by two o'clock.

Kelleher rolled off the ferry shortly after noon. It occurred to him that a pre-trip nap might not have been a bad idea, given his lack of sleep the previous night — but he was too wired to sleep, no matter how exhausted he felt.

The traffic was light. Kelleher passed the time listening to the St. John's–Villanova game on the radio. Rollie Massamino and Looey Carnesecca had been gone three years, but it was hard to think of Villanova without Rollie and St. John's without Looey — even though their successors, Steve Lappas and

Brian Mahoney, were good guys and good coaches. St. John's had Felipe Lopez, the super-hyped freshman from the Bronx, but was struggling anyway, and Villanova was hammering the Red Storm. That was another thing Kelleher was having trouble getting used to: St. John's not being the Redmen anymore. They had changed their nickname the previous spring to avoid charges of political incorrectness.

Kelleher was passing through Hicksville on the Long Island Expressway as the game wound down. He was only half listening when Cal Ramsey, the color commentator, said, "It will be interesting to see how the Red Storm bounce back tomorrow afternoon when they play the University of Louisiana at Alumni Hall in a nationally televised game."

Kelleher sat up straight. He hadn't realized that Louisiana was going to be in town the next day. It might be worthwhile, he thought, to go to that game — if only to see whether Miles Akley was on hand.

He hit traffic crossing the Triborough Bridge and cursed himself for not taking the Midtown Tunnel. He had figured if there was one place he might hit traffic, even on a Saturday, it was the tunnel, which was always undergoing some kind of construction. Instead, there was an accident in the middle lane of the bridge, and it took him twenty minutes to get by. It was 2:10 by the time he swung onto 65th Street — and, of course, found no place to park. Annoyed, he pulled into a garage, knowing he would get killed, even on a weekend.

"I'll be an hour," he told the attendant.

"Ten bucks all day, weekend rate."

"*Ten* bucks?"

"Yeah. That's all."

Only in New York could you pay ten dollars to park on a Saturday.

The skyscrapers blocked the sun in Manhattan; the two-block walk to the restaurant was freezing. Siddons was waiting for him in a booth in the back.

"Fifteen minutes — not bad for you."

"Accident on the Triborough."

"Why didn't you take the tunnel? I mean, it is Saturday — "

"Don't start. It doesn't matter which way I go in this town, I'll *find* the traffic."

He brought Siddons up to speed on the last month of his life, going light on the details about leaving the *Herald* and heavy on the Buzelis/Harrison story. When he was finished, Siddons said nothing for a full minute. The pizza, Kelleher's favorite pizza in the world, thin-crust, New York–style, arrived. He dove into it as Siddons started to talk.

"I don't want to sound like your mother, but the first thing I'd say to you is, what makes you think these guys won't kill you if you go running around trying to find out what happened? The second thing I'd say is, if you *are* going to run around trying to find out what happened, you clearly *have* to find Nikki Buzelis. The problem is, she's probably terrified right now."

"With good reason. But you're right — I do have to find her."

"Bobby, all kidding aside, don't you think you should be careful here?"

"Yes. But I also think the best way to protect myself is to find out just what these guys are up to."

"Can't you let the cops do that?"

"Larry, I realize you're an editor now, but do you know what you sound like?"

Siddons took a bite of pizza. "I know I can't talk you out of this, but at least promise me you'll be careful. Whoever did this, Akley or anybody else, plays for keeps."

"What do you mean, 'anybody else'? Akley did it."

"You can't convict a man on circumstantial evidence, Bobby. Maybe he *was* in the bathroom."

"Then why did he lie to the cops about when he came back?"

"Don't know."

"Exactly. Which is why I have to find Nikki Buzelis."

"You don't want to chance just calling her on the phone?"

"No. I think this is a show-up-on-the-doorstep job."

"But you need to find the doorstep."

"Which means I need to come into your office and use the crisscross directory."

Siddons nodded. "Of course. But those things aren't infallible, you know. Especially if it's a brand-new number."

The crisscross directory was a phone book that matched phone numbers with their addresses, and vice versa. They came in handy when some kind of news event was unfolding and you wanted to call around a neighborhood to try to find out what people could see from their houses or apartments. You would go to the crisscross, look up an address, and start calling the number or numbers listed, hoping you found someone home. It was also useful in a situation like this — if you had only a phone number. Kelleher had already called information for listings under the names and initials of Vida and Nikki. Nothing. The crisscross often carried unlisted numbers matched with their addresses.

Kelleher didn't want to hassle reparking his car in the Rockefeller Center neighborhood where the AP office was located, so they paid for the pizza and took a cab downtown. They saw a few frigid-looking skaters on the ice as they got off at 50 Rockefeller Plaza, a half block down from the NBC building at 30 Rock.

Siddons guided Kelleher past security and upstairs to the quiet newsroom. Kelleher had always loved the newsroom on weekends. It was quiet but hummed with just enough life to let you know work was being done. Siddons sat Kelleher down at an empty desk with a crisscross and then went off to get coffee for them.

Kelleher called Mearns to check in before digging into the crisscross. The cops were still questioning witnesses from the game. She wasn't sure if anyone had confirmed Akley's story. She had called friends at both local food markets, asking them to call her immediately if Nadia Buzelis came in.

Siddons returned with the coffee. "You need any help with this? If you do, I'll call Lauren and tell her I'll be late."

Kelleher waved him off. "Go home and see your family. But there is one thing you can do."

"Name it."

"Call St. John's and get me a credential for tomorrow's game. I don't think saying I used to cover politics for the Washington *Herald* will get me in."

Siddons laughed. "I'll even get you a seat next to Occ. By the time the game's over, you'll know everything you never needed to know about college hoops."

Occ — Jim O'Connell, the AP's legendary college sports reporter — was the only man in the history of sportswriting to cover the Maui Invitational every year who not only never saw the beach but never even put on a short-sleeved shirt. He sat in the gym, watched twelve games, and flew home. Being a St. John's graduate, he would definitely be in town for a nationally televised game against the ninth-ranked team in the nation.

Kelleher was poring through the crisscross — it was slower going with just a phone number — when Siddons, wearing his coat, came back and said, "Pick it up at Will Call. The game's at Alumni Hall — *not* the Garden . . ."

"I know," Kelleher said.

"Call me if you need anything," Siddons said. They shook

hands. "I won't say it again, I promise, but one last time — be careful. *Please*."

"I promise. No hero stuff."

Kelleher thought about getting more coffee but decided the ten cups he'd had so far were enough for a while. He turned another page. Halfway down, he saw it: "555-2346: 425 East 58th Street — PH."

Penthouse. Nikki and Vida were apparently doing quite well. What's more, 425 had to be near the East River, since the numbering system in Manhattan started in the middle and worked toward the two rivers. One East 58th Street would be right off Fifth Avenue — the dividing line between east and west — and the higher you got, the closer you were to the river. In all likelihood, 425 was over near York Avenue, in the swanky neighborhood known as Sutton Place. Either Vida was making a lot of money on Wall Street — always possible, he supposed — or Nikki's modeling career had really taken off. Or money was coming in from another source.

He sat back in the chair and looked at his watch. It was a little after four. He knew the next thing he needed to do was take a taxi to the apartment building and try to get in to see Nikki. No doubt there would be a doorman. If he just showed up and announced himself, he probably wouldn't get in. After all, Nikki and Vida Buzelis had either never heard of him or had been warned by their father to watch out for him.

He considered the old pizza delivery trick but thought better of it. For one thing, he would have to call ahead to make sure someone was home. Even if someone were home, when the doorman called upstairs to say the pizza was there, the Buzelis sisters would say they hadn't ordered any pizza.

So how did he get in? He cursed himself for telling Siddons

to go home. What he needed was a partner who could distract the doorman long enough for him to get to the elevator. Finally, he decided to do what he always did: let his instincts carry him. He would go over there, check out the situation, and then decide what to do.

Regretfully, he left the newsroom — it was so warm and comfortable and safe — and hailed another taxi. As the cabbie turned the corner at 57th Street onto First Avenue, Kelleher saw a pay phone and had an idea.

"Let me off here." He paid the driver and hopped out, the wind cutting through him like a knife. The closer you got to the the river in Manhattan, the colder it was.

He pulled the phone number out of his pocket, found a quarter, and dialed.

On the third ring, a female voice answered.

"Miss Buzelis?"

"Yes."

"Nikki or Vida?"

There was a pause. "Nikki."

"Detective Sulahian, Suffolk County police. Sorry to bother you, ma'am, but has my partner been in touch with you?"

"You mean Detective Tonelli? I spoke with him this morning on Shelter Island."

"So he didn't get a chance to call you back?"

"No. Why?"

"There are a couple of items we wanted you to take a look at, if possible. I can't really go into it on the phone. I'm in Manhattan right now, using the NYPD's computer system. Would it be all right if I dropped by your apartment? Only take a few minutes."

"Well, I do have to go out in about an hour — "

"I can be there in ten minutes. It is 425 East 58th, right?"

"Yes, it is."

"What's the apartment number, ma'am?"

"It's the penthouse."

"Oh, okay, fine. Would you do me a favor and call your doorman to let him know that Detective Sulahian will be coming to see you in about ten minutes?"

"Okay, sure."

He hung up, triumphant. He looked in his wallet to make sure his D.C. police pass, the one all *Herald* reporters were issued annually, was still there. The pass had his picture and said, in block letters, 'POLICE.' Beneath it, in smaller letters, it explained that the person pictured was an accredited member of the media and should be allowed inside police lines at a crime scene. If you glanced at it quickly, you would think the person in the picture was a cop. The only ones who knew for sure that the pass was only for the media were the cops.

He walked around the block to kill ten minutes. The building had a driveway straight through from 58th to 59th Street, with the entrance smack in the middle. He went through the revolving door, his coat pulled tight around him so the doorman wouldn't see the UVA sweater he was wearing underneath.

"May I help you?" the doorman asked.

Kelleher pulled out his wallet just as he had practiced during his walk and flipped it open to his police ID.

"Detective Sulahian. I believe Ms. Buzelis told you I'd be coming."

He flipped the wallet closed before the doorman could even think about taking a closer look.

"Yes, detective. First elevator on your left. I'll call and let her know you're here."

"Thanks."

He walked around the wall of mirrors and found one of the

two elevators open. He stepped in and pressed 'PH.' Nothing happened. He pressed again.

He stepped off the elevator and shouted back at the doorman. "Is there something wrong with this elevator? I'm pressing 'penthouse,' and nothing happens."

"Give it a second," the doorman called back. "She has to press a button up there to allow you access to the floor."

Fancy stuff. He stepped back on and pressed the button again. It lit up. He breathed a sigh of relief as the elevator rocketed up at supersonic speed, covering twenty-eight floors in about 2.6 seconds. The door opened and Kelleher found Nikki Buzelis, dressed in a pair of running shorts and a Minnesota State sweatshirt, standing in front of him.

Kelleher had seen supermodels on television and in magazines for years, but he had never in his life stood face to face with a woman quite this stunning. He remembered a letter he had read once in *Sports Illustrated* after the annual swimsuit issue: "These aren't really women. They can't be. Mortals can't possibly look this good."

Nikki Buzelis fit that description. Her long blond hair cascaded down her shoulders and, although she didn't look to be wearing any makeup at all, her blue eyes were hypnotizing. Even in bare feet, she appeared no more than an inch shorter than Kelleher. He took a deep breath, searching for his voice.

"Ms. Buzelis?" he managed finally, stepping off the elevator into the apartment.

"Yes. Detective Sulahian?"

"Yes, ma'am."

"You have identification, of course?"

Whoops. Kelleher hadn't expected that. Why would she let him up here and then ask for ID? Oh well. He pulled out his wallet, flashed the "POLICE" ID as quickly as possible and snapped the wallet shut.

Nikki Buzelis smiled. "That's quite good. You know, I haven't been in this country for so long, but I would guess that pretending to be a police officer when you're a reporter is against the law — isn't it, Mr. Kelleher?"

Kelleher almost fell backward into the elevator. She couldn't possibly have read the fine print so quickly. "Kelleher?" he bluffed lamely. "Who's that?"

She laughed, turned on her heel, and walked back into the huge living room. "Would you like something to drink?"

This was too strange. He followed her into the living room. It had a bar on the far side — near the picture window that looked north, up the East River. She walked behind the bar and opened a bottle of Perrier.

"May I call you Bobby?" She poured the fizzy water into a glass.

It was time to abandon the charade. "How did you know?"

"Tell me what you want to drink and I'll tell you."

"Coke."

Reaching under the bar, she produced a can of Coke. She pulled some ice out of a bucket, dropped it into a glass, and poured. Handing him the drink, she led him to one of the couches and sat, curling her legs under her in that way that made even unattractive women look sexy. Kelleher sat in an armchair across from her, trying not to stare.

"So tell me — do you pretend to be a policeman often?"

"Actually, I've never done it before. I've been a pizza delivery boy, but never a cop. Now please, before I lose my mind, how did you know who I was?"

She smiled. "To tell you the truth, I wasn't sure. I knew you were going to call, but I was surprised you knew my address."

"How did you know I'd call?"

"My brother phoned a few hours ago. He said he had spoken to you this morning, before my father and Miles Akley found you. He said he gave you the phone number because he thought you were honest and you were a friend of Scott's."

Kelleher was pleased to hear that he had connected with Rytis Buzelis. "So when I called, how could you know it was me? I mean, it could have been a cop."

"At first I thought it was. But when you asked me if I was Nikki or Vida, I knew you couldn't be the police, because Vida gave them her own address and phone number. I guessed that it had to be you, since this number is not listed."

"What do you mean, 'her own address and phone number'? She doesn't live here too?"

"No. My parents and brother think we live together, because that way they worry less about me. She lives in Greenwich Village. My parents were not there when we were questioned, so she gave them her real address."

Nikki said "Grenich." Unless you knew she hadn't grown up in this country, you wouldn't even notice the tiny trace of an accent.

"What happens when they call looking for Vida?"

"I give her a message and she calls them back. Or they get the tape, which says Nikki and Vida are not home. It's not that difficult."

Kelleher finished his Coke. "Quite a place you have here. You must be doing well as a model."

"Actually, yes. I've signed three magazine contracts in the last three months, and I'm supposed to tape a television commercial next week. I only wish I enjoyed the work more. It's boring, but the money is good, so it's hard to say no."

Kelleher stood up. "Mind if I refill my Coke?"

She looked at her watch. "Please, help yourself. Will thirty minutes be enough time for you to talk to me?"

"I would think so. More Perrier?"

She shook her head. He poured the Coke and reseated himself.

"My brother says you knew Scott Harrison well." She had cut to the chase before he could.

"I knew him in college. He was a coach of mine for two years, even though I didn't play very much. We kept in touch." He paused. Time to turn the tables and take a chance. "How well did you know him?"

She looked out the window for a moment. The last rays of the sun setting on the far side of Manhattan reflected off the river.

"I didn't know him very long." She paused. The blue eyes looked a little misty. "I'm not sure how to describe our relationship. I liked Scott. He was nice. But to be honest with you, I was with him only for — " She stopped again.

"Only for a short time." He finished the sentence for her.

"No." She shook her head. Now she was smiling. "I'm sorry to say this, especially to someone who was his friend." She stopped again.

This was maddening. "Don't worry about that. You were with him only for basketball games?"

Now she was laughing. "I'm sorry, Bobby, I don't mean to laugh. I was with him only for sex."

Now it was Kelleher's turn to laugh. Talk about the ultimate irony: Scott Harrison being used by a woman as a boy-toy, after all his years of womanizing. Of course, if you were going to be looked at as a sex object by someone, Nikki Buzelis wasn't a bad choice.

"This is funny?"

"It's more ironic than funny. Do you know the word ironic?"

She looked at him as if he were mentally retarded. "It's ironic, isn't it, that a brainless model would be smarter than a brilliant reporter?"

"Sorry — I just figured the language thing . . ."

"My English really isn't very good, is it?"

"It's only slightly better than mine," he replied, embarrassed that he had been patronizing someone whose IQ was probably at least as high as his. Being bright seemed to run in the family. "Tell me how you got involved with Scott."

She shrugged. "Fairly simple. He began coming to my brother's games in December. Like the other coaches, he would hang around after the games. He was quite handsome, so one night, I just walked up and introduced myself. He got very flustered and said he would really like to talk to me but it was against all the rules. I said I understood. A few minutes later, when we were leaving, he sort of jumped out of a bush outside and asked if he could have my phone number. I gave it to him. He called me and came to see me here several times, usually the day he flew in for a game or the day after."

"Did you tell the police you were involved with him?"

"Why not? I'm not ashamed."

"What about your parents?"

For the first time since he had walked into the apartment, her look of absolute self-confidence faded just a bit. "Mother. Not father. He's as old-fashioned as he is bullheaded. He might have killed Scott."

"Nikki, someone did kill Scott."

"I didn't mean it that way. American slang."

"I understand. But you're certain your father doesn't know?"

"One hundred percent sure."

"What about Miles Akley?"

She pursed her lips, then shook her head. "If he knew, he would either have told my father or blackmailed me to not tell him. No, he couldn't have known."

He had thought that bringing up her relationship with Scott would be delicate. It had turned out to be easy — she had brought it up. Now came the really delicate part.

"Nikki, what were you and Scott talking about last night before the game?"

"When?"

"Outside. Behind the building. About thirty minutes before tipoff."

She pulled her legs out, stood up, and walked to the bar. "How could you know about that?" For the first time, her voice had the tiniest hint of a quaver.

He stood up and walked to the bar. She was pouring another Perrier. He leaned on the bar.

"It was purely by accident, but I saw you. I don't know exactly what was said, but it was an intense, emotional conversation — not the kind you expect between two people who meet just for some good old-fashioned casual sex."

She took a long swig of her drink. "It was personal."

"Nikki, nothing's personal anymore when someone is dead."

She looked at her watch and sighed. "You're going to have to give me a minute to call my date and tell him I'm going to be late."

For a second Kelleher thought he had gone too far and she was going to call the cops or building security. "Can't you just answer my question?"

"It's not a simple answer. You aren't going to just nod and say, 'That's fine, thanks for the Coke,' and leave."

"Try me. Just tell me what you two were talking about."

"He wanted my help."

"To recruit your brother."

She shook her head. "No. Well, yes, he did, but that wasn't what we were talking about last night."

"What, then?"

She put the drink down and looked him right in the eye. "He said someone was trying to kill him."

Kelleher took a deep breath. "Go call your date."

SEVEN

THE COACH

THE STORY that Nikki Buzelis laid out for Kelleher over the course of the next hour was both chilling and stunning. She had known from the very beginning of their relationship that Scott Harrison wasn't interested in her just because of her looks, and she found that refreshing.

"He wanted me to help convince Rytis that he didn't have to go to Louisiana. He knew that would be hard, because my father was in so deep with Akley, but he had also figured out that if anyone could convince Rytis to go against my father, it would be me or my mother."

Kelleher asked Nikki to walk him through the conversation the night before the game in as much detail as possible. Her memory was very good. Scott had called the apartment that morning sounding nervous. He had said it was very important that he see her someplace away from Shelter Island after the game that night. She had told him that was impossible, since her whole family was supposed to go out with Akley after the game. He had asked if there was any way she could get out of it. No. Okay then, he had said he would stay overnight and meet her the next morning when she was supposed to drive back to the city.

"So then why did you meet before the game?"

"When I got to the island, my mother said Scott had called the house. That was very unusual, since coaches aren't supposed to call at all — especially on the day of a game. But he had said he wasn't calling about Rytis — he needed her to get a message to me to meet him behind the building near the jungle gym thirty minutes before the game. My mother asked me what was going on, and I said I had no idea."

"So you went and met him."

She nodded. "I knew something was wrong right away. As cold as it was, he was actually sweating. He started talking about how it had all gotten out of hand, that he had never meant for it to get this crazy. I kept asking him what he was talking about. Finally, he said he had been told a week ago that someone might want to kill him. He hadn't really believed it. Then he had gotten another warning that day, which was why he had taken the chance and called the house. Now, he said, he was certain it was true, because they were here."

"*They?* You're sure he said *they?*"

"Absolutely. I asked him who *they* were. I even asked him if he was talking about Miles Akley and his people. He just laughed and said that Miles Akley was the least of his worries."

That really threw Kelleher. If Akley hadn't done it, then who the hell had? Who were *they?* He pressed her again.

"He said there wasn't time to explain — he was afraid if he didn't get back inside, you or those other coaches might come looking for him. He told me we had to meet the next morning at his hotel, a Holiday Inn near Riverhead — he would tell me the whole thing then. And he also said that if something happened to him, the only person I should trust was you. So you see, you didn't have to go through that policeman routine. You had my brother and Scott on your side."

"But didn't know it."

He kept at her to try to remember more details — anything. She had told him everything, she said. "Oh — the last thing he said was that he had to go back to his car to get his cellular phone. He had to call his boss and tell him what was going on, but he didn't want to do it in front of anyone on the lobby pay phone."

"Which is where he went at halftime. He couldn't do it before the game, because he ran into me in the lobby." Kelleher was still having trouble digesting all this. Who in the world would Scott Harrison think might want to kill him, if not Akley? "You're sure he was convinced someone other than Miles Akley was trying to kill him?"

She nodded.

"Of course, that doesn't mean Akley didn't do it. He and your father lied to the police about how long Akley left the game for at the start of the third quarter."

"I know. My father told Vida, my mother, and me to tell the same lie."

What was interesting to Kelleher as she talked was that Scott hadn't been selling Minnesota State to Nikki as much as he had been selling Scott. She said he had never once suggested Nikki talk Rytis into a campus visit at Minnesota State or even a meeting with his boss, Bobby Taylor. It had always been Scott.

"You think that's significant?" Nikki asked when he started probing for details.

"Maybe, maybe not. Scott was very ambitious. It's possible that he saw Rytis as a way to get a head coaching job, either at Minnesota State or someplace else, and someone was on to him."

The doorman's buzzer rang. "Ms. Buzelis, there's a gentleman here to see you."

She looked at her watch. "Oh my God. I told him an hour — it's been an hour and a half. I have to get dressed."

She buzzed back. "Please tell him I'll be down in ten minutes."

"Yes ma'am."

"You have to do me a favor," she appealed to Kelleher. "Stay here until I'm gone. It would be too awkward to explain."

He put up a hand. "No problem. I'm flattered that anyone might think, even mistakenly, I was a candidate for a date with you."

She gave him the knockout supermodel smile. "Oh, come on, Bobby Kelleher — my guess is you do just fine."

"If you'll forgive me for sounding corny, Nikki, you are way beyond just fine."

She laughed at that one, then disappeared into the bedroom. Five minutes later, she was back — it amazed Kelleher how quickly women could dress when they *had* to — in a long dress, with her hair combed out and just enough makeup to make her even more gorgeous, if that were possible.

"You are certainly worth waiting for."

"Thank you," she replied with an indulgent smile, flattered by his admiration. "Please help yourself to food or anything else to drink. Where will you stay tonight?"

Kelleher hadn't given that any thought, since he had initially planned to drive back to Shelter Island. But now, with the game at St. John's tomorrow and all the information Nikki had given him, that was out of the question.

"I'm not really sure."

"There's an extra bedroom here."

"What about your date?"

She laughed. "It's one of those modeling-agency setups. Dinner at some restaurant, where we'll be seen and photographed, and that's it. Straight back home. He's a perfectly nice guy, but . . ."

"No Scott Harrison."

She shook her head sadly. "As a matter of fact, no. Stay. There are extra sweatshirts in my bottom drawer for you to sleep in if you need one."

It was a hell of an offer, even if he, too, was no Scott Harrison.

"Okay. If you don't mind, I'll order some Chinese and make some phone calls."

"I'll tell the doorman to send up anyone with Chinese food, but no pizza boys or police."

They both laughed. "Be home by eleven," he admonished as she stepped onto the elevator.

He sincerely hoped she would be.

Kelleher found a Chinese place he had heard of in the phone book. He pulled a comfortable-looking sweat suit out of the bottom drawer, changed into it, and sat down at the desk in the den, adjacent to the living room. He resisted the urge to look through the apartment for further clues. He wouldn't have known what to look for, and to do it after she had trusted him enough to leave him alone seemed gross.

He called Mearns. "Where have you been?" she demanded.

He told her. "So, the night has potential," she said when he finished.

"Stop it," he said, blushing in spite of himself. "She's just being nice."

"No doubt," she said. "But her niceness aside, it sounds to me like we need to talk to Bobby Taylor and find out if Scott ever made contact with him that night."

"And to find out if he had any notion Scott might be recruiting the kid for himself rather than for Minnesota State," he said, relieved she wasn't pursuing the topic of Nikki any further.

"You really think that's possible?"

"Tamara, anything's possible at this point."

"You know, Scott's funeral is Monday. I imagine Taylor will be there."

"Where is it?"

"Chicago. Actually, some suburb where he grew up."

"Hinsdale." Kelleher remembered Harrison's telling him he had grown up there, the star basketball player in one of the few places in America where swimming was bigger than basketball. "I wonder if I should go." He felt a pang of guilt, realizing that going to Scott's funeral had never crossed his mind until the moment it appeared to be something he needed to do to advance the story. Then again, he didn't know anyone in the family. It wasn't as if his presence would lend comfort or his absence cause pain.

"There's a very early flight on American out of Islip that gets to Chicago at something like eight o'clock in the morning," she volunteered.

"A jet?"

"Yeah. American has jet service out of there to Chicago. It's one of their hubs."

Tamara would go to church in the morning and try to talk to Nadia. She might even try to find out what Rytis was doing and talk to him, since he seemed to be on their side. Kelleher would go to the Louisiana–St. John's game and see who showed up. Then they would make a decision on whether he should go to Chicago.

Kelleher hung up and thought briefly about trying to call Bobby Taylor, then decided against it. This was another one of those conversations that had to take place in person. The question was whether his assistant's funeral was an appropriate setting.

He spent the better part of an hour writing down everything he could remember from his conversation with Nikki and then called George Ferrer to tell him he was at Siddons's house. He then called Siddons, gave him Nikki's phone number, and told him to say he was in the bathroom if Ferrer called, then call so he could return Ferrer's call. He figured it would be easier to tell Siddons that he was at Nikki's than it would be to tell Ferrer — who would have the number for the penthouse. At eleven, he watched the news and then the first thirty minutes of *Saturday Night Live*, a show he had given up on several years earlier. It was still as unfunny as he remembered.

At midnight, he went to bed. He wasn't exactly sure what he had thought or hoped might happen when Nikki returned, but he knew waiting up all night for her was foolish. He couldn't keep his eyes open another minute anyway. In his wildest fantasy he imagined the two of them, thrown together by the trauma of Scott's death, seeking comfort in each other. Kelleher had enough ego to think there was perhaps one chance in a thousand of that happening. When she wasn't back by midnight, he knew he had been too generous in assessing the odds.

He tossed and turned for a few minutes, finally forced himself *not* to think of Nikki or Scott, and fell into an exhausted sleep.

When he woke up, sun was streaming under the bottom of the window shade. He rolled over and looked at the clock: it was almost nine. He had slept for nine straight hours — a world record for him.

Jumping out of bed, he walked into the living room and heard her calling him from the kitchen. She was wearing a Wake Forest sweatshirt, shorts, and running shoes. "I was getting worried about you. I knocked on your door when I got in last night, but you must already have been asleep."

"When did you get in?"

"Checking up on me?"

"No, not at all," he assured her hastily, feeling guilty for asking. "I went to bed a little after midnight. I was wiped out."

"We must have just missed each other. I got in about twelve-thirty."

He wanted to kick himself for not hanging in a little longer, even though he wasn't exactly sure why he thought staying up would have mattered.

"Would you like coffee? I'm about to go for my run, but it's already made. There's cereal here, and if you want eggs or something, I'll fix them when I get back."

He smiled. "The cereal and coffee sound great. You fix eggs?"

"Remember where I grew up. All the girls learn to cook in Vilnius."

He had forgotten. It was hard to connect this stunning woman to a poor city in an embattled country. "Did you have a good time last night?" He hoped he wasn't probing too much.

"It was okay. He's a nice guy. We went to Elaine's."

"I didn't think anyone went there anymore."

She shrugged. "I do what I'm told. There were photographers there, and Woody Allen with his stepdaughter."

"Shows you what I know about the New York social scene."

She laughed, took a last sip of orange juice, and headed for the door. "I'll be back in forty minutes."

"How far do you run?"

"Four miles. Ten minutes a mile. Nothing Olympian."

Thank goodness, he thought, she wasn't all-world at *everything*. He had just sat down with his coffee and the newspaper when the phone rang. Resisting the urge to answer, he heard the tape come on announcing that Nikki and Vida weren't home, then heard Siddons's voice.

He grabbed the phone.

"Jesus, Bobby, what happened?" Siddons said.

"What do you mean?"

"I called you three times last night to let you know Ferrer called to check on you. I told him you were asleep. He told me to tell you to call this morning."

Strange, Kelleher thought, that Ferrer would check on him, then take Siddons's word that he was there but asleep.

"When did you call?" he asked.

"I called three times — one, two, and three in the morning. I left a message the first time."

"I fell into a sound sleep about midnight. Nikki wasn't back yet, but I'm surprised you didn't get her. She said she got in about twelve-thirty."

He thanked Siddons and hung up. Something Siddons had said was bothering him. What was it? The previous phone calls. Why hadn't Nikki answered? Maybe she turned her phone off at night. He pressed the "play" button on the message machine and, sure enough, heard Siddons's message. But the first one hadn't come at one o'clock — it had been at 12:40. If she had gotten in at 12:30, surely she wouldn't have been in bed asleep with the phone turned off that quickly. Then again, maybe she had been a little off in her estimated time of arrival.

Probably nothing, he thought. Then again, he couldn't take anything for granted. Then again, maybe she *had* been out all night with this guy and didn't think it was any of his damn business.

He was showered and dressed when she came back from her run. He told her about Siddons's call and his calls during the night.

"I always turn my phone off in the bedroom," she said. "Sorry about that."

"No big deal. Everything's okay now." He decided not to press her on when she had actually come in.

He left the apartment about 10:30, promising to call if he learned anything new. "I'll call your house on Shelter Island and leave a message if I hear anything from my family," she said. They shook hands at the elevator as he left. Even though absolutely nothing had happened between them, part of him couldn't help but feel like Shirley MacLaine in *Sweet Charity* — "If that little gang of mine could only see me now . . ."

It was a spectacular Sunday morning, sunny and chilly, but a good deal warmer than it had been all week. A hint of spring was actually in the air, which reminded Kelleher that Tuesday was the first of March. Shelter Island would be playing its first state playoff game ever on Tuesday night at home.

The first round was today. Shelter Island was one of eight teams in the twenty-four-team field that had a first-round bye. According to what he had just read in *Newsday*, Shelter Island would host a second-round game Tuesday night, the winner advancing to a quarterfinal game at Madison Square Garden on Thursday. The semifinals and the final would both be played on Saturday — New York had decided to copy Indiana's format of playing the last three games on the same day. That would make for a hectic week of basketball, the paper noted, but it would be the same for everybody. Several thousand fans were expected to attend the first state championship held in the city in almost forty years.

The guy at the garage was grumpy when Kelleher arrived. "You said one hour," he accused, looking at the back of the ticket.

"I lied," Kelleher replied blandly, seeing no reason to explain himself.

"Twenty dollars."

"Twenty? The guy yesterday told me ten."

"Ten for yesterday. Twenty for overnight."

Kelleher sighed, muttered something about usury being a

crime, and paid up. The guy took ten minutes to bring his car. Kelleher was sorely tempted to stiff him, but he had worked for tips for too many years to do it. He handed the guy a dollar as he got out of the car.

"You're welcome," he remarked when the guy couldn't even come up with a thank-you.

The guy looked at him as he climbed into the car. "You expect 'thank you' for a buck?"

"What'd you do, wash and wax the thing? You charge me twenty bucks, you take your sweet time bringing it up, I still give you a tip, and you can't even say 'thank you'?"

"Go fuck yourself."

Kelleher had a sudden urge to jump out of the car and demand the dollar back. At the same time, he realized he was acting as much like an ugly New Yorker as this ugly New Yorker. He smiled as sweetly as he could. "You have a real nice day now."

"Your ass," the guy replied.

Kelleher blew him a kiss and pulled out, glancing in the mirror on the chance the guy was chasing him down the street. He breathed a sigh of relief when he saw nothing. It was amazing how complicated the simple act of parking your car could be in the city.

He opted for the 59th Street Bridge, figuring he would recoup three dollars of the twenty-one he had spent parking by avoiding the toll at the Triborough or the tunnel. There wasn't a hint of traffic, and Kelleher remembered how much he had loved Sunday mornings as a kid. No traffic, no hassle. The city felt almost clean.

On a Friday night, it would have taken him at least an hour to get to St. John's. Now, it took less than twenty minutes. It was just after eleven o'clock, and the parking lot at Alumni Hall was still half empty when he pulled in. St. John's was one of the few places left in America where you could watch big-time college basketball and pay nothing to park. Same city. Different borough.

His pass, as promised, was at Will Call. He walked down the steps to floor level and searched out the press room, which turned out to be the sports information office with coffee and donuts on the desks. That was fine with him. He devoured a donut and was about to walk out to the floor when he noticed someone in the next office sitting at a computer. It was Jim O'Connell: the legendary Occ. He recognized him from his own playing days, when Occ's presence on press row — then as now — was proof that a game was important.

Occ — like Kelleher — had put on a few pounds since then. He had a round Irish face, thinning hair, and an easy smile. When he talked, he sounded like someone doing an imitation of a guy with a New York accent. Occ didn't say "with"; he said "wid." He didn't say "definitely"; he said "def-fanly." Kelleher walked over to introduce himself.

"Oh yeah, Larry told me you were comin'," Occ greeted him. "Let's take a walk out on the flaw, where there's no one around. You can fill me in a little. Maybe I can help."

"You don't have work to do here?" Kelleher glanced at the computer.

"Nah, it's just notes stuff. No problem. You want coffee?"

He did. They each poured themselves a cup and walked out of the makeshift press room. Seeing a sign that said "Floor," Kelleher turned left.

"Not that way," Occ corrected him.

"But the sign?"

"Yeah, I know. It's about twelve steps from here to the flaw. But to get there, you gotta pass the St. John's locker room. We can't do that. They're afraid one of us might breathe on Felipe." He pronounced it "breed."

Kelleher had heard something about St. John's closing its locker room to the media in order to "protect" Felipe Lopez, its overhyped freshman. But he hadn't heard anything about the hallway *outside* the locker room being off-limits. "Isn't that a bit ridiculous?"

Occ shook his head. "It's beyond ridiculous. It's not worth fighting, though. They're all out of their minds these days."

They walked the long way down to the floor and saw a couple of Louisiana players out for early shooting. The arena was empty. Kelleher glanced around to see if any familiar faces were there. No one. They sat down in the front row.

"Larry tells me you knew this Scott Harrison pretty well," Occ remarked. "What do you t'ink happened to him?"

Kelleher hesitated. Even though he felt like he knew O'Connell, having seen him at games and having read him for years, he didn't. How much could he share with him without forcing O'Connell, if only out of responsibility to the AP, to start pursuing the story himself? Siddons he could tell. Siddons was his pal.

Occ read his mind. "Listen, kid, I understand if you don't wanna tell me everything. But I'll be honest wid you — I got no time to chase a story like this, even if I t'ought it would win me the Pulitzer Prize. I just told Larry if I could help you, I would."

Kelleher nodded. Some people you inherently trust. Occ was one of those people, even the first time you met him. It was, no doubt, one of the reasons he was a good reporter. People felt comfortable telling him things. He laid out most of the story, watching as O'Connell's eyes grew wider by the minute. When he was finished, Occ took a last sip of the coffee and put the cup under his seat. He sat back and waved at Ron Rutledge, a St. John's assistant who had just come on court with a few of the Red Storm players.

"First of all, I t'ink your instinct to go to Chicago is absolutely right. You gotta talk to Taylor and maybe some of the other MSU people too. I t'ink the key to the whole story is finding out who Scott was double-crossing. 'Cause if Akley didn't do it, then someone he pissed off did. And if he was trying to steal the kid for someone else, the trail may lead you back to Minnesota State."

Kelleher was about to answer when he heard someone behind him yell, "Occ baby, you been killing me, Occ. Why are you killing me?"

He turned, expecting to see Dick Vitale, the loudmouthed but lovable ABC/ESPN hoops analyst. Only it wasn't Vitale, it was Nick Angellini, the equally loudmouthed but not nearly as lovable Vitale wanna-be who had become the number-two network analyst behind Vitale, with much of the same schtick. Angellini wasn't as funny or as knowledgeable as Vitale, but where Vitale played off being a bald, one-eyed, once-fired coach only a mother (and America) could love, Angellini was Mr. Style, wearing Rick Pitino—like Armani suits, slicking his dark hair back, and making all the ladies swoon. He sounded like Vitale but looked a lot like Pitino, the suave, street-smart Kentucky coach.

Occ shook his head as Angellini approached. "Guy's a pain in the ass," he whispered. Then he stood up to greet Angellini. "Hey Nick, you had it wrong on Krzyzewski giving a million bucks to Duke. It was two hunnerd an' fifty grand, which is a lot of money, but it's not a million bucks. When you exaggerate, I have to call you on it."

"But you never call Dickie V. on it, do you? Why not? Because he's your buddy?"

In those three short sentences, Kelleher saw a side of Angellini he hadn't seen before. This wasn't the smooth, bear-hugging, everybody's-pal Nick Angellini the public saw. This was a jealous, trying-to-hide-how-pissed-off-he-was Nick Angellini showing just a little bit of a vicious streak.

Occ ignored the dig. "Nick, meet Bobby Kelleher. He's with the *Washington Herald.*" Whether Occ knew that wasn't true anymore or not, Kelleher wasn't sure. But there was no point in contradicting him. He stood and shook hands with Angellini.

"Hey Bobby, yeah, good to see you. Love your stuff, babe," Angellini said. "Your buddy, though, whatsisname, he kills me."

"Doug Doughty?"

"Yeah, Doug. He's my man, but he kills me."

Angellini was right about that. Doughty did kill him, every chance he got — usually with good reason. As for Angellini loving his stuff, Kelleher would have willingly bet a million dollars that Angellini had never once read a word he had written.

"You know, Bobby played at U. Va.," Occ said, no doubt trying to embarrass Angellini, who tended to only know stars and superstars.

Angellini looked shocked, but he recovered. "Sure, yeah, I remember now. You were on the '84 Final Four team."

"Graduated in '83."

"Oh yeah, right. You and Ralph Sampson — right, kid? I remember you now. You're the kid from Boston."

"New York."

Angellini gave up. He turned back to O'Connell. "So what's the scoop, Occ? What's the matter with your boys? Give me a line or two I can use."

"You mean steal."

"I only steal from the best, baby."

Kelleher had seen more than enough of this guy's act. He waved at O'Connell and indicated he was going back to the press room. Occ nodded. Kelleher walked up the ramp back to the hallway. His head was down and he was lost in thought, wondering if he should call American right then to make a plane reservation for the next day. As he turned the corner, he bumped into someone.

"Sorry," he said.

"Keep your head up," a voice snapped. A voice he knew. Kelleher looked up and saw the familiar sneer of Miles Akley.

EIGHT

THE COACH

"YOU JUST CAN'T TAKE A HINT, can you, Kelleher?" Akley growled as the two men untangled.

"Hint?" Kelleher repeated. "Is there some reason I shouldn't be at a basketball game?"

Akley glared at him. "Look, I don't give a shit what you do. Just stay out of my way. You already caused me enough trouble with the cops."

"Gee, Miles, I feel really bad about that. Great guy like you having to deal with that sort of nuisance."

"Kelleher, I told you once, I'll tell you again. All I do is try to help kids."

Kelleher laughed. "Kids who can run, jump, dunk, and shoot. Why don't you help some ghetto kids who are five-six and can't play a lick? Rytis Buzelis needs your help as much as he needs a recommendation from me to get into college."

For a moment Kelleher thought he and Akley were finally going to have the fight they had seemed destined for since the first time they met. Instead, Akley mumbled a couple of obscenities, walked around Kelleher, and continued down the hall.

Kelleher took two steps in the direction of the press room, then stopped. "You came here to see what Miles is up to, so let's see what Miles is up to," he said to himself.

He followed Akley down the dimly lit hallway, keeping a respectable distance. His guess was that Akley was heading for the Louisiana locker room, to check in with his buddy Fred Murray. To his surprise, Akley stopped at one of the portals leading to the floor and turned into it. Kelleher followed. He peered around the corner at the portal to make sure Akley wasn't lying in wait for him, then walked down the slight incline leading to the bright lights of the playing area.

Kelleher stopped just short of the entranceway when he saw Akley walk over to Nick Angellini. The TV loudmouth had parted company with O'Connell and was standing in front of the ABC broadcasting table talking to his partner, Roger Twibell. When Akley approached, Angellini looked less than thrilled to see him. There were no hugs or warm handshakes. Angellini did, Kelleher guessed, introduce Akley to Twibell, because the two men shook hands briefly. Akley glanced back over his shoulder, which caused Kelleher to duck back into the shadows. Akley pointed to a portal at the far end of the court. He and Angellini began walking in that direction, their body language screaming that this was not a social occasion.

Kelleher stood for a moment, trying to figure out whether to follow them or circle the hallway and get close enough to hear them. Quickly noting that he would not have to pass the off-limits area in front of the St. John's locker room, he decided on the circle route.

He sprinted up the portal, turned left and went down the hallway, almost colliding with several Louisiana players coming out of their locker room and ducking under their arms. Approaching the corner, just shy of the portal that Akley and Angellini had exited, he slowed. At the corner, he stopped and peered around it. There they were: Angellini leaning against the wall, smoking a cigarette, Akley almost in his face.

"I'm telling you, Miles, back off!" The hallway's acoustics carried Angellini's angry whisper.

Kelleher peeked around again. With no one else in sight, the two men thought they had complete privacy. The St. John's locker room was around the far corner. He could see a lone security guard down there, too far away to hear anything.

"Back off, my ass!" Akley snapped. "I got cops all over me thinking I killed the little SOB. And I got this pain-in-the-ass reporter snooping around everywhere I go. He's even here to-day."

On cue, Akley peered around. Kelleher snapped his head back, thinking for a moment that Akley might have spotted him.

"What reporter?"

"Name's Bobby Kelleher. He thinks he knows what the hell's going on because he played two minutes in four years at Virginia."

"Just met him. *Washington Post* or something?"

"*Herald.* Only he's not there anymore. Got fired or something — but he used to cover politics, so he knows his way around. Listen, fuck him, Nick. Just tell me the truth, for once in your life. Was the kid double-crossing you?"

"I don't know — he might have been or he might not have been. But it wasn't me or any of my people. God's truth."

"Then who the fuck killed him?" Akley snarled, furious.

"If you don't know, how the hell should I know? Hell, you were there."

"No shit I was there. How do you think I found out what you're trying to pull?"

"Well, you don't have to worry about it now, Miles, do you? Harrison's death doesn't exactly break your heart, does it? Means the kid's all yours."

"We'll see. The old man's giving me trouble."

"Holding out?"

"You might say that."

"Come on, Miles, you've got more money than God. Quit whining."

"Fuck you, Nick."

Kelleher heard footsteps. Apparently having decided that this was the right note on which to end the conversation, Akley walked back to the floor. Angellini took one more drag on his cigarette, dropped it on the floor, and followed. Kelleher leaned against the wall. What the hell had he just overheard? Scott had told Nikki that *they* were going to kill him. Could *they* be Angellini and Akley? Judging by what he had just heard, the answer was an emphatic "no."

But what was Angellini's connection to this whole thing? Why would Akley think a TV announcer would want to kill Scott Harrison? And how could Scott possibly have doublecrossed Nick Angellini? The more he knew, the less he knew. One thing was certain: if Akley had killed Scott Harrison, he was one great actor. The man he had just been listening to was as baffled — though not as sad — about Harrison's death as he was.

Kelleher walked back to the press room and tried to call Mearns. No answer, which he hoped meant she was with Nadia. He called to check his messages, in case Nikki had called. Nothing. Well, he'd been gone less than two hours. He broke down and ate another donut. A roar outside told him the game was about to start. He walked back to press row and sat down next to O'Connell.

"You findin' anythin' out?" O'Connell asked over the starting lineup introductions.

"If I told you what I just heard, you'd say I was nuts. And if you didn't say I was nuts, I'd say *you* were nuts for not saying it."

"Try me."

Kelleher sighed. "Let me ask you a question. Can you think of any reason why your pal Nick Angellini would have been involved with Scott Harrison?"

Occ shrugged. "Maybe Scott was tellin' him what was goin' on with Buzelis — you know, bein' a source." He stopped and shook his head. "That doesn' make sense, though, 'cause Akley could do that for him."

"Why Akley?"

"Are you kiddin'? Angellini's on the Brickley payroll. Check out the little Brickley sneaker on his lapel. You think he does that gratis? Listen to him sometime — all he ever does is praise Brickley coaches and talk about how lucky kids are to go to those schools. 'Course, he never says it's because they work for Brickley."

"He probably just wants to help kids," Kelleher remarked dryly.

"Yeah, right. Hey, wait a minute. I wonder if Harrison was on the NYU short list. Maybe that's the connection between him and Angellini."

The game was underway, and Felipe Lopez had just dunked, meaning that Kelleher could barely hear O'Connell. "What the hell are you talking about?" he shouted over the din.

O'Connell leaned closer so Kelleher could hear. "New Yawk University is upgrading next year, goin' back to Division One ball — first time since the sixties. Angellini went ta NYU. He's on the search committee — in fact, he basically *is* the search committee. Maybe Harrison was a candidate for the job."

"Jesus!" Kelleher shouted. "Jesus!"

"What?"

"Nothing. I'll tell you later."

He sat transfixed, not sure what to do next. Nikki had wondered if Scott was recruiting Rytis for himself or for someone else. That someone else had to be NYU. He was hoping to use Rytis to get the NYU job. Clearly, he had double-crossed *someone*. The question was whether it was his boss, Bobby Taylor, or Angellini. His guess was Taylor. After all, if Taylor thought Scott was using Minnesota State money, time, and entrée to recruit the kid for another school — especially when Taylor desperately needed a player like Buzelis to rescue his sinking program — he would have every reason to feel betrayed.

Still, was murder the next step in such a scenario? Why not just fire Scott and denounce him publicly? That would end any chance he had to get Buzelis, but if Scott had been planning to take him away to NYU — assuming Akley didn't succeed in buying him — he had no chance to get him anyway.

The game had stopped for the first TV time-out. Louisiana led, 9–7. O'Connell turned back to Kelleher. "So, you t'ink Angellini's involved in this somehow? Boy, wouldn't the basketball would love that!"

"I don't know, Occ. The only thing I know for sure is that you're right about tomorrow. I have to go to that funeral."

He left at halftime. It was a good game, tied at 39, but it occurred to Kelleher as the buzzer sounded that he hadn't seen a single play. There was no point sticking around to not watch the second half. He patted O'Connell on the back, thanked him for his help, and headed back to the parking lot. One good thing about leaving a game at halftime: no traffic.

All the way back to Shelter Island, Kelleher kept playing out the possible scenarios in his mind. It amazed him, but he was now almost certain that Miles Akley hadn't killed Harrison. Kelleher guessed that for once Akley had been telling the truth when he said he didn't kill people. He bought them, traded them, took advantage of them, but apparently he didn't kill them.

He stopped at the McDonald's in Riverhead and tried Mearns again. This time he got her. "I talked to Nadia," she reported. "Any luck with Akley?"

"More than you'd believe. I should be at the ferry in twenty-five minutes. Why don't we meet at the Dory" — he looked at his watch — "at 4 o'clock."

"Fine."

He was five minutes late and found her sitting at a table in the back. The place was empty except for a few people sitting at the bar watching an NBA game.

Mearns had spent an hour with Nadia after church. Nadia was still extremely shaken, not only by Harrison's death but by what Rytis had told her about the scene at the gym the previous morning. "She's worried that Arturas is going off the deep end with this whole deal."

"She's got reason to be worried."

The most significant piece of news, given what Kelleher had learned at St. John's, was that Bobby Taylor had called the house Saturday morning to ask if there was any point in Minnesota State's continuing to recruit Rytis in light of Scott's death.

"Doesn't sound as though he's too distraught to go on, does it?" Kelleher asked. "What did Nadia tell him?"

"She said she didn't know what to say and that, to be honest, she was so heartily sick of everything that had happened, she almost wanted to tell Rytis never to play basketball again."

"Whoo! That would cause a few upset stomachs, wouldn't it?"

"Starting with her husband."

Mearns had done some homework for her trip to Chicago.

The American flight left Islip at 7:20 and arrived at O'Hare at 8:30, picking up an hour with the time change. The funeral was scheduled for eleven. Mearns had the name of the church and the funeral home.

"The question is, what do I say to Taylor? 'So, Bobby, Scott was double-crossing you, and you had him killed?' "

"You do what you always do — follow your gut."

She was right, of course. In more ways than he wanted to think about, Mearns reminded him of Maureen McGuire. She was smart and funny and a very good reporter. Not to mention the dimples. Kelleher knew he had to keep his hormones in check right now. Even if Mearns *was* interested in him — which, he conceded to himself, was at least slightly more plausible than Nikki's being interested in him — this wasn't the time or place for that kind of complication.

"What're you thinking?"

"You don't want to know."

She nodded. "You're right. I was going to offer to fix you dinner, but maybe I shouldn't."

"Compromise. I'll fix *you* dinner. I'm never anything but a perfect gentleman when I'm under my mother's roof."

"Deal. I'll shop so you can go home and make your plane and rental car reservations."

That sounded fair. Kelleher fixed steak — what else? — and resisted all his various urges, including the one to open a second bottle of wine. The last thing he needed was a hangover when he had to wake up at five o'clock. They exchanged life stories, and platonic kisses on the cheek shortly after ten. Kelleher was in bed by 10:30. Naturally, he didn't sleep a wink. Every five minutes he rolled over and looked at the clock, thinking it had to be morning. By the time the alarm went off, he was exhausted and ready for sleep. He rolled into the shower, sucked down two mugs of coffee, and caught the 5:40

ferry by a whisker. During the summer, the first ferry was always packed. Now, his was one of three cars.

He spent most of the flight trying to envision himself talking to Bobby Taylor. How would he broach the subject of Scott's involvement with NYU? In fact, he wasn't absolutely certain that Scott *had* been involved with NYU. He was still rehearsing questions in his head when the "fasten seatbelt" sign came on. Looking out the window, he saw three planes lined up parallel to his, approaching the adjoining runways at O'Hare. No airport was busier than O'Hare, and sometimes it seemed as if the planes were bumper to bumper as they came in. That's why experienced fliers called it "O'Scare Airport."

There were no scares on this flight. The weather in Chicago was cold but clear and, best of all, almost windless. It was, Kelleher thought as he picked his way through the always-crowded American terminal, a beautiful day to be alive. Certainly not a day to be buried.

He made it out of the airport in surprisingly fast time, stopping first to pick up his rent-a-car, then to call the funeral home for directions to the church. It was only a little after nine when he pulled off the National rent-a-car lot and followed the signs for 90 and 94 West. He would find the church, then go get some breakfast. It was an old trick he had learned from his coaching friends: when early, find where you're going first, then worry about how to kill time. If you kill the time first, you may end up lost and late.

He found the church without any problem and went searching for a McDonald's. As he drove past the huge Hinsdale houses, with their perfectly manicured lawns, it occurred to him that this was not a McDonald's kind of neighborhood. He drove back in the direction of the interstate and found a McDonald's one exit up. He bought a *Chicago Tribune* out of a machine outside and sat down with an Egg McMuffin, coffee, and the sports page.

In the bottom left-hand corner on the front was a headline: "He Would Have Done Great Things." It was a profile of, and a tribute to, Scott Harrison.

The reporter had done a lot of homework. He wrote about Scott's days as a star at Hinsdale High School and his popularity in school. Scott had been class president as a senior and, in his high school yearbook, had been chosen "Most Likely to Date Miss Universe." They hadn't been far wrong with that assessment. The piece went on to chronicle his playing days in college and his coaching career. The most glowing quote in the story came from Bobby Taylor.

"With all that has gone on here in the past couple of years, I don't know if I could have hung in this long without Scott," Taylor had said. "His loss is beyond devastating for all of us. It makes me sincerely question whether I even want to continue. It's as if all the fight has gone out of me. I feel as if I've lost a son."

"We'll just see about that, won't we?" Kelleher said, folding the paper up.

The story also noted that while Suffolk County police investigators were pursuing several leads, they had no suspects. What that really meant, Kelleher assumed, was that with so many different suspects, they hadn't been able to pick just one. He wondered if they had any idea about Nick Angellini's possible involvement. Or Bobby Taylor's.

He parked a block from the church and was at the front steps by 10:30. People were already starting to trickle in. Rather than go in and claim a seat, Kelleher decided to find a spot off to the side somewhere, so he could watch people as they arrived.

Most of the early arrivals were unfamiliar — local Hinsdalians, no doubt. They looked prosperous and, in many cases, devastated. Scott Harrison had left here as a golden boy fifteen years earlier, Kelleher recalled. This wasn't the way he was supposed to come home.

The coaches came in groups. Bob Knight and his entire staff arrived with Johnny Orr, the former Iowa State coach, and Jim Crews, the Evansville coach who had played for Knight at Indiana. Dean Smith and John Thompson came together. So did Mike Krzyzewski, Jeff Jones, and P. J. Carlesimo. Rick Pitino, Jim Boeheim, and Gary Williams were close behind them. It struck Kelleher that this was quite a turnout for an assistant coach's funeral, especially at this stage of the season. But Harrison had been well known and well liked in the coaching community, and the notion that one of their own had actually been murdered and that the recruitment of a player might be the reason was the kind of thing that would send shock waves through the coaching community.

Amaker arrived a few minutes after Krzyzewski, accompanied by the other Duke assistants, Mike Brey and Pete Gaudet. Tom Perrin and Pete Herrmann from Virginia were with them. Stepping out from the shade of the tree he had been leaning against, Kelleher called to Amaker and Perrin.

"What's the matter, you guys can't walk in with the bosses?" Kelleher gibed as they walked over and shook hands.

"Someone has to park the cars," Amaker shot back.

"You here to mourn or to report?" Perrin wanted to know.

"Both."

"You find anything out?" Amaker asked.

"Plenty. What are you guys doing after?"

"We'll go to the cemetery, then there's a reception at the Harrison house," Perrin said.

Kelleher wasn't eager to crash an event like that, but he *had* been a friend, so he wasn't really crashing. "Make sure you talk to me there."

They went inside. The church was going to be packed. Shortly before eleven o'clock, the hearse pulled up to the front curb. Harrison's parents and two sisters climbed out. One other person had ridden with them: Bobby Taylor.

Kelleher almost gagged. If Taylor had been involved in Scott's murder, he had remarkable gall. Either way, his proximity to the family was going to make it difficult for Kelleher to talk to him.

Kelleher waited until the family had walked in, then followed them up the steps. A number of people were already standing around the back of the church, which made it apparent that no seats were left. Kelleher found a spot in the corner as the Harrison family was led to their seats in the front row. Bobby Taylor appeared to be holding Mrs. Harrison up. The sight of the coffin made Kelleher feel a bit weak-kneed himself.

Any hope that the ceremony would be brief was quickly dashed when the minister made reference to the three eulogies to come. The eulogists were Harrison's father, Scott Sr.; his best friend from high school; and — Kelleher should have known — Bobby Taylor.

Taylor was easily the most eloquent of the speakers. He told funny stories about Scott and how he had never met a mother who could resist him. He talked about his doggedness and his dedication and what a great head coach he would have been. Finally, he talked about what Kelleher figured most of those in the church had to be thinking about.

"How can something like this happen?" Taylor asked. "How can a future so bright be snuffed out in a single instant by an act of complete insanity? That's what this is: an act of complete and total insanity. We all have questions now, and no answers.

Even when we have the answers, it won't change the way we feel. Scott will still be gone. We'll all be left with the same void."

His voice was rising. "If, as some suspect, this is somehow connected to the recruitment of a basketball player, then all of us here, especially those of us in the basketball business, *must* take a serious look inward at what we do and who we are and what we have become. The message out there is that basketball is *important* — so important that cheating and lying and stealing are okay as long as you win. Have we now added killing to that list? All in the name of winning games?

"To me, there is no rhyme nor reason in the death of someone young. I have heard members of the clergy talk about God having a plan, or it's being someone's time. With all due respect, I cannot accept that. This was *not* Scott Harrison's time. Not even close. Insanity killed him. The question we all must address is whether we are part of that insanity. Sadly, the answer is probably yes. For my part, all I want now is to find a way to be part of a solution. I am disgusted knowing that I have been part of the problem."

Kelleher was moved, both by Taylor's words and by the passion with which he delivered them. He certainly didn't sound like a man who had plotted to kill Scott Harrison. But who? Who had been so insane? He had to find out a way to talk to Taylor before the day's end.

Leaving the church, mourners were greeted not only by bright sunshine but by the harsh glare of TV lights. Kelleher had forgotten that this would be a major media event. Since no cameras were allowed in the church, the TVs, local and national, had set up outside the church to get a minute or two with some of the famous coaches as they came outside. Several stopped and talked.

Bobby Taylor walked out of the church not with the family,

Kelleher noticed, but with Phil Wynans, his other assistant coach. Seeing a couple of cameras heading for Taylor, he decided to follow along. When he walked up, Taylor was pleading with the crews to let him pass without a comment.

"Please, guys, not today. You've got half the Hall of Fame here — you don't need me."

"Coach, he *did* work for you," a voice said. It sounded familiar. Kelleher searched the crowd. It was Dick Schaap from ABC, one of the class acts in TV. Taylor looked at Schaap and nodded sadly. "Okay, Dick, you're right. But please, quickly. We've got to get into line for the procession to the cemetery."

Taylor turned to Wynans and pulled a set of car keys from his pocket. So — he wouldn't be riding to the cemetery with the family. Kelleher wasn't sure if that helped him or not.

Schaap asked Taylor the first question. "Coach, you said in church that you didn't want to be part of the problem anymore. Does that mean you're considering quitting?"

It was a good question, a logical one. "Dick, I've considered almost everything since Friday night. I've gone from thinking the best thing for me to do is really upset all these insane people by going out and following up on the work Scott was doing and getting the kid, to thinking I don't want to coach another game or be in this business for another minute. It's all so emotional for me right now. That's why I finally decided not to make any decisions until I'm a little less emotional — whenever that may be."

"*Coach, what about the rumors that there was a woman involved in all this?*"

Predictably, this came from one of the tabloid-TV types, a tall, blond woman wearing enough makeup to sink the *Titanic*.

"I'm trying hard not to listen to any rumors, because that's all they are," Taylor replied. "When there are facts, they'll come from the police, and then I'll listen."

Kelleher had to strain to hear the next question. It came from near the front, and it was almost a whisper. Leaning forward on tiptoe, Kelleher could see that the questioner was Bob Verdi, the longtime *Chicago Tribune* sports columnist, one of the most thoughtful men in the business. Kelleher couldn't hear the whole question but he did hear the end of it: ". . . the toughest thing you've ever done?"

"Oh, Bob, easily." Kelleher guessed Verdi had asked about giving the eulogy. "There were so many things I wanted to say to so many people — Scott's family, his friends, all the coaches, all the sickos in college sports today. But there was also a part of me that wanted to say nothing — that just wanted to be here because I need to be here, and then get going."

He paused as a cacophony of voices shouted more questions. "Guys, really, I have to go. They asked us to be in line in ten minutes, and it's been almost twenty. Please understand."

The cameras parted, almost by magic, opening a path so he could get to the curb. Wynans had pulled up; all the way down the block, Kelleher could see cars lined up to follow the hearse to the cemetery.

In fact, they were starting to move out. No way was Kelleher going to get to his car and back here in time to follow the procession. He had no idea where the cemetery was. And he had no chance to get to Taylor in this mob scene.

"Dammit." Looking around desperately, he heard someone call his name. Tom Perrin, behind the wheel of a car that also contained Jeff Jones and Pete Herrmann, braked to a halt.

"Tom — you guys following the procession?"

Perrin nodded.

"Let me hitch with you."

"We aren't coming back here — we're going straight to the house and then the airport."

"That's okay. I'll worry about getting back later."

He jumped in the back seat with Herrmann, who had once coached David Robinson at the Naval Academy. It had been a while since he had seen Jones, his old teammate, but Perrin had obviously kept him abreast of what was going on. During the forty-five-minute ride to the cemetery, the four men traded theories about what had happened to Harrison — with Kelleher, for once, listening more than talking.

At the cemetery, everyone walked slowly down a hill to the burial site. Seeing the coffin mounted on the machine that would lower it into the ground made Kelleher sick to his stomach. He didn't like funerals, but he absolutely couldn't stand cemeteries.

"Makes you stop and think, doesn't it?" Perrin remarked softly.

It did. And, Kelleher knew, it made almost everyone stop and think the same thing: my day in a place like this will come. He shook his head to push that disturbing thought away and looked for Taylor, whom he saw standing near the front. It looked as if at least three hundred people had come to the cemetery. There were four chairs in front of the coffin for the family. Everyone else stood.

"We will be brief," the minister said. "The Harrisons have asked me to remind everyone that all are invited to their home when we are finished, and to again thank you all for being here. It has meant a great deal to them."

He read several brief prayers, then walked over and spoke quietly to the family. By now, each of them was sobbing. Kelleher remembered the last time he had been in a cemetery like this — at his grandmother's funeral. He remembered that the most difficult moment for everyone, but especially for his father, aunt, and uncle — the three children — had been getting up and walking away. Awful. But to have to do that for your own child . . .

Kelleher felt his own tears. Looking around, he saw he wasn't alone. He knew that coming to the cemetery was supposed to give everyone a feeling of closure. The problem was, Scott Harrison's life wasn't supposed to close for another fifty years.

Standing now, the family began walking to the hearse, the minister and Mr. Harrison supporting Mrs. Harrison. Slowly, everyone followed up the hill to the cars. Bobby Taylor hadn't moved. A number of people walked up to the casket, knelt, and crossed themselves, or stood quietly for a moment. Several placed flowers on the casket.

"You coming, Bobby?" Perrin asked.

Taylor still hadn't moved. "You guys go ahead. I'm going to stay a minute."

"You sure?"

"Sure."

The crowd thinned. Finally, only two people — Taylor and Kelleher — were left, other than the cemetery crew, who stood a respectable distance to the side, waiting for the last mourner to leave before lowering the coffin into the ground. Kelleher stood well behind Taylor, leaving him alone with the coffin and his thoughts.

Finally, Taylor let out a soft, sad, wailing sound and walked up to the casket. He put his hand on it, then put his head on top of his hand. He stood there, unmoving. Then he patted the coffin with his left hand, sobbed again, and turned around. Clearly he had thought he was alone, because when he saw Kelleher, he did a double take.

"Coach, I'm sorry to intrude at a moment like this — "

Taylor looked at him sadly. "Do I know you?"

"No. But Scott did. My name's Bobby Kelleher."

Recognition flashed in Taylor's eyes. "You were there, weren't you? You found Scott." He started to cry once more.

Then, very softly, he said, "Scott said you were the best reporter he ever knew."

That made Kelleher choke up all over again. He knew his eyes were glistening with tears, but he didn't really care. "Bobby, you aren't here to interview me, are you? I just can't ..."

"No, Coach, I don't want an interview. But if you really want to know who killed Scott, I need your help."

Taylor looked surprised. "*You* need help? What about the police?"

"I don't think they know as much as I do."

Taylor took his arm. "Phil Wynans went to get the car. Why don't you ride with us to the Harrisons' house? We can come back for your car later."

Kelleher didn't bother to explain where his car was. Taylor was still choking back tears as they walked up the hill. At the top, Kelleher couldn't help turning around one last time.

The casket had already been lowered into the ground. Four men were shoveling dirt into Scott Harrison's grave.

NINE

DEAD ENDS

WYNANS DROVE; Taylor and Kelleher sat in back.

If he were going to get Taylor to really talk, Kelleher realized, he had to prove he knew more than the cops.

He started with Nikki Buzelis, figuring Taylor knew all about her. He did. In fact, he asked Kelleher if she were really as beautiful and brilliant as Harrison had claimed. "You know, normally I tried not to know what Scott was doing socially, especially if it involved a recruit's family. It was one of those 'If you don't tell me, I won't know' things. But he couldn't stop talking about this girl."

It surprised Kelleher — and, he thought, would probably surprise Nikki too, given her description of the relationship. "Scott wasn't exaggerating," he assured Taylor. Then he asked the sixty-four-dollar question: "Did Scott's relationship with her give you a real shot at getting this kid?"

Taylor looked at him for a moment, as if studying him. "It was us and Louisiana — no doubt about that. I know what Scott thought — that in the end, it would be the mother, the sister, and the kid against the father, and three would be better than one." He took a deep breath. "Judging by what happened, I'd say he was on to something."

Kelleher pressed ahead. "Coach, was Scott in line for any jobs that you know of?"

Taylor looked at him quizzically. "No, not that I know of. He got a call from the NYU search committee early on, but he told them no thanks. I think he might have been interested, except that Nick Angellini was running the show. Scott hated Angellini — he'd been such a thief when he was coaching."

Taylor was right about that. On more than one occasion since Angellini's rise to TV stardom in the last five years, Kelleher had heard Harrison rail about how much it galled him that a "glorified bagman" was now treated as one of the important voices in the college game. Taylor's bringing up NYU surprised him. If he believed Scott had been trying to steal Buzelis and take him to NYU, that would make him a suspect.

Taylor leaned forward so Wynans could hear him. "Phil, did Scott have anyone courting him he didn't tell me about?" His voice was still hoarse from crying.

"No, Coach, I don't think there was anyone."

"Why do you ask?" Taylor inquired.

Kelleher explained that at first he had been convinced Miles Akley was behind the murder, but now he wondered. Akley had an excellent alibi and, from everything Kelleher had heard on Shelter Island, felt very comfortable that he had the father wrapped up. Kelleher had also heard rumors that Nick Angellini was involved. He watched Taylor closely for a reaction.

"How would Angellini be involved?"

"What if he secretly had something going with Scott? What if Scott didn't turn down NYU and was planning to deliver Buzelis to NYU in return for the job?"

For the first time all day, life flashed in Taylor's eyes: anger.

"Where the hell do you come up with a theory like that? You knew Scott. You have to know he wasn't capable of something like that — *especially* with scum like Angellini!"

Kelleher said nothing. Every cell in his brain, every reporter's instinct, told him that Bobby Taylor hadn't done this. But the last three days had been too strange for him to give up on any theory that was even the tiniest bit plausible.

"Coach, forgive me for asking this, but how true are the rumors about your job being in jeopardy?"

Taylor shrugged. "I've got two years left on my contract. A group of alumni wants to buy me out. The president has been fighting them, but some of them are real fanatics. They say they'll run him out too if he doesn't get rid of me. The sad thing is, we aren't far from being very good again."

"Would Rytis Buzelis be the difference?"

"We get Rytis, we win at least twenty next year. We're a Final Four contender in two years. Legit. Plus, our recruiting next year and the year after gets a huge boost."

"He can make or break you."

Taylor looked out the window for a long time. Finally he murmured, "Make or break. One kid."

Kelleher remembered something. "Coach, did Scott call you Friday night? He said at halftime he was going out to call you on his cellular phone. Did he?"

Taylor shook his head. "The last I heard from him was that afternoon, when he landed at the airport. He said he might stay an extra day. The sister had told him Akley might try to close something with the father, and he wanted to keep an eye out."

"Were you home Friday night?"

"At the office, watching tape. With my coaches."

"And Scott would have known to call you there?"

"Absolutely."

"No message? No voice mail? Nothing?"

"Nothing at all."

"When he called you Friday afternoon, did he say anything about feeling like he was in jeopardy? Or had he said anything about it before then?"

"Never said a word. All he talked about was Akley. Why?"

"Nikki said he told her before the game that someone — actually, some *they* — was trying to kill him."

Taylor sighed. "So he did know something was going on. I wonder why he didn't call."

"But he told her he was going to call. If he thought someone was going to kill him, why would he go out to his car in a dark parking lot, especially if he wasn't going to call you?"

"Maybe he never got the chance," Wynans volunteered.

"Possible," Kelleher agreed. "The phone was still in his hand when I found him."

"Might be worth getting hold of the records for his phone," Taylor suggested. "That way you can find out who he called that night — or, for that matter, all day."

Taylor was not acting like a guilty man. Why mention the records if he were lying about the phone call?

"Can you get me those records?"

"Sure, if he was using our cellular account. I'll have my secretary check into it tomorrow when we get back."

"Coach, do you have any theories on who did this?"

"Mine has been Akley all along. That's what I told the police. Someone said he might actually have the audacity to show up today. That's why I wanted to be sure and make the point about sickos in our sport in my eulogy. That was directed at the coaches, but also at him."

"I don't think he was here. I don't think he dared."

"But you don't think he did it."

"Coach, I don't know what to think. There's evidence that he didn't."

Taylor leaned back in his seat. "Well then, it must be someone we haven't thought of yet. Someone who's even more insane than any of us can imagine."

Kelleher didn't stay at the Harrison house long. He introduced himself to the Harrisons, told them how sorry he was, and talked briefly to a few of the coaches. He heard one of the coaches make a crack about a reporter having a hell of a nerve showing up at a time like this, and he was tempted to say something, but resisted.

Shortly after two, he called a taxi to take him back to his rent-a-car near the church. He made the four-o'clock flight and spent the trip writing notes about the day. If Bobby Taylor didn't do it and Nick Angellini didn't do it and Miles Akley didn't do it, then who?

He wanted to see whom Scott had called on his cellular phone in those last hours: it might provide a clue. He also wanted to find out more about the NYU short list. Had Scott really turned them down at the beginning, or had he just told Taylor that? Of course, if Taylor believed Scott had said no to NYU, then what was Taylor's motive? Lots of questions still, and no answers.

As soon as he landed, he called Mearns. It would be after nine o'clock before he was back on the island, and he was exhausted. He told her he had plenty to tell her but suggested they talk over breakfast. "Did the cops come up with anything new?"

"Nothing major, but a couple of interesting tidbits."

"Like?"

"Like they still haven't found anyone other than Arturas who can verify Akley's story about coming back from the bathroom midway through the third quarter."

"And they *won't* find anyone, since they're both lying."

"Right. But that's not the most important thing. They *have* found two people who say they saw Akley talking to Scott near the end of halftime."

"Whoa! Any names?"

"Not yet. But I think I can get them tomorrow. Billy Hollister was off today."

"Great. Now what about — "

"Hang on. I haven't told you the most important news yet."

"You haven't?"

"No. It looks like tomorrow's the big day. Nadia called me this afternoon. Akley and his people are coming for the game tomorrow night, and she says they want to finalize the deal afterwards."

"Finalize what deal?"

"She's not even sure. But there's a big powwow planned, and Arturas told her it would all be over by Wednesday morning, one way or the other."

Kelleher whistled. "We need to find out more."

"Nadia told me she would try to call tomorrow when she had any details. It might be worth putting a call in to Nikki."

She was right. He wondered if Nikki was coming out for the game. Still standing in the airport baggage claim area, he dialed her apartment and got the machine. He left a message asking her to call him on Shelter Island, no matter how late she got in.

Seized by a craving for a pizza on the drive back to the island, he stopped at Sergio's in Riverhead, the closest thing to New York street pizza you were going to find on the East End. When he hit the back road, he felt a surge of exhaustion, mingled with relief at being almost back to Shelter Island. The long day had been unnerving — the lengthy, bitterly sad service in the church, the sight of Bobby Taylor at the cemetery, and the sight of the casket disappearing into the ground. He still didn't feel anywhere close to figuring out who had killed Scott. Mearns's news about witnesses having seen Scott talking to Akley seemed to point to his original suspect.

He stayed up late watching Nevada–Las Vegas play New Mexico State on ESPN and found himself amazed at how far Vegas had fallen since the glory years under Jerry Tarkanian. It was remarkable, he thought, how thin the margin for error was in college basketball. One or two players could turn a whole program around. Which was why Rytis Buzelis meant so much to so many people. Clearly, Miles Akley felt Louisiana had to have him to stay viable on the national scene. Just as clearly, he was the player who would probably save Bobby Taylor's job. And he could easily be the player to launch a reborn program like the one at NYU. One player. One seventeen-year-old kid.

He fell asleep listening to Barry Tompkins talk about how fired up he knew Dick Vitale must be to be doing Indiana–Michigan the next night.

When he woke up, still stretched across his father's chair, Sportscenter was on. He got up and looked at the kitchen clock: it was almost eight. He put coffee on and headed for the shower. Halfway up the steps, he heard the phone.

"Bobby, I'm sorry I didn't call you when I got home, but I didn't check my messages until just now."

"No problem, Nikki. Are you coming to the game tonight?"

"Yes. Mother called yesterday and said Akley was coming to make a deal with father. She wants both Vida and me there."

"Nikki, I need to find a way to be at that meeting."

"That's impossible. You know that."

"I don't mean sit at the table. I mean somehow know what's going on."

"How can you do that?"

"I have no idea. But if I come up with one, will you help?"

"Of course. I'll come back here just before three o'clock — before Vida and I leave to drive there. If you need me, call then."

He called Mearns to see where she wanted to meet for breakfast. She suggested the Inn-Between.

"I didn't know they served breakfast."

"New thing. I guess it's an experiment for the spring. They just started last week. It's actually pretty good."

The Inn-Between was exactly halfway "in-between" the North and South ferries. It was more spacious than the Dory and had a comfortable upstairs dining room. What it lacked during the summer was that back porch right on the water. They agreed to meet at nine o'clock.

Kelleher stopped to pick up papers at Carol's and walked into the Inn-Between just before nine.

"Power breakfasts on Shelter Island — I never would have dreamed it," Kelleher announced, shaking hands with Billings. Eddie Billings was an old friend — someone he had spent a lot of late nights with, drinking an extra beer and wondering why none of the O'Brien girls understood what great guys they were.

"Hey, if it's good enough for ace reporter Bobby Kelleher, why not?" They had known each other close to two decades. If they talked three times a year, it was a lot. But they were still friends, because the bonds of growing up together are never broken.

"How's business?"

"Go upstairs and see for yourself. People seem to like the idea of sitting at a table and spreading out rather than sitting at the counter at Carol's or the drugstore. It's a change of pace."

"Jamie and the kids okay?"

"Perfect. Danny reads me the sports pages in the morning."

"At five?"

"He's six. Time flies."

That was for sure. Kelleher walked up the steps and saw what Billings was talking about. Only two tables were empty. Mearns was already there, sitting up against the far wall, reading *Newsday*.

Kelleher told her about his conversation with Nikki. She had already been to the police station and seen Billy Hollister. One of the people who had seen Harrison and Akley talking was from Sag Harbor. The other was Josh Mothner, the manager up at Gardiner's Bay. Mearns would try to find the person in Sag Harbor; Kelleher would approach Mothner.

"What about tonight?" Mearns asked.

"Our best bet is to hope Arturas will tell Nadia what happens."

"Yeah, but even if he does, can we write that? I mean, putting the murder aside for just one second, we started out on this story convinced Miles Akley was trying to buy Rytis, right?"

"Right."

"So we need something solid to nail him with. Nadia repeating to us what Arturas tells her might be okay, but we need something more solid."

She was right — as usual. And while Arturas might feel compelled to tell Nadia about what had gone on as it related to Rytis, if any discussion of the murder took place, he might not mention it to her at all. He was about to concede her point when a sudden crash echoed under their feet.

"What's that?" Mearns asked.

"There's a storeroom right below us. Used to be a big makeout place when I was a teenager. You'd come up here or hang out at the bar, and if you'd had enough to drink, you might coax a girl back there. Lots of dark corners. This floor is the storeroom's ceiling."

"Sounds charming."

"Yeah, well, the good part of it was that unless you knocked something over, no one up here could hear you. But you could hear everything people were saying up here. Watch this."

He leaned down a little and, in a voice no louder than the one he had been speaking to Mearns in, said, "Everybody okay down there?"

"Just fine," came a muffled reply.

"Gee," Mearns remarked. "I never would have thought this breakfast could be so enlightening on the subject of Shelter Island lore."

"Stick with me, kid, and you'll learn — "

He stopped in mid-sentence and smacked himself on the forehead. "My God — that's it! That's how we nail Akley!"

Mearns looked at him uncomprehendingly. "What are you talking about?"

"What if Akley and Buzelis had their meeting right here, and what if one of us was downstairs in that storeroom with a tape recorder? We might not pick up every word, but I bet we'd pick up a lot of it."

Her eyes widened. "Sounds great, but how do you get Akley and Buzelis to sit here? Do you explain to them this is the only place where you can listen to them without being in the room?"

"Ha-ha. Look, there's got to be a way. We'll need help from Nadia and Nikki, though. They have to find out where Akley and Buzelis are planning to hold their meeting and then manipulate it so they end up here."

Mearns looked at her watch. "Arturas should be at work by now. I can call Nadia."

"Tell her to meet us somewhere. We need to do this in person."

"She might be afraid to meet us in a public place."

"Tell her to come to Kissing Rock."

"To *where?*"

He smiled. "You do need a lesson in Shelter Island lore. Kissing Rock was the place you took someone special. It's down past the end of Looey's Beach, at the dead end. You drive straight down the hill there and you come to this big rock on the beach. You can't miss it."

"Let me go call her."

"I'll talk to Eddie. We're going to need his help too."

Kelleher found Billings in the kitchen downstairs, finishing cooking an omelette.

"Geez, Bobby, the food'll be right up. Are you that hungry?"

"Actually, I am. You got a minute?"

Billings flipped the omelette onto a plate and handed it to a waitress. "Now I do."

"What time do you close tonight?"

"Restaurant at ten, bar at eleven."

"So upstairs is pretty much cleared out after ten."

"Usually before then. Occasionally we get people lingering until ten-fifteen or so."

"If some people came in here at ten or a little after, would you seat them upstairs?"

"Normally, no."

"Would you do it as a favor to me?"

Billings shrugged. "Sure, Bobby, for you. How many you got?"

"It's not me. It's Arturas Buzelis and Miles Akley."

"Akley. The Brickley guy, right? I've seen him hanging out at the games a lot lately."

"Exactly."

"So you want me to seat them upstairs if they come in tonight?"

"I want them to have absolute privacy up there."

Billings gave Kelleher a sidelong look. "What're you up to, Bobby?"

"Do me one more favor and don't ask. At least not right now."

Billings nodded. "Tell me what to do."

Kelleher did, emphasizing that he shouldn't offer them seating upstairs but should make sure they sat upstairs. He knew Billings was dying for details but that all the years of friendship kept him from asking. Mearns was halfway through her omelette when Kelleher got back.

"My end is done," Kelleher told her. "What about Nadia?"

"She'll meet us at your rock at noon. She's very nervous."

"That's okay. So am I."

After breakfast, Kelleher stopped at the golf club looking for Josh Mothner but was told he wouldn't be in until the afternoon. He went home and killed time until noon reading the papers and cleaning up the house. He was convinced that if he could listen in on Akley's meeting with Buzelis, he would know a lot more about what had happened to Scott Harrison — not to mention having the chance to catch the two of them red-handed brokering a deal.

En route to meeting Nadia at Kissing Rock, he stopped at the hardware store to buy a new tape recorder — just in case. He tested it, and was pleased to see that the mike could pick up voices across the room.

He had many memories of the Rock, almost all of them fond ones, although he had once been summarily dumped by a girl there. "There's someone else," she had told him in a scene straight out of a bad movie. Nadia and Mearns were already there, standing with their backs against the Rock, when he arrived.

"Beautiful spot," Mearns said. The Rock was about twelve feet high and covered with graffiti, most of it heart-shaped stuff with names inside the hearts. "I didn't realize kids did this sort of thing anymore."

"On Shelter Island they do."

He shook hands with Nadia Buzelis, who appeared to be shivering slightly, even though the sun was out and it was a mild, windless day. "Thanks for coming, Mrs. Buzelis. I know this is hard for you. But it's very important."

"I am so tired of all of this. I wish it would go away. But I need to know who killed Scott Harrison. I am frightened by what we may learn."

"Do you think your husband was involved in some way?"

She shook her head. "I do not think Arturas is capable of such a thing, and he swears to me that Miles is not. But Miles did ask him to lie to the police about where he was during the third quarter. He cannot explain to me why this was necessary."

"Which is why it's so important that I be able to hear what they're going to talk about tonight."

She spread her hands. "But this is impossible. I could not possibly invite you into my house at this point."

"Is that where they're planning to meet?"

She nodded. "After the game."

Kelleher thought for a moment. "Any ideas?" Mearns asked.

"One. Mrs. Buzelis, do you think you could throw them out of the house? Could you work up some kind of outrage that they would be discussing matters like this in your home and say you won't allow it? That if they have to do this, they won't do it under your roof?"

The phrase "not under my roof" was a favorite of his mother's. It usually referred to the sleeping arrangements that were not permitted when he and his brother brought girls home for the weekend in college.

"I could do that, yes, I think I could. Arturas knows I am not comfortable with any of this, even though he keeps insisting he is doing the right thing and a good thing. I could say that to them, but what if I did?"

"They'd need a place to go — which is where Nikki enters the plot. She could tell her father that the Dory is bound to be packed after the game, but that she's been to the Inn-Between a couple times and it's almost always quiet late at night."

"You think they'll buy that?" Mearns asked.

Kelleher shrugged. "They don't have many options, do they? They could go sit in a car together, I suppose, but that's not very comfortable — especially if Akley brings some of his people along, which I imagine he will. They could also go off-island, but the last ferry back is at eleven-thirty, and that would mean they'd be pretty short on time. It's not a lock, but it's a good bet."

"And what would you do then, Bobby?" Nadia Buzelis asked.

"It's hard to explain. But if they go to the Inn-Between, I think I can find out what they're talking about. And if I can do that, we may finally get some answers to our questions."

She looked at Kelleher, then at Mearns.

"Tamara, you approve of this?"

Mearns didn't hesitate. "One hundred percent, Nadia. I think Bobby's right."

Mrs. Buzelis nodded her head slowly. "All right then, I will do it. When Nikki and Vida get here, I will tell Nikki what must be done." She shook hands formally with them and walked to her car. Opening the door, she turned back in their direction.

"Promise me no one else will get hurt."

"I promise," Kelleher said.

It was a promise he sincerely hoped to keep.

In mid-afternoon, Kelleher went up to the club and met with Josh Mothner. Mothner told him what he had told the cops: that he had seen Harrison and Akley talking near the front door just before halftime ended. He had noticed them only because he knew who Akley was and remembered briefly seeing Harrison with Nikki Buzelis at a couple of earlier games. Harrison had waved an arm at Akley — Mothner thought maybe in disgust but obviously couldn't be sure — and then headed for the front door. Akley had turned and walked the other way.

Mearns went to Sag Harbor and came back with a similar story. The guy, whose name was Tom Shupe, was a recruiting junkie, so he knew both Akley and Harrison. He described their conversation as "animated" but said he wasn't standing close enough to hear anything.

Shortly before five o'clock, the phone rang. It was Bobby Taylor's secretary. "Coach Taylor asked me to call for your address. We were able to get a copy of Scott's phone calls from the cellular company today, and he wants to mail it to you."

Mail would take too long. He asked her to hold, dialed Mearns at the office, and got her fax number. Then he asked the secretary to fax the records to Mearns.

"Well, I suppose that's okay," she remarked dubiously.

"It's very important."

She said she would do it right away. Kelleher called Mearns back to tell her to expect the fax, then jumped into his car and raced to the *Reporter*. Mearns was holding two pages in her hands when he walked in.

"Lots of calls," she informed him. "But Taylor's telling the truth. The last call to the 612 area code was at four o'clock that afternoon."

He took the two fax pages from her and sat down at an empty desk. Harrison had used the phone eight times on the last day of his life. Several of the calls were to his direct line — no doubt to check messages. The 4 o'clock call was to a similar-sounding number — probably the call to Taylor.

Two things intrigued him. None of the calls was to Nikki or the Buzelis house. Nikki had told him Harrison called her apartment and then left a message with her mother. Of course, it was entirely possible that Scott had called her from the plane, where he couldn't use a cellular, or from a phone booth, to save Minnesota State a few bucks.

Far more important was the last call. It had been made at 8:43 P.M. and had lasted seven minutes. Kelleher wasn't sure what time he had found Scott, but it couldn't have been more than twenty or thirty minutes later than that. The phone number was in Connecticut.

"See this?" he said to Mearns, pointing to the last call. "This may be the key to the whole thing."

"Should we call?"

"Why not?"

He dialed the number. On the fourth ring, a message tape answered: "Hiya, sports fans. Not here right now. Leave a message, though, and I promise I'll call you back!"

There was absolutely no question to whom the voice on the tape belonged: Nick Angellini.

"Taylor's telling the truth about Scott not calling him that night. We also know that not long before he died, Scott called Nick Angellini and spoke to him — or someone — for seven minutes. What does that tell us?"

Mearns was rehashing what they knew for a fifth time as they finished dinner at the Dory. It was an old reporting trick to repeat the facts you had over and over and hope that something clicked the fifth or sixth time that hadn't clicked the first four. Kelleher shook his head.

"Logic says he was in cahoots with Angellini, right? My gut says that if he was, Taylor didn't know. If Taylor did know, why does he send us phone records that link Scott to Angellini when he insisted to me that Scott hated Angellini?"

"Okay — what if Taylor didn't know? Scott's in this thing with Angellini; he's going to deliver the kid to NYU. Who wants him dead for that?"

"Akley."

"Who still doesn't have an alibi."

"Or Arturas Buzelis."

"Who lied on Akley's behalf."

Something was gnawing at Kelleher. He looked at the phone records once more. It reminded him of the two non-calls to Nikki. He ran that past Mearns.

"This is crazy," she acknowledged, "but — what if that conversation you saw out back wasn't what Nikki told you it was? What if Scott was dumping Nikki and she got mad at him?"

"Woman scorned? Doesn't make sense. First of all, Nikki was in the gym the whole third quarter. And second, based on what Taylor told me, Scott liked her even more than she knew."

"Then who? It almost has to be Akley."

"Let's hope we find out tonight."

The gym filled early for the game, partly because Shelter Island had never hosted a state playoff game before, but also because Oswego High School had brought close to three hundred fans — an amazing number, considering that it was at least a six-hour drive from upstate New York to Shelter Island.

A few coaches from smaller schools were in the gym, probably looking at a couple of the Oswego players. Most of the big-timers no doubt figured they could see Rytis that weekend in New York. Perhaps they also thought that showing up at the game after one of their own had been murdered was a bit much.

But Akley was there, along with Fred Murray and one of Murray's assistants, Rudy Jefferson. Kelleher pointed the threesome out to Mearns during warmups. "Not a single ounce of decency among the three of them. Jefferson's been the bagman for Murray even longer than for Akley."

The game was competitive. Oswego double-teamed Rytis whenever he touched the ball, and for most of the first half he was forcing things. Midway through the second quarter, he began to find the open man. It was 44–34, Shelter Island, at the break.

At halftime, Mearns went into the lobby to bump Nadia and Nikki — to make sure everything was still "go" after the game. Kelleher stayed in his seat and chatted with Bob De-Stefano, who wanted to know why Kelleher hadn't been up to the club for almost a week.

Mearns came back to report that Nikki had given her a thumbs-up in the lobby — to indicate everything was "go."

The second half was a rout, Rytis scoring 24 of his 36. Shelter Island pulled away for an 88–66 victory. That put them into a Thursday night quarterfinal in Madison Square Garden against Bayside High School, from Queens. Kelleher couldn't believe it: Shelter Island High School playing in the Garden.

A fairly sizable press contingent had appeared for the game, and a small press room had been set up in one of the downstairs classrooms. Several reporters had come from Oswego; a number of New York–area writers were also on hand. Newschannel 12, the Long Island all-news station, had sent a crew. The two coaches came in and spoke briefly, but no one really cared what they had to say. They all wanted to talk to Rytis.

He came into the little classroom and talked about what a thrill it was to win, to be part of Shelter Island's first twenty-victory season — they were now 20–1 — and how much he looked forward to playing in the Garden.

"Rytis, how close are you to making a decision about college?" someone asked.

Rytis smiled. "Not too close, not too far. After my season is over, I will visit schools and see which one I like the best."

"A lot of people think you're already locked up for Louisiana." This came from one of the Oswego reporters.

Rytis shrugged. "People can think what they want. When I make my decision, I will tell you all."

Malcolm Moran, the veteran *New York Times* reporter who normally covered college basketball, raised his hand. "Rytis, I know it's tough to talk about this, but how well did you know Scott Harrison, and are you aware that some people think his death may have been connected to your recruitment?"

"I am very sad about Coach Harrison," Rytis said, before Joe Dierker, standing off to the side basking in his reflected glow, stepped in.

"Rytis isn't here to talk about that. He's here to talk about basketball. He doesn't know anything about what happened to Harrison."

Moran looked at Rytis as if Dierker weren't there. "Is that so, Rytis?"

"I only know that he was a very good man."

Again Dierker interrupted. "Maybe you didn't hear me the first time."

"I heard you," Moran answered. "But I think Rytis is entitled to talk about Scott Harrison if he wants to."

"I'll decide what Rytis will talk about," Dierker declared, pointing a finger at Moran.

"No you won't."

It was Rytis. Dierker looked at him as if he had seen a ghost.

"What did you say?"

"I said, if I wish to talk about Scott Harrison, I will. No offense, Coach, but I am old enough to make these decisions. I don't need to be told what to do with my life all the time."

Dierker glared at Rytis for a moment, opened his mouth as if to say something, then turned around and walked out. Rytis smiled uncomfortably. Kelleher was tempted to lead a round of applause, but resisted. Then Rytis talked for several minutes about Scott and how much he and his family had liked and respected him and how sad his death was, whether it was connected to his recruitment or not.

Kelleher was struck once more by how mature the kid was. He was also interested in his comment about not wanting to be told what to do with his life all the time. That sounded an awful lot like someone who didn't want his father ordering him to go to school someplace when perhaps he wanted to go someplace else.

Rytis was answering a question from the Newschannel 12 reporter when the door opened and Arturas Buzelis walked in, followed by Joe Dierker and Miles Akley.

"Enough," Arturas Buzelis said, apparently unfazed by the rolling TV camera. "Rytis, it is time to go. No more talk tonight."

This time, the kid didn't argue. "Thank you very much," he said to the reporters. Then he followed his father and Akley out the door. Dierker lingered.

"I don't ever want to see you around here again," he said to Moran, who was standing up and putting his coat on.

Moran was hardly the confrontational type, but he had clearly had enough of some high school coach who would never be heard from again once Buzelis was gone. "Coach, let me just tell you one thing," he said. "I've been in the business a long time, but I've never seen anyone humiliated the way that kid humiliated you tonight. So don't come in here and pick a fight with me because you can't even control your own player."

He walked past Dierker, who stood spluttering into empty air. Kelleher followed Moran out the door, but as he went by Dierker, he couldn't resist: "Don't worry Joe. He's just with the *New York Times*. No big deal."

Dierker spluttered something about "fucking reporters," but Kelleher was halfway down the hall.

Kelleher looked at his watch: it was a couple of minutes before ten. The timing was just right if Nadia and Nikki could pull off their part of the job.

Mearns had been in the Oswego locker room, picking up a few quotes about Rytis. She met Kelleher back on the gym floor. The plan was to drive to the Buzelis house and wait outside in the hope that the Akley/Murray contingent would be shown the door by Nadia.

They drove past the house to a section of fence about a quarter mile down Burns Avenue. Akley's Cadillac had been parked in the Buzelis's driveway, right behind Arturas's van. Kelleher swung a U-turn, parked next to the fence, cut the lights, and turned off the engine. "If it gets too cold, I'll turn it back on. I'd rather not chance someone coming out and hearing it idling."

"We're a ways down the road."

"Let's not take chances unless we have to."

They sat in silence for a few minutes. Kelleher started to go over the plan one more time, but Mearns put a hand up: "Bobby, we've been through this a dozen times."

"I know. Sorry." Then he smiled. "First time you called me Bobby."

He saw her smile in the darkness. "I won't let it happen again."

The Buzelises' porch light came on. "Crack the window," Kelleher whispered, rolling his down a few inches. They could hear voices but couldn't make out words. Kelleher wished he had parked a little closer, but it would have been too risky. Still, they had a clear view of the driveway, now lit by the porch light. Murray and Jefferson were walking toward the white Cadillac. Akley and Arturas were heading for the van. Kelleher could see Nikki talking to her father. He hoped she was giving him directions or reassuring him that the Inn-Between was the place to go.

The Cadillac backed out of the driveway toward Kelleher and Mearns.

"Down," Kelleher commanded.

Peering up across the dashboard, he saw Arturas's van in front of the Cadillac, leading it in the direction of town. After they paused at the stop sign on the corner and proceeded, he turned on the engine.

"Don't get too close," Mearns cautioned. "No sense spooking them now."

Kelleher didn't answer. His heart was pounding; the game was really on. A couple of hundred yards before Rte. 114 he slowed, in case their prey had been forced to wait for a passing car. Nearing the corner, he saw the Cadillac pulling away.

"So far so good," he murmured.

He stopped at the sign, turned right, then followed several hundred yards behind. Arturas veered left, heading for the town center. Unless the van went past the Inn-Between and headed for the Dory, they were in good shape. The van and the Cadillac passed the school, turned right, and went by Town Hall. At the stop sign in front of the IGA, they paused and turned left. Once they had made the turn, Kelleher sped up. Ahead, he saw both vehicles turn left into the Inn-Between's parking lot.

"They did it!" he exclaimed. "Nikki and Nadia pulled it off."

"Now it's Eddie's turn."

"Don't worry about Eddie." He looked at his watch. It was 10:35; the upstairs should be empty by now. He drove past the Inn-Between, so as not to turn into the parking lot and run smack into their friends. At Reiter's Fish Market, he hung a U-turn and went back. The Cadillac and the van were parked next to each other out front. Taking no chances, he pulled around to the back of the building.

"Okay, kid," he said to Mearns. "Remember, if anyone comes downstairs, get up like you're going to the bathroom and come back as fast as you can and pound on that storeroom door."

"Got it." She leaned across and squeezed his neck. "Good luck."

"To both of us."

Taking deep breaths to keep himself calm, he got out of the car and stuffed the tape recorder into his pocket. In the other pocket he had some masking tape. While Mearns circled around front, he headed for the delivery entrance in the rear. Walking in, he heard voices from the bar area and ducked into the storeroom, which Eddie had left unlocked. He couldn't turn on a light, but Eddie had left a bar stool for him in the far corner. After a few seconds to adjust to the darkness, he began walking carefully in that direction. He saw the stool just before he bumped into it.

Pulling himself onto the stool, he heard voices directly above him. "Nikki was right," he heard Fred Murray say. "This is perfect. Can we order some drinks?"

"Absolutely." It was Eddie.

Everyone seemed to be ordering beer. "If you have a bottle of champagne, put it on ice for us," Miles Akley said. "We're planning to celebrate before the night is over."

"My pleasure," Eddie answered. Kelleher heard his footsteps crossing the room, back to the stairs. Chairs were scraped; people were sitting: time to get to work. He pulled himself to a standing position on the stool and, the tape recorder still in his pocket, pressed the "play" and "record" buttons simultaneously. Removing the recorder from his pocket, he pressed it to his ear to make certain he could hear the tape spinning. Satisfied, he pulled the masking tape out of his other pocket and, as quietly as possible, began pulling tape off the roll. It sounded terribly loud. He glanced upward and heard small talk: they were oblivious to him.

He stuck two lengths of tape under the recorder so that they stuck out on both sides. Then he put the recorder against the ceiling, the microphone pointing upward, wrapped the tape tightly around the recorder, and pressed it against the ceiling. This way, he wouldn't have to hold his arms over his head. He had sixty minutes before the tape had to be flipped.

"I apologize again for my wife," he heard Arturas say. "This has been a difficult time for all of us, and she is just a little uncomfortable."

"Say no more, Arturas," Fred Murray assured him. "She's a fine lady. And anyway, this place is quite pleasant. Lots of room, quiet. And here come our beers."

He heard Eddie's footsteps again, heard him putting beers on the table, then leaving.

"Before we begin," Arturas said, "I must tell you gentlemen that I am very, very uncomfortable with what happened to the Harrison boy."

"So are we," Fred Murray replied.

Arturas went on as if Murray hadn't said anything. "Miles

has told me why it was necessary to lie for him to the police. I know the stakes are very high for all of us in this, but I must have your word that you know nothing about any of this."

"Arturas, I already told you — " Akley protested.

"Tell me again, Miles. Tell me why you had to talk to him."

He heard Akley sigh. "Do you really want to hear this again? It wasn't painful enough the first time?"

"It was. But tell me again. Tell me so I believe."

Kelleher hardly dared breathe.

"I found out that Harrison was involved with your daughter."

"From?"

"I told you, I can't tell you."

"Tell him, Miles," Murray said. "No sense protecting anyone now."

"Okay then," Akley continued. "I found out from Nick Angellini."

Kelleher slapped a hand over his mouth and said "Jesus!" into it.

"I thought Harrison was trying to use Nikki, Arturas, to convince Rytis not to listen to you about where to go to college. I wanted to let him know he was making a mistake."

"So you threatened him."

"I didn't threaten him, I told you that. I just told him there was no way Rytis was going to end up at Minnesota State."

"Or NYU," Murray put in.

"He told me he wasn't involved with NYU," Akley said. "He said he was never involved with Nick."

"Then how," Arturas asked, "did Nick know about him and my daughter?"

Good question, Kelleher thought. Arturas could have been a reporter.

"Nick knows a lot of people — he has a lot of contacts in a

lot of places," Akley said. "He told me the word on the coaching grapevine was that Harrison was trying to use Nikki to get to Rytis."

That was a lie. It hadn't been on the coaching grapevine. If it had been, one of the coaches Kelleher was friends with would have heard it, or at least heard something about it. Arturas bought the story anyway.

"I am still not comfortable with all this. A murder because of my son. We left New York to escape this sort of thing."

"Which is why our campus is the perfect place for Rytis," Murray countered. "There's nothing in the world farther removed from New York City than the U of L."

"I am listening," Buzelis said. "Do you have answers to my requests?"

"Yes, I do," Akley answered. "The company is more than willing to make the kind of commitment you want, as long as we are guaranteed that when Rytis becomes a pro, he will be committed to us."

"What if he does not become a pro?"

"We'll cross that bridge when we get to it."

"What, then, do you offer?"

Kelleher strained upward, wanting to make sure he didn't miss a word. He couldn't believe he was hearing all this.

"Exactly what you asked: a one-million-dollar commitment each year he stays at Louisiana. That includes the whole package — everything you asked for."

Kelleher gasped. One million a year! He had heard about players getting a hundred grand — maybe in some cases a hundred grand plus a car for themselves and one for their parents, and maybe even a job for the parents. But a million dollars a year!

"And what about the TV?"

"We're still working on that. I can't really pursue it until our deal is locked in, but obviously it benefits us at least as much as you to get TV involved, since we want his name spread not just in this country and Lithuania but in all of Europe."

"TV is very important," Arturas declared. "People these days do not believe something is real without TV."

"We understand. The TV will be there. I'll put it in writing if you want."

There was a long silence. Kelleher guessed Arturas was considering the offer. Kelleher was still in shock at the numbers he was hearing. He wondered exactly what kind of TV they were talking about, but that didn't really matter right now. He had just heard Miles Akley make a four-year, four-million-dollar offer to the father of a basketball player. And as long as the tape recorder was working, he had it on tape.

"One more question," Buzelis said. "What happens if he goes pro after two or three years?"

"We would renegotiate. We will still be committed though, Arturas, one way or the other. We believe in every aspect of this project. We want Rytis at Louisiana, we want him to help promote Brickley/Europe, and we want the things you want too. There's not going to be a problem here."

"As long as my son performs."

"That's the least of our worries," Murray interjected. "He'll perform."

"What is it you say here?" Arturas remarked. " 'I think we have a deal'?"

"That's what we say," Akley agreed.

Chairs scraped; Kelleher guessed they had stood up to shake hands. "Find that waiter," Murray said. "Let's get that champagne up here."

Kelleher had heard enough. It was time to leave. Excited, he reached for the tape recorder, pulled it off the ceiling, and lost his balance. Before he could catch himself, the bar stool toppled backward. Kelleher, clutching the tape recorder, twisted like a diver going off the platform to keep from landing on his head.

He heard a crash, felt a twinge of pain in his shoulder, and jumped to his feet. They would have heard the crash upstairs. Panicked, he wondered if he should sprint for the door or try to hide. While he was deciding, the door swung open.

Kelleher was stunned. They couldn't have moved *that* fast.

It was Eddie. "Get behind that stack of boxes over there," he hissed, pointing to the corner.

"But what about — "

"Shut up. I'll take care of it."

Kelleher sprinted for the corner and heard the door swing open again. The light clicked on. Peeking through the boxes, he saw Eddie lying on his back next to the bar stool.

"Boss, what happened?" It was Matt, the bartender. Right behind him was Rudy Jefferson.

"Oh Christ, Matt, I was trying to get a case of wine out from behind this bar stool, and I fell right over the damn thing.

"Why didn't you turn a light on?"

That question came from Jefferson, who was peering around the room.

"Excellent question. I come in here all the time and never turn the light on. It disturbs people sitting upstairs, and I know my way around my own storeroom."

Matt was helping Eddie to his feet. Eddie winced and rubbed his elbow. "Fell on my funny bone."

Rudy Jefferson was still looking around. "Nothing broken?" Matt asked.

"No. But I hope when I open that case, I don't find a cracked bottle or two."

Matt turned to Jefferson. "Thanks for your help."

"Yeah," Jefferson said. "Sure. Fine. You're okay then, huh buddy?"

"I'm fine."

Jefferson turned to leave. "I'll clean this stuff up, Matt," Eddie said, and then, to Jefferson: "Tell your friends I'll only have the light on down here for another minute. Matt, get that champagne up to them, okay?"

"Right away, boss."

The door shut behind them. Kelleher felt himself starting to breathe again. Carefully, he stepped around the boxes.

"Jesus, that was quick thinking," he whispered in Eddie's ear.

"When I heard the crash, I figured right away it was you, Eddie whispered back. "Good thing I briefed Matt a little beforehand."

"He was perfect."

"The guy saw Tamara sitting there."

"That's okay. If she's sitting there, they won't think I'm here. 'Least, I don't think so."

"You better get out of here."

"Right now. I got what I came for."

They were at the door, still whispering.

"Promise me one thing," Eddie said.

"Name it."

"Someday you'll tell me what this was all about."

"Guaranteed."

"Let me make sure it's clear out here."

He walked into the hall and looked around. Then he beckoned to Kelleher, who stepped into the hallway, patted Eddie on the shoulder, and sprinted for the door. Looking around to make sure no one was in the back parking lot, he made his way to the car. About to drive away, he remembered Mearns, still inside.

"Damn."

He couldn't leave without her. He pulled the door shut, pushed the driver's seat as far back as it would go, and lay back, so he wouldn't be visible from outside the car.

He pulled the tape out of his pocket and hit the "rewind" button. When it had spun back to the beginning, he hit "play" and waited. Finally, he heard the voices; first Buzelis, then Murray, then Akley. He stopped the tape so he could play the whole thing for Mearns. He was pouring sweat but so hopped up he didn't care.

A tap on the passenger-side window made him jump in fright. He smiled with relief, seeing it was Mearns. He popped the lock, and she jumped in.

"What the hell happened in there?" she demanded.

"I got so excited that I toppled over," he admitted, embarrassed.

"Arturas came downstairs after Jefferson went looking for you in the storeroom and read me a polite version of the riot act."

"How so?"

" 'What are you doing here, are you following me, why can't you reporters just leave us alone.' Usual stuff."

"What'd you say?"

"That I was having a beer with my good friend Eddie."

"He buy it?"

"Enough that he turned around and went upstairs. That's when I got out of there. So what's the deal? Did it work?"

He smiled, starting the engine. He handed her the tape recorder. "Hit the 'play' button and see for yourself."

Mearns had heard most of the tape by the time they reached Kelleher's house. Occasionally she let out a gasp or a whoop or an "Oh, my God." It was, Kelleher knew, powerful stuff. They now had Akley cold. He would finally be revealed to the world as the glorified pimp that he was, a buyer and seller of teenage boys. But they still didn't know who had killed Scott Harrison.

Mearns finished listening to the tape while Kelleher made coffee. "What's your gut tell you about Akley's disclaimers on the murder?" she asked as he handed her a mug with "NCAA West Regional, 1983" printed on it — one of the few tangible reminders of his playing days.

"Good question." He sat down. "Obviously, if he did do it, given Arturas's concerns, he wouldn't just say, 'Yeah, we did it, Arturas, now do you want the money or not? On the other hand, he *did* know about Scott and Nikki. If Scott was involved with Angellini, which his phone records indicate, then Angellini telling him might make sense."

"Why would he be dealing with Angellini?"

"That's the next question. Right now, I think we need to get this story in print. That might flush some people out into the open."

"Not to mention ruin Akley."

He smiled. "Not to mention."

The phone rang. "Oh God," Mearns exclaimed. "I'll bet that's Nikki or Nadia. I told them I'd call as soon as we knew anything."

It was Nikki. "You're back," she said to Kelleher. "I was going to leave a message for you to meet me at the Dory. What happened?"

"We got 'em. Cold. On tape. Akley offered your dad a million bucks a year for Rytis."

She gasped. "A million dollars! You have this on tape?"

"Word for word."

"What about Scott? Did you find out anything about that?"

"Only that he was involved with Nick Angellini in some way. We're still trying to figure out exactly how."

"I have to hear this tape."

"Why don't you come over here?"

There was a long pause on the other end. "You're there with Tamara?"

"Yes."

Another pause. "I was hoping . . . no, forget it. . . . It's just that I thought maybe you and I . . ."

His heart started pounding again. "Well, that would be, um, okay. I can manage that."

He looked around at Mearns, who was staring out the window.

"Maybe we can meet at that rock where you met my mother. I think that would be safer than your house."

He was feeling pretty confident about safety, especially since no one knew what they had done, but he didn't want to start arguing about locations with Mearns there.

"Okay. When?"

"Half an hour?"

"You know where it is?"

"Mother will tell me."

He hung up and returned to the living room, trying to keep a straight face.

"Hot date, huh?" Mearns asked.

She had heard every word.

"Nothing like that. She just wants to hear the tape."

"Alone."

"No, not at all."

She stood up. "Oh come on, Kelleher, nothing to be ashamed of. She's a beautiful woman. You're probably her hero right now. I just wish she had a brother."

"She does."

"You know what I mean."

She patted him on the arm and picked up her coffee. "Just take good care of the tape. Bring it into the office first thing in the morning so we can copy it and transcribe it. Is she coming here?"

"Actually, I'm meeting her at Kissing Rock." He blushed.

"Whoo boy. I won't expect you before noon."

"Come on, Mearns, there's nothing to it."

She smiled, which always reminded him how pretty she was. "Enjoy it. You're entitled. We'll talk strategy tomorrow."

TEN

LONG GONE

KELLEHER DECIDED he needed a shower before going to meet Nikki, even though he kept telling himself not to expect anything more than a conversation about the evening's events. By the time he dried his hair, he was a few minutes late.

Her car was at the bottom of the hill when he pulled up. Seeing his lights, she came to meet him. When he got out, she threw her arms around him and kissed him. "Congratulations. You're a genius."

"No one's a genius," he protested, hoping he sounded modest. "You did this and your mom did this and Tamara did this and Eddie Billings did this and I did this. It was a team effort. Did you tell your mother?"

She sobered. "Yes. She's happy you have evidence, but very upset. After all, she's been married to my father for almost thirty years. She didn't think he could be involved in something like this."

Understandable, he thought. But he was — and he had the evidence right here in his hot little hand. He glanced at the water. The moon was three-quarters full; there wasn't a breath of wind. "Why don't we go sit by the rock and you can hear the tape?"

She gave him the full-treatment smile. "Okay."

They sat with their backs against the rock and he rewound the tape. Nikki listened quietly, not reacting, except for an occasional shake of the head. When it was finished, she stared straight ahead.

"How sad it all is," she said finally. "So many bad things have happened because my brother can play basketball. We all thought it was such a fun thing, such a joyful thing, in the beginning. There's no joy in any of this. Only sadness."

He edged a little closer to her and put an arm around her shoulder. She rested her head against his. He waited a little, then turned her head toward his and leaned forward. His lips brushed hers, and she smiled. He brought his other arm around to pull her toward him, wondering when he was going to wake up in bed and realize he was fantasizing. He closed his eyes to kiss her and then heard a car. Startled, he looked up and saw headlights coming down the hill very fast.

"Who the hell is this? Did you tell anyone we were coming here?"

"No one. Except my mother."

The car pulled up next to his. Two people got out. In the darkness, Kelleher couldn't see them. "Hello?" he called out.

"That you Bobby?" an unfamiliar voice came back.

"Yeah. Who's there?"

They were walking onto the beach now. As they approached, the moonlight hit their faces, and Kelleher knew he had a problem: both wore ski masks. He thought about grabbing Nikki by the hand and sprinting up the beach, but the chances of outrunning them were zilch. Instinctively, he stuck the tape recorder into the pocket of his pants.

"What do you guys want?"

"Nothing big," the taller of the two men answered. "Just give us the tape and we'll get out of here."

Give us the tape?! How could anyone know about the tape? It was an hour old, and the only ones who knew it existed were him, Nikki, Mearns, and Nadia Buzelis.

"Tape?" he asked innocently. "What tape?

"Fine, play it that way," the taller one said. "Buster, check him out, head to toe. And if he hasn't got it, I'll check the babe."

Buster took a menacing step forward.

"Okay, okay," Kelleher said. He reached into his pocket and pulled out an extra tape he had been carrying all night. "Stay calm, Buster."

He turned as if to toss it to Buster's partner, only he flipped it high and wide. As the two men turned instinctively in the direction of the toss, Kelleher took off, racing up the beach in the direction of the Hicks house, on the hill overlooking Kissing Rock. He had no intention of deserting Nikki. All he wanted to do was toss the tape someplace where he could come back for it later.

As he took off, the tall one yelled, "Hey, asshole, get back here!"

He sprinted as hard as he could toward the dunes. He assumed one of them was following him, but he didn't turn to look. When he had gone about fifty yards, his feet churning in the sand, he pulled the tape recorder out of his pocket and glanced up at the Hicks house to mark his spot. Trying not to use too much arm motion, he flipped it toward the hill up near the Hicks property. Glancing over his shoulder, he saw Buster in pursuit. From behind, he heard another voice.

"Hey, Kelleher, you want your girlfriend's face busted up?"

He ran three more steps and stopped. Okay, fine, he thought; you got me. But you haven't got the tape. He turned and faced Buster, arms in the air. "All right, Buster, you got me."

Buster huffed up to him, exhausted from the pursuit. He grabbed Kelleher by the collar and practically lifted him off the ground.

"Fucking wise guy," he growled, pushing Kelleher in front of him back the way they had come. Non-Buster was standing behind Nikki with an arm wrapped around her neck, the extra tape in his free hand.

"Okay, Kelleher, I'm going to say this once: where's the tape?"

Still breathing hard, Kelleher pointed at the extra tape. "That's the only tape I got."

Non-Buster nodded at Buster, who gave Kelleher a thorough and somewhat painful patting down. When he was finished he looked at his partner. "Nothing, Tommy."

"Shut up, asshole." Tommy was clearly not pleased that Buster had used his name, even though he had used Buster's a moment earlier. He tightened his grip on Nikki's neck. "I don't have time for these games, Kelleher. Now are you going to give me the tape, or do I hurt your friend here?"

Kelleher would have lunged at Tommy, but Buster still had a firm grip. "Look, Tommy, I don't have this tape — whatever it is — you're looking for. You want to check my car, go ahead. You've already checked me. I haven't got it."

He couldn't bluff much longer. If Tommy started beating Nikki up, he'd have to tell him what he'd done. As if reading his mind, Nikki suddenly struck backward with her leg, kicking Tommy hard in the shin. He grabbed his leg for a second, then took off after her as she sprinted toward the cars. If it had been five yards less she might have made it. Tommy brought her down just short of the spot where beach became pavement, and they struggled briefly. Buster had grabbed Kelleher's arms the second Nikki made her move and was holding him firmly.

Tommy and Nikki rolled in the sand for a couple of moments before Tommy came up holding her by the arms. He half-pushed, half-shoved her back to Kelleher and Buster.

"Try that again and I *will* hurt you," Tommy snarled. "I don't care how beautiful you are or who you model for."

Christ, Kelleher thought, the guy knows all about Nikki too. How was all this possible?

"Okay, here's what we're going to do," Tommy said. "My guess is that you tossed the tape on the beach someplace during your little run, Kelleher. So Buster and I are going to get our flashlights out of the car and look for it. In the meantime, to make sure neither one of you tries anything again, we're going to put you in your car and Nikki in our car."

"How we gonna do that?" Buster asked. "We haven't got any rope."

"You ever hear of a trunk, asshole? One in each. Now come on, I haven't got time for any more games. Let's go."

He pushed Nikki toward the cars, while Buster did the same with Kelleher.

Can't let them lock us up like this, Kelleher thought. He had one chance and one chance only. "You're going to need the keys, Buster."

"Right," Buster said. "Give 'em up."

"You just patted me down. You know I haven't got them on me. They're in the ignition."

"Shit." With his arm around Kelleher's neck, Buster maneuvered himself to the driver's door and pulled it open. Behind him, Kelleher could hear the trunk of the thugs' car pop open. As Buster tried to reach into Kelleher's car with his free arm, Kelleher yanked his right elbow back as hard as he could, hoping to land a solid blow to the stomach. He heard Buster say

"Aaah!" and felt his grip loosen. He pulled himself free and, as Buster tried to regain his balance, put both hands around his throat and banged his head as hard as he could on the open car door. Buster sagged. Kelleher let him go, turned, and ran right at Tommy, who had started to push Nikki into the trunk.

"What the — " was all Tommy got out when he saw Kelleher come around the corner of the car and dive at him. They tumbled to the ground, Kelleher on top. Wanting to ensure that this would never be a fair fight, Kelleher pulled his left hand free and swung it as hard as he could across Tommy's face. Pain went right up to his shoulder as he connected; he saw Tommy's eyes roll up into his head.

Pulling Tommy to his feet, he rolled him over his shoulder and, before his back broke under the dead weight, shoveled him into the open trunk. He pulled off Tommy's ski mask. Tommy had a heavy beard and long black hair. Nikki was on her feet, staring at Kelleher openmouthed.

"Come on and help me with this other guy before he comes to," Kelleher said.

"What are you going to do?"

"I'm going to put them both in the trunk so we can go get the cops."

"What about the tape?"

"Tommy was right, I tossed it on the beach. We'll come back for it. Come on!"

She followed him around to where Buster was lying next to Kelleher's car. Kelleher noticed some blood coming from the back of Buster's head and he worried for a second that he had done serious damage. He pulled the ski mask off. Buster had blond hair and looked to be about Kelleher's age. He was breathing fine and his pulse sounded strong. He was also much too heavy for Kelleher even to consider lifting. Kelleher picked him up under the arms and ordered Nikki to drag his feet. Together, they managed to get him to the other car. With great effort, Kelleher propped him against the trunk, then rolled him into it, after pushing Tommy far enough to the side that they wouldn't be on top of one another. Tommy was starting to stir, so Kelleher slammed the trunk.

He sat against the trunk, gulping air, trying to catch his breath. Nikki stood there, hands on hips, shaking her head.

"You're really something, aren't you?"

"Yeah, right. I just hope I didn't kill old Buster. I needed to hit his head hard or he wouldn't even blink. Nikki, something went very wrong here. These guys not only knew just who we were, they knew about the tape. How is that possible?"

She shook her head. "I have no idea. The only person I told was my mother."

"And the only other person who knows is Tamara. We screwed up somewhere, but I don't know where."

"What now?"

He sighed. "Let's go get the cops and then come back here and start looking for the tape."

"Don't you want to wait until it's light out?"

"No. I won't sleep until I have that thing back." He snapped his fingers. "Wait a minute. Tommy said they had flashlights."

He opened the driver's door and searched the front seat. Nothing. Then he checked the back seat. Still nothing. Damn! They were undoubtedly in the trunk, which he wasn't about to open.

"No luck?"

"Must be in the trunk."

"You don't want to chance opening it?"

"Absolutely not. We can pick some up at my house after we go get the cops."

"We could also probably use another set of eyes."

"You mean Tamara."

"If you still trust her."

Kelleher trusted her. His gut told him there was no way

Mearns was behind this. He wasn't quite as certain about Nadia, although he couldn't figure out why she would help them get the tape, then try to steal it from them. The same was true of Nikki.

"I trust her. Look, we can call her from police headquarters. Let's get going. I want to make sure they get Buster to a doctor and then start looking for the tape."

"What about the flashlights?"

"I told you, I've got some at my house."

"Why don't we split up to save time? You go to the house, call Tamara, and have her meet you here. I'll get the cops and bring them back to get Buster and Tommy."

It made sense, especially the part about Nikki going to the cops. The odds were she would get a far quicker response at this hour of the night than he would.

"Okay. Let's get going."

She turned to walk to her car, then stopped, came back, and hugged him. "Thanks for saving me."

He felt himself blushing. "Aw shucks, ma'am," he started to say, then stopped himself. This wasn't a time for movie star imitations.

"See you in a few minutes" was the response he finally opted for.

He jumped in his car, the keys still in the ignition. Thank God, he thought, he hadn't stuck them in his pocket when he arrived. Turning around, he went back up the hill. She was right behind him. At the corner, he turned right to go to his house, and she went straight, to the town center. Kelleher looked at the car's digital clock. It was 2:20. It was going to be a long night.

Mearns was still at the *Reporter* when he called. "Didn't expect to hear from you again tonight," she said cheerfully when she heard his voice.

"Listen, I haven't got time to explain anything right now, but I need you to meet me at Kissing Rock right away."

"What's wrong? You sound awful. What the hell happened?"

He took a deep breath. "We got ambushed. Two thugs in ski masks. They knew our names, and they knew about the tape."

"But how? That's impossible."

"I know. Only it isn't."

"So they got the tape?"

"No. That's why we have to go back. I'll tell you the whole story when you get there."

"Ten minutes."

He hung up and went to the garage for flashlights. His mother always insisted on having several in the house in case of a power outage. He found two but had no luck finding a third. The cops would have flashlights; maybe they would lend him one.

He walked back into the living room and sat down in his father's chair. He needed to regroup. He was still shaking from the terror and the fight. Kelleher had been in fights before, but he didn't think of himself as a fighter. He knew that either Tommy or Buster would have kicked his butt in a fair fight, but that didn't matter. What did matter was who the hell had sent them. With luck, the cops would figure it out.

He pulled himself out of the chair, feeling exhausted, terrified, and wired all at once. There was no doubting the stakes here. One person was already dead. Whoever had killed Scott would probably kill again if they felt it necessary.

He jogged to the car, tossed the flashlights on the front seat, and started the engine. During the ten-minute drive back to the Rock, he kept replaying the evening in his mind. He could think of only one reasonable possibility: that Jefferson had spotted him in the storeroom and chosen to say nothing, then reported back to Akley and Murray. Even so, where the hell had they come up with a pair like Buster and Tommy so fast? And that still wouldn't explain how they knew about the tape, unless they had taken a wild guess that he had been recording them in the storeroom. It was the longest of long shots, and the scary part was, it was the only one that made any sense at all.

Mearns was leaning against her car, waiting, when he pulled up. Tommy's and Buster's car was alongside. Kelleher was a little disappointed that Nikki wasn't back yet, but maybe the cops had needed to get organized. Probably only two guys were on duty when she got to the station.

"Whose car?" Mearns asked as he got out.

"The two guys who jumped us. In fact, they're both in the trunk."

"How did you manage that?"

"Long story." He handed her a flashlight. "We've got work to do. The tape is on the beach someplace."

"*What?*"

"I tossed it there to keep the thugs from getting it. Don't ask me to explain the whole thing right now. We've got to get to work."

He looked up and saw a flashing red light coming over the crest of the hill. "Boy, it took them long enough."

Billy Hollister and Ronnie Johnson jumped out of the front seat, Nikki out of the back.

"Where's your car, Nikki?" Kelleher asked.

"At Town Hall."

"Took you guys long enough," he said to Hollister and Johnson.

Hollister shot him a look. "Jesus, Bobby, we came right away. What'd you want us to do, helicopter?"

"Okay, okay. Sorry. I'm uptight. Look, at least one of them's probably conscious. The key's in the ignition."

Johnson reached into the driver's side, pulled out the key, and flipped it to Hollister. "Let me get back there, just in case they try something." He pulled his gun, as did Hollister.

"Bobby, did you check them for weapons?" Hollister asked.

Kelleher shook his head. "Sorry."

"Okay then, Bobby — you, Tamara, and Nikki get back behind our car. Ronnie, get off to the side. I'll pop the trunk with the key."

"Kind of a risk, Billy," Kelleher pointed out.

"I think I can turn the key almost from the side."

Kelleher, Mearns, and Nikki walked behind the police car. Johnson positioned himself on the driver's side, both hands on his gun. Hollister stood on the passenger side. "On three," he said softly. Leaning against the rear corner of the car, he reached with his left arm and stuck the key in the trunk lock. "One," he whispered, "two . . . three!"

He turned the key and the trunk popped open. "Don't make a move and no one gets hurt!" Hollister ordered.

Nothing. Cautiously, Hollister shone his flashlight past the rear window and open trunk lid into the gaping compartment. "Jesus Christ!" he exclaimed. "What is this, some kind of joke?"

Kelleher stood up from a crouching position. "What is it, Billy?"

"Oh, nothing much — except the only thing in this trunk is a spare tire."

They spent the next twenty minutes explaining to the cops, step by step, what had happened. Kelleher was beginning to believe in ghosts.

"There's no way they got out of that trunk themselves," Hollister said. "Houdini couldn't get out of that trunk. Someone had to help them."

"But why'd they leave the car here?" Kelleher asked. "I

could almost see Akley or Murray coming along to check on what was going on and finding their boys, but why leave the car?"

"Who knows?" Johnson said. "Doesn't matter, really. The problem you got, Bobby, is there's absolutely no proof it was Akley and Murray. In fact, there's no proof these guys were here."

"Except for the car," Mearns pointed out.

"Which we'll run through the computer. But even so, my guess is it won't trace back to Akley or Murray. Bobby, what did you have on this tape that's so important?"

Kelleher hadn't explained how the tape had come to be, just that he had a tape he believed Akley and Murray wanted to get their hands on.

"Recruiting stuff that could make them look bad, I think," he said, wanting to low-key it.

Hollister shrugged. "Well, ordinarily I'd say, why would anyone send two thugs out for a tape like that, but someone's already been killed out here because of Nikki's brother, so nothing is impossible. My suggestion is you get a good night's sleep and come back here to look for your tape in the morning."

Kelleher shook his head. "Gotta look now. I have a pretty good idea where I tossed it. If you'll loan us a third flashlight, it shouldn't take all that long."

Hollister nodded. "Long as you bring it back in the morning."

Nikki yawned. "Bobby, I hope you won't hate me, but I have a shoot at ten o'clock in the morning. I have to get up to drive back to the city with Vida in a little more than three hours. Do you think you can get by without me?"

"We could use help," Kelleher said. "I don't suppose you officers want to help."

Johnson shook his head. "If I was off duty I would, Bobby. But we can't. The station is unmanned right now. We had to flip the emergency radio over to Chief Ferrer's house, and he's none too happy about it as is."

Kelleher held up his hand. "I understand. You too, Nikki. Call me in the morning and I'll let you know what happened."

She gave him one more hug before following the cops back to their car. "I'm sorry about this," she said. "But it'll be all right."

"I know. I just wish I could figure out how it happened."

"You will," she assured him. Then she kissed him on the cheek. He stood and watched her climb into the police car.

"Kelleher. Earth to Kelleher."

It was Mearns, standing behind him. "Sorry," he said. "I just got distracted there for a second."

"No kidding. Listen, when we find this tape, you and I are going to each get some sleep, and then you're going to tell me everything that happened out here tonight."

"That's fine. Why?"

"Just because. Now let's get the flashlights and get to work."

Kelleher had hoped his sprint toward the dunes had left enough tracks to show where he had tossed the tape. But the sand was so thick in that area that only a few signs remained of the churning made by his and Buster's feet.

Even so, Kelleher had a pretty good idea where to start looking, since he had used the Hicks house as a marker. He and Mearns walked about fifty steps up the beach in that direction, then began combing toward the dunes. It was slow work, even with the flashlights, because of the large area they had to cover. Twice, Kelleher thought he had it: the first time it was a piece of washed-up log, and the second, a beer can. Mearns also had one false alarm herself.

By five o'clock, Kelleher was so exhausted that he was tempted to suggest they stretch out on the beach and nap for an hour. By then the sun would be coming up, and they wouldn't need flashlights.

"Tired?" he called to Mearns.

"What do you think?"

"Let's rest for a couple minutes."

They made their way back to their starting point and sat down. Kelleher lay back and closed his eyes. For a second, he thought he might doze off.

"You think we'll find it faster when the sun comes up?" Mearns asked.

"Suppose so. I just hope it isn't lodged in a bush or something."

"Even then, we should see it. It isn't like it's a needle."

"Or this is a haystack." He pulled himself up. "Come on. Let's switch sides. You look up that way. I'll go back down where you were."

"You check up by the sea wall yet?"

He shook his head. "It isn't there, though. My arm's not that strong, and I didn't even throw it with all my might."

"When you've checked all the right places, it sometimes pays to check the wrong ones."

He didn't argue. He headed back the way he had run, trying to slow himself so as not to miss anything. Twenty more minutes went by. Kelleher noticed a few streaks of sun on the eastern horizon. He was happy to see light coming but also disgusted that they still hadn't had any luck. He was about to make a comment about it to Mearns when he heard a shriek.

"Bobby! Quick!"

She was on the far side of the sea wall, kneeling over something. There was just no way he could have hurled the tape recorder that far. Then again, adrenaline, heat of the moment —

He raced up, breathing heavily. "You got it?"

She pointed her flashlight. Half-buried in the sand was, without any doubt, a tape recorder.

Gingerly picking it up, he checked that the tape was still inside. Seeing it, he breathed a sigh of relief, popped it out, and made sure no sand was lodged inside the recorder.

"Play it," Mearns said. "Let's make sure it's okay."

He was certain it was, but he popped it back in anyway and hit the "play" button. The tape whirred for a few seconds but produced no sound. Kelleher panicked. "Wait — let me rewind it. Nikki heard almost all of it when Tommy and Buster showed up."

He hit "rewind" and was surprised when the tape went backward for a few seconds and stopped. Now he was really worried. He hit "play" again. This time, after a second of silence, they heard a voice:

"This extra tape came in handy, Kelleher. Next time, you'll be the one in the trunk. I promise."

Kelleher felt nauseated. No question whose voice was on the tape: Tommy's.

Mearns stared at him. "Who's that?"

"One of the thugs. Somehow, they got out of the damn trunk, found the real tape, took it, stopped to put this one into the recorder, and left."

"All in thirty minutes."

"All in thirty minutes. I don't understand it."

Mearns stood up. "Neither do I. But I'll tell you one thing. They didn't do this without help."

He looked at her. "Who?"

"I don't think you want to know."

His mind was so blank and he was so tired, he couldn't even come up with an idea, much less a name.

"Haven't you figured it out yet?" she asked.

"Not even close."

She sighed and crouched down so she could look him in the eye. "Bobby, only one person could have done all this. Only one."

Again he was blank. "Who?"

She shook her head sadly. "Don't hate me," she said finally. "But it had to be Nikki Buzelis."

Sitting on the beach, he stared in the direction of the sunrise, which was streaking the sky with red. He knew she was right. Nikki had to have set him up, and Nikki had to have let Tommy and Buster out of the trunk. As sad as it made him, knowing she had led him on to get what she needed confused him far more.

"I'm not arguing with you. But the question is, why? Why would Nikki help us make the tape, then go to all that trouble to get it from us?"

She looked at him. "I don't know. But my guess is, if we figure that one out, we'll know who killed Scott."

More questions, he reflected. Just when he thought he had some real answers, more questions. Without the tape, they had no story. They were back where they had started: full of suspicions and questions, but running on empty when it came to answers.

ELEVEN

NEW YORK,
NEW YORK

THERE WAS NO SENSE DOING ANY-
THING except going home and getting some sleep.
Even if Kelleher had felt the urge to confront Nikki and
demand she tell him what was going on, he knew he would
never get into the Buzelis house at such an early hour — if
ever. It occurred to him that they could wait for her to come
out on her way back to the city, but it seemed pointless.

At least it seemed pointless right then. After agreeing to
talk that afternoon, he and Mearns drove off in different directions. Kelleher dropped into bed about six-thirty, tossed and
turned for a while, and then fell asleep. He dreamed that Miles
Akley, Nick Angellini, and Nikki were sitting upstairs at the
Inn-Between, laughing at him for thinking he could outsmart
them.

It woke him up. He sat up in bed and looked at the clock: it
was almost two. He was not surprised when he went downstairs and found several messages on the tape.

One was from Larry Siddons, wanting to know if he was

coming into town for the state championships. One was from Mearns, pointing out that it was noon and he should get his butt out of bed. The last was from Billy Hollister.

"Just woke up, Bobby, and thought I'd give you a call. Wanted to see if you had any luck with that tape and also tell you something that may interest you. Of course, it may not. Give me a call at home."

Kelleher looked up Hollister's number in the Shelter Island phone book and dialed. Without going into detail, he told Hollister they hadn't found the tape. Then he asked what Hollister had to tell him.

"That girl, Nikki — I know she's drop-dead gorgeous, but I'm not sure she's being straight with you, Bobby."

"What do you mean?"

"Remember she told you she left her car at Town Hall?"

"Uh-huh."

"When we got back in the car last night, she asked if we could take her home. She said she'd pick her car up in the morning. No big deal, we dropped her off. But when we got back to headquarters, there wasn't a single car in the lot. In fact, there wasn't a car parked within a half mile of the place."

"Someone dropped her off when she came to get you guys."

"You got it."

Kelleher had another thought. "Hey, Billy, do you remember what time she came in?"

"Matter of fact, I do. I was a little pissed at you for making that crack about its taking us a long time to get there, so I checked the log when I got back. She walked in here at 3:07. We were at the Rock less than ten minutes later."

Kelleher thanked Hollister and hung up. He now had no doubt that Nikki had gotten Buster and Tommy out of the trunk and helped them find the tape. He remembered looking at the car clock when he pulled away from the Rock after the fight. It had been 2:20. Nikki hadn't gotten to the cops until three-quarters of an hour later. It was a five-minute drive — max — to Town Hall from the Rock. That left her plenty of time to free them, find the tape, and get them out of there. No doubt they had dropped her off and then gone to wait for the first ferry off the island.

Confirmation of Nikki's involvement was extremely aggravating to Kelleher. This was not the first time he had screwed up by deluding himself into thinking he was irresistible to women. If his reporting antenna had been up, he would have wondered why Nikki insisted on meeting him alone and at Kissing Rock. Instead, he had convinced himself she was dying to be alone with him, and he had walked right into a trap.

Of course, the larger question hadn't changed: why had Nikki trapped him? Had she had some sudden change of heart and decided she couldn't betray her father? Unlikely; dialing up thugs like Tommy and Buster wasn't exactly the same as ordering pizza. What happened had to have been prearranged. Nikki wanted the tape made, but she also wanted it to end up in her hands, not Kelleher's.

Why?

He and Mearns discussed the possibilities on their way into the city on Thursday. Shelter Island was playing Bayside that night in the third of the four quarterfinal games that night. The first game of the evening doubleheader was at seven.

The trip produced no answers — only theories, none of which really made sense. That didn't mean one of them wasn't correct.

They arrived at Madison Square Garden shortly before six with no real plan about how to proceed. Mearns had checked with the cops before they left the island to see if any new leads on Scott Harrison's murder had surfaced. They told her the Suffolk people had come up blank: the only suspects of any note — Kelleher and Akley — had alibis. She and Kelleher both knew that Akley's alibi was a lie, but the proof was in the possession, they suspected, of Nikki Buzelis — or someone Nikki Buzelis was working with.

After parking the car in the cheapest lot they could find in the Garden area — a mere fifteen dollars for the evening — they walked to the employee entrance on 33rd Street and Eighth Avenue to pick up their press credentials. They had decided that Mearns would try to get some time alone with Nadia to review the events of Tuesday and that Kelleher would talk to Nikki, if possible.

He wasn't looking forward to the confrontation, but he knew it was necessary. Although he didn't expect her to simply come out and tell him what was going on, she might provide some clues. If she didn't, and if Nadia didn't have something to tell Mearns, they were at an absolute dead end.

Kelleher breathed a sigh of relief when his credential was waiting for him. It wasn't that he didn't have faith in Siddons, who had arranged the pass for him; it was just that he knew from experience that if your credential wasn't right where it was supposed to be at the Garden, the ushers who manned the employee entrance were about as helpful as a stalled car in the middle lane at rush hour. In New York on vacation once, he had covered a college basketball game for the *Herald*, and his credential hadn't been at the door. When he had asked the usher to phone the PR department upstairs to find someone to straighten out the problem, the guy had looked at him and said, "What do I look like, your fuckin' secretary? There's nothin' here — now get lost."

Kelleher had walked to the corner, dialed the PR department on a pay phone, and, after ten minutes on hold, been told the credential was downstairs at the employee entrance. He had explained that it wasn't. After several more minutes on hold, he finally found someone who agreed to meet him downstairs. When he walked back in, the PR man was digging through the pile and — voila! — produced the credential. The usher — who had refused to let Kelleher look through the pile — had missed it.

Accepting his credential from the PR man, Kelleher had waited for the usher to apologize — or say *something*. What he had said, to the person standing behind Kelleher, was, "Who's next?" Kelleher hadn't been able to resist: "You know, saying 'I'm sorry, I just missed it' wouldn't hurt."

The usher had looked at him scornfully and replied, "You get wise with me, you won't ever use that thing."

Kelleher's retort had been cut off by the PR guy grabbing his arm and dragging him to the elevator. "You can't win that one — he'll have five cops on you in about a second if you say anything."

As the PA announcer always said at the start of a ballgame, "Welcome to the magic world of Madison Square Garden."

This time, no hassles or problems confronted them. The usher found Mearns's pass, handing it to her with a comment about a pretty little lady like her not needing to be going into locker rooms; he dug Kelleher's out without comment. On principle, Kelleher didn't say thank you, then felt bad for descending to that level.

Taking the elevator to the loge, where the press room was located, they dropped their coats and computers off. As much as he disliked the hostile atmosphere he frequently noticed in the building, Kelleher still felt a nostalgic chill whenever he walked into the Garden. Seeing the Knicks' championship banners from 1970 and 1973 brought back memories of his dad taking him to see those great teams when he was a little boy. The Rangers' brand-new Stanley Cup banner reminded him of the days in the seventies when he had honestly believed the Rangers would never again win a Stanley Cup.

They walked down through the almost-empty seats to the

floor. A few players from Shelter Island and Bayside were casually shooting around. Rytis Buzelis was standing under one of the baskets talking to someone. As Kelleher got closer, he saw who it was: Nick Angellini.

"What do you think about that?" he asked Mearns, pointing out the chatting duo.

"What's he doing here?"

"That's the question of the night. He's sure as hell not doing the games on TV, and I'm guessing Shelter Island–Bayside wasn't high on his list of must-sees this season."

"Think we should try to talk to him?" Mearns asked as they reached floor level.

"Very definitely. I wonder if he's still thinking he can persuade the kid to go to NYU, regardless of who they hire as coach. Why don't I go talk to him while you try to find out where the Buzelises are going to be sitting."

She nodded and went off to look for someone from the Garden who could help her find the family seating. They wanted to get to the Buzelises early, while they were still dispersed, waiting for the game to start. That was their best bet.

Thinking about how to approach Angellini, Kelleher worked his way slowly in the direction of the basket where Angellini and Rytis Buzelis were talking. If he came on strong, Angellini would walk away. Flattery was definitely the route.

He stalled for a moment when he got to the end of the floor, not wanting to make Rytis uncomfortable by interrupting his conversation. After a couple of minutes, Angellini gave Rytis a warm handshake and started to walk away. He had gone about four steps when some kids who had arrived early for warmups — just as Kelleher had done as a kid — began calling his name and demanding an autograph.

When Angellini stopped to sign, Kelleher made his move. Angellini looked up as Kelleher approached. Recognition flickered in his eyes, but he clearly couldn't put a name to the face. "How ya doin'?" he asked, in that tone people use when they really don't want to get into a conversation.

"Fine, Nick, fine." Kelleher tried to sound genial. "You may not remember me — I'm Bobby Kelleher. We met out at St. John's on Sunday, before the St. John's–Louisiana game."

"Of course I remember you, Bobby. *Washington Post*, right?"

"*Herald*." He didn't bother with any details.

"Right. Both great papers. How ya doin'?"

Kelleher told him he was doing just fine and wondered if he had a few minutes to chat — he was writing a feature about the state tournament's return to the city and what it meant to high school basketball to be back in Madison Square Garden. He didn't dare bring up Buzelis.

"I got a few minutes right now." Angellini smiled his best TV smile. "I'm just here to watch some good hoops tonight. No work at all, baby. I'd be happy to talk to you."

"Is there someplace we can go?"

Angellini looked around. People were starting to filter into the seats. More kids were calling his name. "Follow me." He walked toward the tunnel to the locker rooms.

At the gate to the tunnel, Angellini stopped to talk to the security guard. "Joe, I need to get back to the hallway for a minute, so I can have some privacy to do an interview."

"Nick, you're always being interviewed." The guard shocked Kelleher by smiling. Never in all his years coming to the building had Kelleher seen a Madison Square Garden usher or security guard smile. Of course, he had never been with a TV star before.

Joe stepped aside to let Angellini and Kelleher pass. They walked back to the turnoff: two locker rooms in one direction, two more the other. The ones to the left were used by visiting teams — in this case, the high school teams. The ones to the right belonged to the Knicks and Rangers. No high school players would be changing clothes in there this weekend.

Angellini turned right and breezed down the hall to the Knicks' locker room. Another guard blocked the entrance.

"Dino, baby, I need five minutes of privacy to do a big-time interview here with the man from D.C." He indicated Kelleher. "How about letting us use Riley's office?"

The guard blanched. "You tryin' to get me killed, Nick? You know how Pat is about outsiders in his locker room."

"Dino, pal, Pat's not around. No one will know. Give you a mention next game I do here."

Dino looked around. The hallway was empty. "Okay, Nick — just because it's you. But for cryin' out loud, don't take too long."

"You got it, baby."

Dino held the door open, and Kelleher and Angellini walked into the plush, comfortable, although not overly large Knicks locker room. Uniforms hung neatly in each locker, waiting for the Knicks' home game Sunday, after the high school kids cleared out. Angellini led Kelleher into Pat Riley's small office just off the locker-room area. Sitting behind Riley's desk, he put his feet up and said, "So what can I help you with, baby? Fire away."

Kelleher asked all the easy questions first, pulling out a notebook and making a pretense of taking notes. Angellini rattled on about the great game of basketball and the atmosphere of the Garden: "Still the Mecca, baby. If you want to play hoops in the big time, you gotta get to the Garden!"

Kelleher nodded, as if soaking it all in. Hoping Angellini wouldn't notice the lack of segue, he brought up Rytis Buzelis. "I noticed you talking to Rytis Buzelis out there. Have you had a chance to see him play?"

"Not yet, but I'm really excited about seeing him tonight. I mean — and you can quote me on this, Billy — the kid can flat out play. He's Grant Hill with a jump shot! Look at his hands! I love him, I love him, I love him!"

Geez, Kelleher thought, ignoring Angellini's botching of his name, how's he going to feel about him when he actually sees him play?

"You have any feel for where he's going to end up next year? Lot of rumors, you know."

The friendly smile faded just a bit. "You been around, kid — you know how rumors are, especially in the recruiting business. I remember when I was coaching — you shoulda heard some of the rumors about me."

Kelleher *had* heard a lot of them — and believed they were all true.

"I'll tell you what, though," Angellini continued, unable to shut up. "Don't believe everything you been hearing. People say he's locked for Louisiana — not so. There are still some surprises left before this thing is over."

"How do you know that, Nick?"

"Sources, baby, I got sources. You're a reporter — you know about sources."

Kelleher knew it was time to move into dangerous territory. "Nick, did you know Scott Harrison?"

Angellini shook his head sadly. "Never met him. Heard nothing but good things about him. A great young man. What a tragedy."

It sounded as if he had given that speech several times this week. Angellini was telling a big-time lie about not knowing Scott, especially since the last phone call Scott had made in his life had been to Angellini's home phone.

"Any theories on what happened to him?"

Angellini shook his head again. "You know, I haven't heard a thing other than what I read in the papers. So sad."

Kelleher took a deep breath. He wanted desperately to tell

Angellini that he had Harrison's cellular phone records showing a call to him, the person he had never met, minutes before
he was killed. Tipping his hand would be a mistake, though.

"Anything else?" Angellini asked, starting to stand up.

"Just one thing." Kelleher decided to take a stab. "How
well do you know Nikki Buzelis?"

The look in Angellini's eyes told Kelleher he had hit pay
dirt. He staggered backward a half-step, as if Kelleher had
caught him flush on the chin with a left.

"Nikki — I mean, you know, we've had a few laughs. I
mean, she's a kid starting out, I know a few people in the business through my TV connections, so I helped her out — you
know, like a big brother."

Big brother, my ass, Kelleher thought. "Just out of the
goodness of your heart?" he asked, still trying to sound ingen-
uous. It didn't work.

"Look, kid, I don't know what you're trying to pull here,
but frankly, my relationship with Nikki Buzelis is none of your
fucking business."

Kelleher smelled blood. "Except for the fact that she also
had a relationship with Scott Harrison. Beautiful woman like
that, you might not want to share her — "

Angellini took a menacing step to get in Kelleher's face.
"You fuckin' crazy or something? You sayin' I killed that cocky
little sonofabitch?"

He stopped, knowing he had said too much.

"If you never met him, how do you know he was a cocky
little sonofabitch?"

" 'Cause I heard, that's why." Angellini stepped around Kelleher and headed for the door. "Let me just tell you something, kid — you better not go spreading your stupid theory
too many places, 'cause I'll kick your fuckin' ass. You don't
mess with Nick Angellini, you got me? Christ, you'd think

fuckin' Nikki was some kind of fuckin' nun the way you talk. So I fucked her — so Harrison fucked her too. Probably a dozen others this month. So what? I don't fuckin' kill people over a broad, kid, you got it? You're so far off base you can't even see the fuckin' field."

He was at the locker room door now. "I'll give you one last warning, kid. Don't fuck with me."

He turned and walked out, leaving Kelleher standing in the door of Riley's office. He had brought up Nikki's name just to see if it threw Angellini at all. Unexpectedly, he had hit a nerve — a major one. Nikki and Angellini's being involved might explain why she had wanted to set Akley up and get her hands on the tape. After all, if Angellini was trying to get Rytis to go to NYU and not Minnesota State, damning evidence against Akley and Murray might clear the way for him.

One thing was evident: Scott had been in somebody's way. The question was whether he had blocked Akley's path to Rytis or Angellini's path to Rytis — or perhaps Angellini's path to Nikki.

Even though he told himself it was silly, it bothered him to think of Nikki sleeping with the likes of Angellini. He was beginning to think he was the only guy she had spent time with recently whom she *hadn't* slept with.

Sitting down on a stool in front of Patrick Ewing's locker, he reopened his notebook and began scribbling the conversation as best he could remember it from the moment Angellini had stood up, since he had stopped taking notes at that point. He was almost finished when the door swung open. Was Angellini coming back?

It was Dino. "Hey!" he shouted when he saw Kelleher. "What the fuck you doin' in here?"

"Sorry, I was just finishing the notes from talking to Nick, and — "

"I give a fuck. Get the hell outta here."

Kelleher didn't argue. What was the point? But as he passed Dino going out the door, he couldn't resist a parting line.

"Thanks for the hospitality."

"Yeah, and fuck you too."

Such a warm place, Kelleher thought, heading down the hallway. As he walked back into the arena, he could hear the PA announcer: "Welcome to the magic world of Madison Square Garden."

TWELVE

VIDA

KELLEHER SPENT MOST of the first half giving Mearns a blow-by-blow account of his meeting with Angellini. He had to stop several times, because the crowd, which had filled about three-quarters of the Garden's 19,000 seats, got so loud he couldn't be heard.

Bayside was a typical city team: smart, bruising, and not the least bit intimidated by the presence of a highly publicized star. They collapsed on Buzelis whenever he touched the ball, figuring he was the only one on Shelter Island's team capable of doing any serious damage.

At the end of the first quarter, the islanders trailed, 21–13. Sitting no more than fifteen feet from the Shelter Island bench, Kelleher could hear Buzelis running the huddle between quarters. "Let me bring the ball up," he said to Joe Dierker. "That gives me more room to operate."

It was smart, logical basketball. If you want the ball in the hands of your star and he's a good enough ball-handler, let him start with it. The thought probably never would have occurred to Dierker.

By halftime, Shelter Island had the game tied at 42. Buzelis gave the ball up only when triple-teamed, and usually he found a teammate so wide open in that situation that the result was an easy layup.

It was during the break that Kelleher finally managed to finish his story. Mearns had only one question: "What made you bring Nikki up? We hadn't even discussed the idea of her being involved with Angellini."

"Just a stab. It probably came out of my mouth about a half-second after I thought of it."

The next step was to talk to Nikki. With luck, he could find her after the game and get to her before Angellini told her about their conversation. Angellini was sitting a few feet away from the TV announcer's position — the games were being televised on cable by the MSG network — and Kelleher hadn't seen him cross the court to where the Buzelises were sitting. He guessed Angellini wouldn't go anywhere near Nikki with Arturas around.

He hoped that if he did get to Nikki, she wouldn't yet know they were onto her. If she did know, the odds were she would avoid any kind of meeting.

Kelleher was so deep in thought, imagining what he would say to Nikki and trying to figure out what their next move should be, that he barely saw the third or fourth quarters. It was only when Shelter Island called time with forty-one seconds left that he looked up at the scoreboard and realized that Bayside had a 77–75 lead.

Mearns, who had to write about the game for Saturday morning's *Reporter*, had been scribbling notes. Seeing Kelleher staring at the scoreboard, she poked him in the shoulder. "You missed a pretty good game sitting there daydreaming."

"You noticed?"

"I noticed when Rytis dunked behind his head and you never moved."

The teams returned to the court. Everyone knew Buzelis would get the ball. The question was, would he try to go inside for a tie or shoot a three for the lead? Kelleher, assuming that Rytis wasn't listening to a word Dierker was saying in the huddle, figured he'd go for three: when playing a team physically stronger than you, avoid overtime at all costs.

Sure enough, Rytis took the inbounds pass and stood at midcourt for several seconds, setting his teammates in a double high-post offense. Someone was going to pop out and screen for him, so he could shoot a jumper. The Bayside point guard read the play, screaming, "Screen, screen!" as Rytis moved to the top of the key, but it was too late. With one giant step, Rytis got behind the screener, and in a split second the shot was airborne.

Swish. The building exploded. Shelter Island was up, 78–77. Eighteen seconds left. Bayside called time-out. Kelleher glanced up at the scoreboard in the end zone that listed individual scoring totals. Rytis now had 44. Not bad for a guy who had been guarded by anywhere from two to four players throughout the game.

"The good news is, both sides are out of time outs," Mearns said. "The bad news is, if Bayside scores, Rytis will just have to make something happen without being able to set things up."

"Sometimes that's better. You get the defense in a scramble situation, they don't know what they're doing."

The teams broke the huddle again. Kelleher had watched closely enough in the first half to figure out that Bayside's offense was just like its defense: nothing happened without their knowing where Rytis was. Right now, he was guarding Chad Browning, the six-foot-eight All-City center who was Bayside's best player. That meant Bayside was likely to set up a play on the perimeter.

Mike Markey, the point guard who had read the previous

play a fraction too late, brought the ball across midcourt and held up one finger. Rytis was fronting Browning, to make sure he couldn't get the ball. Browning, understanding he had no chance to get open, slid to the left corner. Rytis, showing his inexperience, went with him, which was exactly what Bayside wanted. Rytis had been removed from the play.

Markey hesitated a moment, glancing at the clock, which had rolled down to eight seconds. Then he drove the ball hard to his right. As the defense came to him, he calmly slipped a pass to Tony Kornhoser, the three-point shooting specialist who had already nailed four of them. Given room by Markey's drive, Kornhoser caught the ball cleanly in the corner and had his shot underway before anyone from Shelter Island could even think to put a hand in his face.

The ball zipped through the net, barely moving the twine. Again the building exploded with noise. Bayside was back in front, 80–78. Kelleher glanced at the clock, which automatically stopped after a made basket in the last minute. There were 3.4 seconds left. David Doyle, the Shelter Island point guard, picked the ball up and quickly inbounded it to Rytis. As if on cue, the entire Bayside team ran straight at him.

Rytis, who never seemed to lose his cool, faked as if to throw a long pass. That froze the defense long enough to give him a little space to maneuver. He was just across midcourt when the clock hit one. It appeared to Kelleher that three Bayside players were hanging on Rytis, but the officials weren't about to call a foul in this situation.

Rytis took one last dribble, brought the ball up to his chest, and flung it toward the hoop. Kelleher could see that it was too strong. With all his momentum going in the direction of the basket, he had put too much juice on the shot. The ball hit the glass, dropped down, hit the front rim, and hung there for what seemed like minutes as the entire building held its collective breath. Then it took one last roll and dropped through the net.

For a brief moment, Kelleher wasn't even sure what had happened. Then he saw Rytis with his arms in the air and, out of the corner of his eye, noticed the Shelter Island bench emptying as everyone ran to jump on Rytis. From forty feet, Rytis had hit a three-pointer. The final score was on the scoreboard: Shelter Island–81, Bayside–80.

"Jesus!" Mearns screamed. "Can you believe that kid? Maybe all these guys are right. Maybe he is some kind of a savior! How the hell did he do that?"

Kelleher knew Rytis had been lucky. But great players always seemed to be the luckiest ones, because they gave themselves the chance to get lucky. The little pass-fake he had made after catching the inbounds had given him just enough room to get to the other side of midcourt for his heave. That wasn't luck; that was genius.

They watched the island kids celebrate. Kelleher couldn't help but notice the Bayside kids, who had played their hearts out, completely convinced they were going to win the game. They were sitting or lying on the court in a state of complete shock, staring into space as if they couldn't believe what they had just seen.

Slowly, their coaches and backups came out to get them, to help them to their feet, so they could start dealing with a loss they would no doubt remember the rest of their lives. Kelleher knew that was no exaggeration. These were moments that players on both sides — hell, fans on both sides — would never forget. These were the moments that made you forget, at least briefly, the kind of sickness sports brought out in people — the kind of sickness Kelleher had been dealing with during the past few days.

He followed Mearns back to the locker-room area, which

was now jammed with media. The state high school tournament was a big deal in small towns, not only all over New York State but all over the country. Combine all the upstate, small-town media with all the city media and the place was packed.

They announced that Rytis Buzelis would be brought to the interview room at the end of the hall, because the locker room was simply too small to accommodate everyone who was going to want to talk to him. That announcement created a stampede for the interview room.

"I have to go listen to this," Mearns said. "You going to try and find the family?"

He nodded, looking around to see if any of the Buzelises were in the hallway. Sometimes, family members were allowed back in the locker room area to meet the players and walk out with them to the back elevator. There wasn't a Buzelis in sight, but as Kelleher turned to walk back in the direction of the court, he saw Miles Akley coming down the hall. How, he wondered, did *he* get back here? The answer was obvious: he probably gave Joe the guard a pair of sneakers.

"Well, well, still hanging around playing reporter, I see," Akley remarked when he saw Kelleher.

"Yeah, and I guess you're still hanging around pretending to be a human," Kelleher retorted, seeing no reason even to feign cordiality.

"Wish I knew how the hell you got in here."

"Ditto."

Kelleher saw no point in continuing this scintillating exchange. All it was going to do was lead to a fight, and he had already done his fighting for the week. So as soon as he had finished his last comeback, he started walking again. Akley seemed to feel the same way, continuing without another word. Kelleher didn't bother looking back as he rounded the corner to the court.

The teams playing in the second game were warming up. Kelleher scanned the seats behind the benches where the Shelter Island families had been sitting and found them empty. "Damn!" he muttered. He turned around and began looking up in the seats to see if he noticed any familiar faces. Halfway up, in the expensive seats, the Buzelises were talking to some of the other Shelter Island people.

He had to approach cautiously. He didn't want to start something with Arturas — he just wanted to pull Nikki away as unobtrusively as possible and try to talk to her. The conversation wouldn't be pleasant, but after his confrontation with Angellini, he figured he was ready for anything.

Fortunately for him, Arturas and Nadia were standing in the middle of a row of seats surrounded by people. Nikki was up on the walkway talking to a tall blond guy who looked to Kelleher like a male model. Kelleher pasted a friendly, phony smile on his face and took the last rows of steps two at a time.

"Hi, Nikki."

When they turned in his direction, he knew he had trouble. Nikki looked at him as if he were delivering a tax bill. A big one.

"Bobby." She nodded curtly and turned to the model. "This is my friend André."

"Of course it is. Hello, André."

Andre nodded so stiffly, Kelleher was tempted to look behind him for the strings.

"Nikki, you got a minute?" He pretended to ignore the ice coming from her.

"As a matter of fact, I don't. We were just getting ready to leave."

"I understand, but I'm talking sixty seconds."

"Why don't you go spend the time with Nick Angellini?"

Aha! Old Nick had gotten to her first. So she knew exactly

what he was up to, and she wasn't going to play any games. That wasn't good. It meant that any chance she might slip and accidentally help him out was lost.

He shrugged as if it were no big deal. "No problem. But at some point, I do need some answers."

"My guess is you aren't going to get them. Come on, Andre, are you ready?"

"Been ready." He slipped his arm into hers and they walked off, leaving Kelleher with absolutely no clue what he should do next. He watched them turn the corner to the concourse and felt as if any chance of getting the story and finding out who had killed Scott had disappeared with them.

"Nikki can be difficult."

Turning around, he found Vida Buzelis standing behind him. No doubt she had seen her sister blow off enough men to feel sorry for some of them. He forced a smile. "Life in the big city, I guess."

"Mr. Kelleher, you need help."

Kelleher laughed bitterly. "An accurate assessment — no doubt."

She smiled. "I meant with your story and finding out who killed your friend. I'm sure you think Nikki is in the middle of it, but she's not."

What was she talking about? Did she know something, or was she just being a protective big sister?

"How do you mean that?" He hoped the general nature of the question would produce a detailed answer.

She looked around nervously. "We can't talk here. Not now. But we do need to talk. I may even be able to help you get your tape back."

Kelleher did at least a double take. "You know about the tape?" he asked, lowering his voice, even though no one walking past could possibly know what they were talking about.

"I think I know about almost everything. That's why we should talk."

"When?" *Now*, he hoped she would say, *or sooner.*

"I can't do it tomorrow. My company is closing a huge deal, and I'll be in the office all day until late. What about first thing Saturday morning?"

Kelleher wasn't sure he could wait that long. "You sure you can't do it sooner?"

"I understand your impatience. But I have to be careful, and so do you." She looked around to make sure no one was listening. "I'll meet you and Tamara at nine o'clock Saturday morning in the main lobby downstairs. That will be safe. Be patient, Mr. Kelleher. I'll help you if I can. I promise."

Patient? How could he be patient? She knew about the tape, and she knew he was working with Mearns. What else did she know? She smiled at him the way a mother smiles at a little boy who wants a toy back. "I know this is hard. But it's hard for all of us."

"Saturday," he said, resigned to his fate. "Nine o'clock."

When he told Mearns about what had happened with the Buzelis sisters, she sighed. "You know, I almost wish the cops would just arrest somebody and get it over with. I feel like we're destined to keep running into dead ends."

He spent most of Friday thinking about that line. It was a gorgeous day, and Kelleher went for a long walk in Central Park, having stayed at his friend Tom Mayer's apartment on East 81st Street. He could do nothing until the meeting with Vida, so he walked through the park and then went downtown to the AP office. Siddons had arranged for him to use one of their computers to type up all his notes.

He filled Siddons in on the twists the story had taken since they had eaten pizza at John's the previous Saturday. Siddons shook his head in amazement as Kelleher reached each new complication.

"I guess the saddest part of it all is Nikki," Siddons remarked.

"The saddest part of it is that Scott is dead," Kelleher answered. He had put his Nikki fantasies behind him. He had not, however, put behind him the idea that he and Mearns might have dinner together that night.

"I can't," she said, when he called her at the hotel where she was staying. "I have a date."

"A date?"

"Is that against ·the rules? Or are you shocked someone wants to go out with me?"

"Cut it out, Tamara. I just didn't know."

"I suppose I should have told you. We've gone out off and on for a few months."

"A writer?"

"No."

"You want to tell me anything about him?"

"Not really. Look, I'm sorry — I'll fill you in some other time. Okay?"

He told her it was fine, no big deal, but it wasn't. Of course he had no right to feel that Mearns owed him any explanations for her social life. After all, he had barely noticed she was a woman while Nikki was there. Now Nikki steps on him, and all of a sudden he comes sniffing around. Even so, right or wrong, he was hurt. It occurred to him that, at least right now, he felt as close to Mearns as anyone he knew.

He ended up walking to John's by himself for a pizza. Then he walked back uptown and spent the evening channel-surfing. Tom Mayer and his family were away on vacation, so he had the apartment to himself. He flipped on ESPN when Sportscenter came on, and there was Rytis Buzelis hitting the winning shot again. As the tape rolled, Kelleher heard anchor Keith Olbermann say, "And the word is that young Mr. Buzelis will announce his choice of a college on Monday. The finalists: Louisiana, Minnesota State, Duke, and, according to our sources, a mystery school that no one is talking about." Olbermann paused. "Maybe he'll shock everyone and return home to the University of Vilnius."

Olbermann was joking. But it occurred to Kelleher, given Nadia's feelings about the whole process, that going home wasn't out of the question. He was pretty certain that the "sources" Olbermann was talking about were one source, and one source only: Nick Angellini. Undoubtedly he was still pushing to get Rytis to NYU — regardless of whom his choice to coach was. Maybe, Kelleher thought, Nick's going to coach the team himself.

He sat up in his chair. It hadn't occurred to him seriously, but the notion actually made sense. After all, as selfish and self-centered as Angellini was, why would he be so excited about recruiting Buzelis to help make someone else rich? Maybe that was where his relationship with Scott Harrison had broken down? Maybe Scott had found out he was just Angellini's set-up guy for Rytis *and* Nikki. Scott had confronted Angellini, and Angellini had decided to get him out of the way. Was Angellini capable of killing or having someone killed? Kelleher remembered the look he had given him in the locker room that night.

"You bet he is," he said aloud.

It made a lot of sense. And at this point, nothing else did. For the five-hundredth time that day, he wondered what Vida knew.

He went to bed shortly after midnight but didn't sleep much. Finally, at a little after seven, he gave in and got up. Having showered and fixed coffee, he decided to walk to the

Garden to kill time and get some exercise. He walked down
Second Avenue to the Dunkin' Donuts on 43rd Street. He
brought newspapers from the newsstand a block away and read
them while he ate a donut — wiping out the benefit of his
exercise — and drank another cup of coffee.

The *Times*, *Newsday*, and the *Daily News* all had features on
Rytis Buzelis. They all mentioned the mysterious death a week
earlier of Scott Harrison and the "mad dash," as Malcolm
Moran called it, to try to recruit the Lithuanian wunderkind.
All three stories called Louisiana the leader in the Buzelis
sweepstakes but mentioned other schools, including Minnesota State, Virginia, Duke, North Carolina, and UCLA, as
places he might end up.

Kelleher read and reread the stories, sipping the coffee and
glancing at his watch every five minutes. Finally, at twenty
minutes to nine, he tossed the papers, bought one more cup of
coffee to keep him warm on the rest of his walk, and started
west on 42nd Street. It was 8:55 when he entered the huge
lobby of the Garden.

The first semifinal would begin at eleven, with the second
game immediately afterward. The final was scheduled for
eight-thirty that night. The box office wouldn't open for another hour; the lobby was empty. Kelleher noticed a lone security guard at the far end, at the foot of the ramp up to one of
the building's entry portals.

He walked to the glass globe in the middle of the lobby. He
remembered, as a kid, standing over the globe with his friends,
trying to pick the best ticket locations. Inside the globe was a
seating chart, showing every section of the building. By the
time he was twelve, he had the whole thing memorized. He
and his pals always asked for section 406 or 430 of the blue
seats — the ones at the top of the building that had become
notorious, primarily because of the raucous behavior of the
hockey fans who sat there during Rangers games.

Kelleher had been one of those Ranger fans as a kid, and a fan at Knicks games. But his favorites had been the college doubleheaders, when the place was half empty and he and his friends could sneak down to the red seats. The ushers might chase them off once, but usually, by the second or third trip, the boys would find a place to slip in unnoticed.

"Getting nostalgic?" Turning, he saw Mearns coming up behind him.

"Just walked in."

"You're lucky. I couldn't sleep. I spent the last hour walking in circles around the block, drinking coffee."

He held up his almost empty cup. "Me too." He looked at his watch again. It was one minute before nine. "I hope she shows."

Mearns was about to answer when Kelleher saw the door open. In walked Vida. "Okay," he said to Mearns. "Here we go."

They all agreed that standing around in what was bound to be a rapidly filling lobby was not a good idea. Kelleher remembered someone saying that the rotunda area, on floor level, was being used for corporate hospitality. He suggested they go up there and see if they could find someplace quiet to sit.

Mearns and Vida followed him up the hallway to the escalators. The guard didn't bother them: he and Mearns had press passes, and Vida had a pass that said "Team Family Member." They took the escalator up two flights to floor level.

"How do you even know about this place?" Mearns asked.

"When I was a freshman, we played in the NIT. They used this as the press area. I sneaked in a couple of times just to take a look."

The rotunda looked a lot different than it had then. Temporary carpeting had been laid down everywhere. A dozen hospitality areas were divided by eight-foot risers that didn't come anywhere close to reaching the ceiling. Kelleher couldn't resist when he saw the sign that said, "Brickley Shoes Welcomes You."

"Let's go in here."

Almost no one was around — only a few maintenance people and a couple of bartenders setting up shop. No doubt the area would be a lot more crowded that night.

"Are you being funny?" Vida asked.

"I think ironic is the correct term."

They found an area that included a couple of couches and comfortable chairs. Vida and Mearns sat while Kelleher went to the bar. "Anybody want anything to drink?"

"Coke?" Mearns asked.

"Nothing for me, thank you," Vida said. "I've been up since seven o'clock, drinking coffee."

Kelleher laughed. "Welcome to the club."

He pulled two Cokes out from the refrigerator under the bar. He hadn't had Coke at this hour of the morning since college, but what the hell — he was already wired from the coffee. A little more caffeine wouldn't hurt.

He handed Mearns a Coke and sat down next to her on one of the couches. Vida sat across from them in an armchair. "So," he began. "You can imagine what the last twenty-four hours has been like for us."

She nodded. "I think what I did to you on Thursday was what you Americans call a tease. I didn't mean to, but I guessed you needed my help, and I didn't know when I'd be able to reach you again. I'm sorry."

"Don't apologize," Mearns said. "But please tell us what you know. We're both about out of theories."

"I'm not surprised. Unfortunately, while I have some answers for you, I'm afraid I don't have them all. But maybe I can help you find the answers you're looking for."

"Tell us about the tape," Kelleher suggested.

She held up a hand. "Let me tell the story as I know it. It'll be less confusing that way."

Kelleher sighed. They would do it her way.

She told the story slowly, filling it with a lot of details that he and Mearns already knew. Scott Harrison and Nick Angellini had both come into Nikki's life in mid-December — Harrison on Shelter Island, Angellini in New York. Angellini had a brother who owned a modeling agency. Out of the blue, Nikki had gotten a call from the agency. When she went there for an interview, she had met Nick. He had told her, according to Vida, that he was going to make her a star.

"But he wanted something in return," Kelleher ventured.

"You guessed it."

Things had happened very fast. Two weeks after meeting the Angellini brothers, Nikki had gone on her first shoot for the agency. A week later, she had moved out of Vida's apartment in the Village to the one on Sutton Place.

"Did she make that much money that fast?" Mearns wanted to know.

"No. Angellini is paying the rent on the apartment."

Kelleher sat back on the couch. "So basically, her loyalty has been to Angellini — and Angellini only — since day one."

"Absolutely. She got involved with your friend Scott only because he made Nick nervous. Nick knew that my mother and Rytis both liked Scott. He felt that Akley would eventually make a mistake and be open to blackmail, but he knew Scott wouldn't break the rules and was ultimately more dangerous than Akley."

"So Scott wasn't involved with Angellini."

"Absolutely not."

"Why do you think Scott called Angellini a few minutes before he died?" Mearns asked.

"Scott knew Nikki was using him, and he knew what Angellini was up to. He was going to go public with the whole thing as soon as he could convince his boss to let him. That's what Nikki told me."

"So Angellini was using Nikki to recruit Rytis for NYU right from the start," Kelleher said.

Vida shook her head vehemently. "No. Angellini couldn't care less about NYU."

"Then who the hell was he recruiting Rytis for?"

Vida smiled sadly. "You aren't going to believe me."

"Try me."

"Minnesota State."

He didn't believe her. He looked at Mearns. She looked at him. "If this is a joke," he said, "it isn't the least bit funny."

"It's no joke. Just listen."

She spent the next several minutes finishing the story. Angellini had told Nikki he was going to be the next coach at Minnesota State, after Bobby Taylor was fired. The deal had already been made. But if Scott Harrison convinced Rytis to go to Minnesota State to play for Taylor, the deal was off.

"So that's it," Kelleher said when she was finished. "Angellini had Scott killed to get him out of the way."

Vida shook her head. "This is the part I can't answer, because according to Nikki, Nick swears he didn't have anything to do with it."

"Do you believe her? Does she believe him?"

"I believe her. She usually only talks to me about this when she's been drinking, which lately has been pretty often. That's how I found out about the tape."

Kelleher had almost forgotten about the damn tape. Now he asked her about it. "They've told Akley they have it. I think there's some kind of meeting tonight. They're going to give him a copy but keep one of their own. If Akley doesn't withdraw his offer and leave Rytis alone — "

"They'll go public with the tape," Kelleher finished. "Jesus! Talk about slimeballs blackmailing slimeballs. I almost feel bad for Akley."

"But not that bad," Mearns put in.

"No, not real bad at all, to tell the truth."

"We need the tape," Mearns remarked.

"We also need to find out where and when that meeting's going to be. Vida, do you think you can help us?"

"I don't know. I can try."

He looked at her. "I should have asked you this before. Why are you telling us all this?"

She looked at the floor. "My family is in big trouble because of all this. My mother is ready to divorce my father for selling her son to Miles Akley. My sister is involved with bad people, she's drinking too much, and for all I know is involved with drugs. I can't go to the police, because I know nothing about the crime they're investigating — only about crimes against and by my family that aren't illegal. My mother thinks you're both honest and you care about Rytis — maybe more than my father and Nikki do."

Kelleher nodded. "Nikki, even when she's drinking, swears Angellini wasn't behind Scott's murder?"

"She says *he* swears it."

"Then who the hell did kill him?" Kelleher asked. "Jimmy Hoffa?"

They left Vida a little after ten, having come up with a two-pronged plan of attack. Vida would try to leave as soon as the Shelter Island game was over this morning and go to Nikki's apartment. Using her key, she would let herself in and try to find the tape. Kelleher and Mearns would make sure Nikki didn't leave the game too quickly.

At the same time, they would try to find out what they could about the meeting. It was possible, if Arturas were involved, that Nadia would know about it. If Fred Murray were going to be there, maybe some of Kelleher's coaching friends — some of whom would no doubt be present that day — would know something about it. And maybe, just maybe, Nikki would have an early drink and say something to Vida.

"This André is a bad influence," Vida remarked. "I wouldn't be shocked if they were using drugs together."

Vida had to meet her family in the lobby at ten-thirty. Leaving her in the rotunda, Kelleher and Mearns walked through the stands to the press room, which was jammed. Rytis fever had hit the media. The first Saturday in March was the last one before conference tournaments began, and often columnists would go looking for stories off the beaten path before they had to cover the big names and the big teams the following week. It was ironic, Kelleher thought: going to the middle of Manhattan for a story that was different.

"Look over there," Kelleher exclaimed. "Marv Albert!"

Mearns gave him a look. "That's the first time I think I've heard an awed tone in your voice."

"One of my heroes as a kid."

The now rich-and-famous voice of the NBA on NBC was standing in a corner talking to Dick Weiss of the *New York Daily News*, a man who was nicknamed "Hoops" because the game was his life. To Kelleher, Albert would always be the guy he had grown up listening to as the voice of Knick and Ranger games on the radio. He couldn't resist walking over to introduce himself.

"I know you hear this all the time," he told Albert, "but you were my hero as a kid."

"Can't you leave out the part about 'as a kid'?" Albert asked, smiling. He introduced Kelleher to Weiss.

"I remember you from your Philadelphia days," Kelleher told Weiss. "I guess you're both here to see Buzelis?"

"Actually, I'm here to see Hoops," Albert replied with a straight face. "Just don't tell anybody."

Weiss let out a staccato laugh. "There he goes, breaking bad on me again. I'm just vurry, vurry happy to be here to see the kid play. All I try to do is skate my wing, okay?"

Kelleher had no idea what Weiss was saying, but he did note the heavy Philadelphia accent that turned *e*'s into *u*'s. If you grew up in Philly, you were always vurry happy, never very happy.

Walking down to press row, Weiss asked Kelleher if he had heard anything new on Scott Harrison's murder. "He was coaching at Virginia while you were there, right?"

"How would you remember that?"

Weiss smiled gleefully. "I remember you as a player, okay? I saw you in high school, up at Five-Star. If you had asked me, I would have told you to go to George Washington. You could have played there."

"You sound like my father."

"Father knows best, okay?"

Kelleher wasn't sure why Weiss ended all his sentences with "okay," but he knew for a fact that father *didn't* always know best. Maybe his father had, but Rytis Buzelis's father sure didn't.

At press row, Nick Angellini was talking to Jim O'Connell. Kelleher started to walk over to say something, but Mearns put a hand on his arm. "Let's be as low-key as we can. Get the game over with and then get to work."

Getting the game over with was easier said than done. Shelter Island's opponent was Mario Cuomo High School, from outside Albany, a team that pressed and fouled the whole game. Fortunately for Shelter Island, Buzelis seemed to have been touched by magic since his miracle shot Thursday night. He hit his first nine shots of the game, including five three-pointers, and had the crowd — surprisingly large for a Saturday morning — going crazy. It was 44–29 at halftime. The only question in the second half was how many points Buzelis would end up with — 52 — and how many fouls the refs would call — 55. The game ended close to one o'clock. Shelter Island won, 86–75.

Amazingly, the tiny school that had never even been in the state playoffs would now compete for the title. And because of the two-games-in-one day format, they would have two hours' more rest than their opponent. It was a shame, Kelleher thought, watching the two teams shake hands, that the story couldn't be that simple. Shelter Island was Cinderella in sneakers. The problem was that no prince was in sight — only wicked stepsisters.

The Buzelis family got up and made its way to the hospitality area. "Can we get back there?" Mearns asked.

"Yeah — media badges are good there."

Their plan was simple. Kelleher would tell Nikki that if she didn't talk to them, he'd inform her father she was the one with the tape that was making his and Akley's lives so miserable. According to Vida, Arturas and Akley knew nothing of Nikki's involvement, and it was important to her that Arturas not know for as long as possible — *never* being her goal, though that was probably impossible.

To Kelleher's surprise, the Buzelises weren't in the Brickley area. Instead, they were all wandering around the MSG network suite. "Wonder if Nikki's trying to make a deal with MSG and better-deal Angellini," Mearns whispered as they walked in.

"Right now, I'll believe anything."

Nikki, wearing jeans and a blue sweater, was talking to several suits, towering over them in high heels that made her about six-two. Vida, Kelleher noticed, had her coat on and was saying goodbye to her parents. That was step one. Now would come the hard part.

Casually, he walked over to the bar and asked for an orange juice. Turning to check on Nikki's whereabouts, he found himself face to face with Arturas Buzelis. This was not a development he had counted on or welcomed.

"Mr. Buzelis," he said, trying to sound as friendly as possible. "What a remarkable weekend Rytis is having."

Buzelis had no interest in small talk. "I know what you did," he muttered venomously. "You think you are some kind of do-gooder, that you know what is best for my son. You know nothing! You are an interfering fool, and I only wish you could be put in jail for what you have done."

"Can't do that here, Mr. Buzelis. Sorry."

Buzelis was red-faced, but he didn't raise his voice, not wanting to cause a scene. "You will not stop this any more than your friend Nick Angellini will stop this. It is something that must be done, and it will be done."

Kelleher wondered for a second if Nikki had convinced her father he and Angellini were in cahoots. Probably Nikki could convince her father of almost anything. "I can understand why you feel so strongly, Mr. Buzelis. There's certainly a lot of money involved — "

Buzelis leaned down so he could look him straight in the eye. "You simple bastard," he hissed. "You don't have any idea what this is all about."

"Why don't you tell me?" Kelleher suggested, smiling.

"Go straight to hell," Buzelis retorted, then turned on his heel and stormed away.

"I thought that went well," Kelleher said to no one. He sipped his orange juice, regaining his bearings. Tamara, as planned, was keeping her distance from him and talking to Nadia. That was good. It was time for him to make his move on Nikki.

Maneuvering slowly through the crowd, he stood behind Nikki while she chatted with the suits, who were staring at her as though she were a Greek goddess.

"Nikki," he began in a low tone, hoping she'd hear him. Nothing. He tried again, more sharply. "Nikki."

This time she heard him. Glancing over her shoulder, she gave him a look to indicate that if a fly had landed on her, it would be more welcome. "What do you want?"

"I want to talk to you."

"You can't always have what you want, can you, Bobby?"

She turned back to her conversation. He walked closer to her, stood up straight so he could get his mouth near her ear, and said, "My guess is you wouldn't want your father to know about your involvement with Angellini, would you?"

She didn't flinch. But she did say to her admirers, "Would you excuse me for a minute? I'm really not sure why they let the media in here."

One of the suits immediately piped up. "I don't think they're supposed to be in here."

"Check the door, pal," Kelleher replied, smiling sweetly. He put a hand on Nikki's shoulder to turn her away from the suits.

"Now, then, you have a few minutes?" he asked softly.

"What makes you think my father would believe anything you say?"

"Nothing. But he might believe Tamara. You want to risk it?"

She sighed. "Talk fast."

Kelleher shook his head. "Not here. I know there's a lot going on today, with the meeting and all — "

Her expression changed slightly. "How could you know?"

He shrugged. "Just because I underestimated you once doesn't mean you aren't capable of underestimating me."

The look on her face spoke volumes. Then she gave him the

stunning smile. "Yes, but that's all you know. If you knew anything more, you wouldn't be talking to me — you'd be finding some way to show up or hide out or something like that."

"Why, Nikki, why would you think a thing like that?" he asked, giving her the sweetest smile he could conjure up. "I don't really need to be in on the meeting. I know what Akley did, and I also know what you and Angellini were up to." He leaned closer to her. "I also know that conspiracy to commit murder is a serious crime."

Looking her right in the eye for a reaction, he got a blank stare. She glanced at her watch. "I'll get my coat and meet you outside by the escalator."

"I'll go with you."

She put up a hand. "Please. I'm not stupid. If I run out on you, you'll go to my father." She looked around the room to find him. "The point is, I don't want him to see me walking around with you. If he does, you might just as well go talk to him right now, because he'll be furious with me for *that*."

"Okay. I'll give you five minutes."

"Thank you, O lord and master."

She turned and headed in the direction of the coatroom. Kelleher couldn't help but notice the way heads turned when she passed. She was one of those women who are so striking that even other women check them out.

He forced himself to stop staring at her, and looked around for Mearns. She was across the room, talking to Nadia. Interrupting wasn't a good idea. He waited at a nearby food table until he caught Mearns's eye, then he gave her a quick "cut" sign, running his hand across his neck. She nodded faintly. A minute later, she patted Nadia on the shoulder and walked out. Kelleher counted ten and followed.

"And?" Mearns asked.

"She's meeting us at the escalator in five minutes." He looked at his watch. "Two minutes."

"Was Nadia helpful?" he asked as they walked to the escalators.

"Not really. Mostly, she wanted to know why I'm hanging around with you. She thinks Arturas is right — you're a troublemaker."

"Sounds like Nikki got to her."

Mearns smiled playfully. "Why would you think that? I mean, you *are* a troublemaker."

Leaning against the wall near the escalator, Mearns wondered if Nikki would show up.

"She's terrified I might talk to her father," Kelleher assured her. "She'll show up."

Five minutes later, he wasn't so sure. Maybe he had underestimated her again. He was about to tell Mearns he was going back to look for her when she swooped around the corner wearing a camel's hair coat. "Sorry," she said. "I had to go to the ladies' room."

He started to make a remark about what had happened the last time she had disappeared on him, back on Shelter Island, but he resisted.

"Where are we going?" Nikki asked on the escalator.

"No place," Kelleher answered. "It's a beautiful day out. We'll just walk around and talk."

He wasn't exaggerating. It had turned into one of those gorgeous late-winter, early-spring New York afternoons that make you think the place is livable. The temperature had climbed above fifty; the sun was shining brightly. They walked out of the Garden on the Seventh Avenue side. Kelleher steered them up to 34th Street and then east. Across the street Macy's loomed, huge and gray, just as Kelleher remembered it from his childhood. They passed Tad's Steak House, where Kelleher remembered buying postgame steaks with his pals for $1.39.

Walking in silence, Kelleher tried to figure out where to begin. On 34th Street, just beyond Tad's, Mearns spoke up.

"Look, Nikki, here's the deal. Bobby and I don't really believe you had anything to do with Scott's murder. But we do think you know things that can help us — or the police — figure out who was involved."

"What makes you think I haven't told the police?"

"We talked to the cops," Kelleher lied. "They don't know anything about your relationship with Angellini or the fact that Nick was using you to try to get the Minnesota State job."

She gave him a hard look. "What do you mean, 'using' me?"

Kelleher laughed. "This is probably new for you, but Nick Angellini couldn't care less about you. In fact, my guess is he didn't even care about getting you into bed. That was just a bonus. You were never anything more to him than a route to Rytis. And Rytis is his route to millions — contract, TV, radio, shoe deal, camp, speaking. A million, easy. More, probably."

She didn't answer; she just kept walking. The sidewalk was crowded with shoppers and people getting out to enjoy the weather. Kelleher and Mearns knew the thing to do was ride out Nikki's silence. As reporters, they knew that Kelleher had staggered her a little. It wasn't so much the concept that Nick Angellini didn't give a damn about her — Nikki was smart enough to know that and probably had seen Angellini as little more than a cash register and an open door to modeling work — but the notion that they knew she had been used.

They had reached the corner of 34th Street where Sixth Avenue and Broadway crossed. "Keep going," Kelleher directed. "We'll walk over to Fifth."

They had crossed both Sixth and Broadway when Nikki finally spoke. "Even if everything you say is right, so what? You can call me a bad person, but you can't prove a thing — about Nick or me. You don't have the tape, so you can't write anything about Akley. You told me that yourself, Bobby. So we control Akley — you don't. And most important, whatever you think of Nick or me — or, for that matter, of Akley — none of us was involved in Scott's murder."

They turned the corner, walking north on Fifth Avenue.

"You know, Nikki, I believe you," Mearns said, playing the good-cop role. "I don't think you know anything about the murder. But do you really believe Angellini when he says he's not involved? I mean, really believe him?"

She took a while to answer that one too. "I'm not going to tell you these are future Nobel Prize winners." She took a deep breath. "But I saw Nick the morning after the murder. He was shaken up — not because he felt so sad about Scott, but because it put everything at a different level, a dangerous one. He said to me, 'If someone killed Harrison, what would keep them from killing us if they knew we were involved?' He even thought about getting out of the whole thing."

"Did he have any theories on who did it?" Kelleher asked.

"For a while, he thought it was Akley. But when Nick talked to him, Akley was scared too — really scared. He told Nick that for the first time in his life, he wondered whether all this was worth it."

At the light on the corner of 42nd Street, Kelleher glanced at his watch. They had killed forty-five minutes. "Does Nick have any theories now?"

She shook her head. "Not one. Neither do I. He checked to find out if anyone else might be involved that we didn't know about. Nothing. I checked with my mother and Rytis. None of the other schools have done anything to suggest they would do anything so crazy."

"It must be *someone*," Kelleher said. He had a thought. "Who did Scott think was trying to kill him when he talked to you that night? He must have had an idea."

She laughed. "Oh, Bobby, I'm sorry — I completely forgot

that you bought that story. He didn't have a clue that anyone was trying to kill him. I made that up."

Kelleher's face flushed. He didn't like the idea that someone could tell him a bald lie and he would fall for it so completely. But then, he had bought a lot from Nikki Buzelis that he normally would not have gone for. "Okay then." He was still a little angry. "What were you two talking about that night?"

She looked around, as if to see whether anyone was watching them. "He had figured out what was going on with Nick and me. I made a mistake and left an Angellini Inc. modeling bag in the corner of my bedroom. Scott was no fool. He called the agency, posing as a magazine editor, and found out that I was working for them. That was what we were talking about that night. He wanted to know what Nick and I were up to and why I had betrayed him."

"Did you tell him?"

She shook her head. "I only told him that Nick had helped me with my modeling career — "

"And paid for your apartment," Kelleher interrupted.

She smiled. "You do know a lot, don't you? I didn't tell him about that — just the modeling. I tried to tell him that Nick wanted Rytis to go to NYU, but he said to me, 'That's a lie, and you know it.' I swore to him that was all I knew."

"But it wasn't. That's why he called Angellini."

She shrugged. "Scott called him and said he knew what Nick was up to and he wouldn't get away with it. Nick said he just laughed and told him all was fair in love and recruiting."

"An interesting choice of words," Mearns remarked.

Nikki didn't respond. They were standing in front of Rockefeller Center. Kelleher glanced at his watch again. They had more than killed the hour Vida had asked for. But continuing the conversation might shed more light on what Angellini was planning.

"So the deal was, Bobby Taylor had to be fired so Nick could ride in on a white horse, convince Rytis to go to Minnesota State, and save the program?"

"More or less."

Kelleher moved closer to Nikki to look her right in the eye. Since she was wearing heels, he had to stand very straight to do it. "Who was Nick dealing with at Minnesota State?"

"I don't know."

"You never asked?"

"What did I care?"

"Gee, I don't know, Nikki — I would think if one were using one's brother to start her career, one might care at least a little bit about the kind of people he was getting involved with."

She looked past him, as if looking for someone down at the corner. "The people Nick is involved with aren't any worse than Miles Akley."

Kelleher thought about that for a second. "Maybe not, unless they had something to do with killing Scott Harrison."

"I told you, Nick had nothing to do with it."

"So he says."

She took a deep breath. "I've told you what I know. I've got a lot of things to do, and I don't need to stand around here and play games with you. I may not be the best person who ever lived, but I'm fairly smart. If Nick was involved in the murder, I think I'd know it."

"You thought Nick cared about you."

She looked at him as if he were a complete idiot. "Don't you think I know how the game is played? He wants Rytis, I want to be a model, a supermodel. We were the perfect couple. Caring had nothing to do with it."

She looked at Tamara. "Have you ever been in love?"

"Once."

"Painful, isn't it?"

Mearns grunted. "Actually, yes."

Nikki nodded affirmation. "I gave up caring about people a long time ago." she said to Kelleher. "Now excuse me. I have to leave."

She took a few steps, then stopped and turned. "Oh, and let me save you some time and energy in case you're thinking of following me back to the apartment. You won't learn a thing if you do." Kelleher watched her walk off, noticing the heads turn. If Nikki knew, she didn't show it. Head high, she loped down the street, her long legs covering a lot of ground quickly.

Something told Kelleher she wasn't lying about the futility of following her. He turned to Mearns, who was also staring after her. "What do you think?"

"I think someone burned her very badly once."

"You too?"

"Only a little. Come on, let's get some coffee."

"Fine. But first, let's call Vida."

THIRTEEN

THE TAPE

THEY WALKED down to the skating rink, pausing briefly to watch.

"You skate?" he asked Mearns.

"A little."

He thought about how much fun it would be to be skating in circles right then with Mearns next to him. They walked down the steps to the mall next to the rink and found a pay phone. Kelleher dialed Vida's number. He was about to give up on the fourth ring, before the tape answered, when she picked up the phone.

"Vida, you okay?"

"Fine. I just walked in the door."

"And?"

"I got it. Four copies, in fact. I stopped to buy a tape recorder so I could make sure I had the real thing."

Kelleher felt his heart pounding. They had the tape! At the very least, Akley was finished. "You checked each tape?" he asked, anxious to be sure.

"The beginning of all four of them."

Kelleher's mind was racing. What they had to do now was

get the tape to a safe place and start putting a story together. They also had to figure out where and when this big meeting was going to take place.

"Okay, Vida, wait for me there. I'll come right down. Then I need you to talk to your mom, to see if she can find out anything about some kind of meeting today — or more likely tonight. If your father is involved, she should know about it."

"You need my address. It's Nine East Tenth Street. Apartment 4D."

"I'll be there as soon as I can grab a taxi."

He hung up, turned to Mearns, and flung his arms around her. "She did it!"

"What next?" Mearns's voice was calm, but her eyes shone with excitement. She had hugged him briefly in return.

"I'll get the tapes from Vida. I want you to go across the street to AP and wait for me. Siddons told me he'd be there all day, so just ask for him. Start playing with some kind of lead on Akley and the tape."

"Who are we writing this for?" she asked, a logical question.

"I think it should go out on the AP wire with a sentence that says, 'The *Shelter Island Reporter* learned in a story that will appear in its Friday edition . . .' "

She nodded. "Makes sense. But maybe I should come with you to Vida's, just to be safe."

"No. To be safe I want you at the AP, so if something goes wrong, which it shouldn't, I can call you. No one has any idea right now that Vida has the tape. Even if Nikki goes home and discovers it's missing, she won't think of Vida — at least not right away."

Mearns was nodding. "You should get going."

She gave him another quick hug and walked off to the stairs at the other end of the mall. Kelleher was so wired, he practically sprinted up the steps and ran all the way to Fifth Avenue. Getting a cab was no problem, but it took ten minutes to go the first eight blocks downtown. Kelleher squirmed in the back seat, wondering if he should get out and walk a few blocks to get by the traffic.

"Once we're past Forty-second Street, we'll be fine," the cabbie said.

He was right; it took less time to get from 42nd Street to 10th than from 50th to 42nd. Kelleher got out on the corner of 10th and Fifth and walked the half block to the canopy that said "Nine."

Inside the lobby, he tried the door and found it locked. No surprise. Scanning the apartment buzzers to find 4D, he pressed the button. He waited ten seconds, twenty, thirty. No response. He pressed again — twice. Maybe Vida was in the bathroom. Another minute went by — still nothing. Kelleher was wondering if he should go outside and look for a telephone when a young woman in a running suit came in the front door. In the New York way, she barely glanced at him, then took out her key and opened the inside door.

Kelleher followed her through the door. She gave him a look, as if to say, "Where do you think you're going?"

"I think my friend must be in the bathroom," he volunteered, feeling an explanation was probably a good idea.

She gave him a bored look. "Who's your friend?"

"Vida Buzelis. Four-D."

Apparently it was good enough for her; she shrugged and pressed the elevator button. They got on the elevator together. He pressed four and she pressed seven, then they stared at the slowly moving numbers as the elevator lurched upward — anything to avoid eye contact.

Smiling when the elevator hit four, he said, "Have a nice day." She continued to stare at the numbers.

Kelleher turned left and found apartments 4E and 4F. Four-D was at the other end of the floor, the last apartment on the left. Kelleher was surprised to find the door cracked open. Maybe Vida had heard the buzzer and had left the door ajar for him? Cautiously, he pushed the door open.

"Vida?" Nothing. "Vida?" Pushing the door all the way open, he walked a couple of steps into the hallway. He raised his voice. "Vida?"

That was when he heard the groan. Suddenly terrified, he raced the last few steps into the living room. Vida was sprawled next to the couch in a pool of blood. A splintered chair lay a couple of feet from her.

"Jesus, Vida, what happened?" he yelled, kneeling over her. Her reply was another moan. Her eyes were rolled back in her head; she was unconscious. Standing up to find a phone, Kelleher heard a noise behind him. The bedroom door burst open and two men, both wearing ski masks, charged through it.

"Not again!" Kelleher exclaimed.

"Don't make a fucking move and you won't get hurt, Kelleher," the first one snapped.

They knew his name! For a moment Kelleher thought it was his old friends Buster and Tommy from the beach. But these two weren't as big as Buster and Tommy.

"What the hell is going on here?" Kelleher bellowed. "What did you do to her?"

"Just stay where you are," the first one said, holding his hand out in front of him as if to ward off an advance by Kelleher. It was then that Kelleher noticed he had something clutched in his fist. Tapes! *The tapes!*

"Hey," he shouted. Forgetting the manpower disadvantage, he lunged at number one. Grabbing his arm, Kelleher twisted it. The two of them fell to the floor, toppling furniture in the process. Kelleher kept trying to get a hand free to grab the tapes. Just as he did, number two grabbed him and yanked him so hard he screamed in pain and fell backward. That gave number one enough time to wriggle free and push Kelleher onto his back. One of the tapes fell out of his hand. Kelleher, on his back, reached for it. Number two responded by stepping on his wrist.

Kelleher screamed again and reached blindly for the thug. Seizing his sweater, he pulled as hard as he could, hoping to bring him down. He got nothing but a scrap of fuzz. Both men were on their feet now.

"Should we just leave him?" number one asked, breathing hard.

"Fuck him, let's get the hell out of here," number two said.

"But she may not be dead — "

"No time," number two said as Kelleher again tried to get up. They shoved him back down and ran to the door. Kelleher heard it slam. He lay there for a moment, trying to recover. His wrist was throbbing with pain. Then he heard Vida groan again and remembered what they had said: "She may not be dead . . ." Neither voice was familiar. In fact, one had a decided Midwestern twang. Tommy and Buster had sounded pure New York.

They had meant to kill her. These had to be the same guys who had murdered Scott. This time, though, they had been less thorough — no doubt afraid to use a gun in a New York apartment building. He got slowly to his feet, checking himself for other cuts or bruises. Nothing. Chasing them — especially alone — was pointless. Opening his left hand, he saw the fuzz he had pulled off one of the attackers' sweaters. It was purple. They had both worn purple sweaters. Purple and white were Minnesota State's colors.

Looking around, he saw that the phone had been knocked to the floor. He picked it up. Relieved to find that it worked, he dialed 911. On the second ring, the dispatcher answered —

also a relief; he had heard stories about dialing 911 in New York and getting no answer.

"Hello, I need an ambulance," he said, aware he was breathing hard.

"Is someone ill, sir?"

"No, someone has had the hell beaten out of them and they're lying here bleeding to death."

"Okay, sir, stay calm. Tell me where you are."

For several seconds, he blanked on the address. Then he got it: "Nine East Tenth Street. Apartment 4D."

"And your name, sir?"

"My name? What difference does that make? Kelleher, Bobby Kelleher. Would you please send an ambulance, for crying out loud, before this woman dies!"

"Okay, sir, you stay right there and wait for the ambulance. It'll be there shortly."

He hung up and looked at Vida, who appeared to be unconscious. He went into the bathroom and looked for a towel to stanch the blood oozing from her head. Returning, he tried to put the towel under her head; it turned completely red in a matter of seconds. "Come on, Vida!" he yelled — pointlessly, he knew. Every minute or so, he looked at his watch. "Come on!" he hissed when seven minutes had gone by.

Finally there was a loud knock on the door. He jumped up, ran down the hall, and opened it. Two paramedics and a police officer were standing there. "You call 911?" the cop asked.

"Yes, she's in the living room. Please hurry."

The paramedics hustled by him. "What happened?" the cop asked, following Kelleher into the living room. "You two get into a fight?"

The question baffled Kelleher for a second. Then he remembered his days as a police reporter. More often than not, the person who placed a 911 call to report a crime was involved in the crime. The natural thing for the cops to think was that he had beaten Vida up.

"No, we didn't get into a fight. She's a friend of mine. She was lying here like this when I came in. Two guys who just took off did it."

"This woman's a friend of yours? What kind of friend?"

Before Kelleher could reply, one of the paramedics interrupted. "Charlie, she's in bad shape. We gotta get her out of here right now."

They lifted her gently onto the stretcher. "Is she going to make it?" Kelleher asked.

"Don't know," the paramedic said. "I hope so. At least you called quickly."

Kelleher understood the implication. "We'll need you to come with us," the cop said. His badge identified him as Officer White. "I need to ask you some more questions."

"That's fine. Can I make a quick call before we go?"

White nodded. The paramedics were on their way out the door with Vida as Kelleher picked up the phone and dialed Larry Siddons's number at the AP office. He breathed a deep sigh of relief when Siddons answered. "Thank God you're there. Is Tamara nearby?"

"Yeah, right here. What's up?"

"Can she pick up another line so I can tell you both at the same time?"

"Hang on."

A few seconds later, Mearns was on the line. "Where the hell are you?"

"Just listen." He launched into an explanation of what had happened, not mentioning the tapes in front of White.

When he was finished, Mearns asked the question immediately. "And the tapes?"

"Gone. They got them. That's obviously what they came for."

White, who had been listening, was growing impatient. "Come on, Kelleher," he said, apparently having gotten his name from the 911 call. "We have to go."

"Right. Where are we going?"

"St. Vincent's."

"Tamara," Kelleher said into the phone, "can you meet me at St. Vincent's right away? I may need you to vouch for me. I made the 911 call, so the cops consider me a suspect."

He looked at White. "Right?"

"We need some answers," White replied.

"I'll meet you there," Mearns said.

Kelleher hung up. As they headed out the door, White said, "I heard you telling your friends what happened. I'll need you to repeat that in an official statement, but you're saying these two guys came here to kill this woman?"

"It's a complicated story, officer, really complicated."

White put up a hand as they stepped onto the elevator. "Save it for when we sit you down at the hospital."

The ride was brief. Kelleher sat in the back seat with White while White's partner, Jamison, drove the squad car. Kelleher tried to figure out how the attackers had known Vida had the tapes.

In retrospect, it wasn't hard. Nikki had sandbagged him again. Probably she had guessed, based on what Kelleher the big mouth had said, that Vida had talked to him. When she went off to get her coat, she had told someone — Angellini perhaps — that Kelleher and Mearns were onto her. Suspecting that Vida might be up to something, they had followed her from the Garden back to her apartment, gotten in, and, after beating her up, found the tapes.

No other explanation was possible. Kelleher had given away too much in his conversation with Nikki.

He was still kicking himself when they pulled up at the emergency entrance to the hospital. Vida was being hustled inside. Kelleher was taken to an examining room so a doctor could look at his wrist. "Wait here," White said.

"I won't go anywhere," Kelleher reassured him, in case he was thinking of putting a guard on the door.

Two minutes later, White returned with a young doctor.

"Any word on Vida?" Kelleher asked the cop.

"Not yet," White said. "My partner's with her, though. If she's well enough to talk at any point, we'll see if she'll confirm your story."

The doctor looked at Kelleher's wrist and probed a few places that caused Kelleher to wince. "You got off a lot luckier than your friend," he said finally. Kelleher had the impression that the doctor, too, thought he had beaten Vida up. "You may have torn something in here, but it should heal fairly quickly. I'll wrap it for you."

"I don't need a cast?"

"It's not that serious. As I said, you were lucky."

Kelleher was getting tired of people acting as if he were some kind of wife- or girlfriend-beater. He knew that his future, both short-term and long-term, might hinge on when or if Vida regained consciousness.

"Okay," White said as the doctor finished wrapping Kelleher's wrist. "You ready to give a statement?"

"Sure."

White took him into a small office, turned on a tape recorder, and began to talk. He told Kelleher he didn't have to talk to him if he didn't want to, and that he could call an attorney.

"Am I under arrest?"

"No, not right now. That's why I haven't read you your rights."

"But I can't just get up and walk out of here if I want to, can I?"

White shook his head. "No, you can't. Right now you're being held for questioning."

"Just want to have it all straight."

Kelleher began to tell the story, deciding there was no longer any point in withholding details from the cops. In fact, having them call the Shelter Island cops to confirm the existence of the tapes and the fight over the original would probably help his case. About halfway through the story, someone knocked on the door. Tamara Mearns poked her head in.

"May I help you?" White asked.

"This is Tamara Mearns," Kelleher said. "She's the other reporter I was telling you about."

"I checked with your partner," Mearns said to White. "He said they're going to take Vida into surgery in a few minutes, but the doctors think he may be able to talk to her for a few seconds beforehand."

"Is she going to make it?" Kelleher asked.

"They think so. But she's lost a lot of blood."

White eyed Kelleher, checking him for a reaction to what Mearns was saying. "I guess if she can talk, your situation will be a lot clearer." He paused. "One way or the other."

Kelleher was praying that Vida would be okay and able to talk. It was getting close to five o'clock. He was convinced it was critical they get to the Garden as soon as possible. The big meeting Vida had told them about had to be sometime tonight — this was the last time for a while that all the players in the soap opera would be in the same place at the same time. He wondered if the two attackers were Akley's people or Angellini's people. Given the purple sweaters, his money was on Angellini. That made it likely the original Angellini plan — using the tapes to blackmail Akley — was back on.

"How soon did Officer Jamison say he might be able to talk to Vida?" he asked Mearns.

"If it happened at all, it was going to be soon. They couldn't afford to delay surgery once she was stable."

Kelleher sighed. If he couldn't get out of here, he would call Siddons and see if he could help Mearns out at the Garden. But Siddons didn't even know what a lot of the key people looked like. Kelleher needed to be there.

"You want to keep telling your story, Kelleher?" White asked. "There's really nothing else for you to do until Jamison comes back and tells us if — "

On cue, the door opened. Kelleher prayed it was Jamison. It was, but the look on his face communicated nothing. "What's the word?" White asked his partner.

Jamison looked at Kelleher. "She was real weak, so they only let me have a few seconds with her." Kelleher groaned. Jamison put a hand on his shoulder to indicate he should be patient. "I asked if she knew who did this to her. She said it was two men in ski masks. I asked if there was any chance Bobby Kelleher was her attacker. All she said was, 'He saved me.' Then they took her away."

White stood up and came around the desk. He put out a hand. "Sorry we had to put you through that. You understand — "

Kelleher put up a hand. "I covered cops years ago — I know how it works. But maybe you guys can do us a favor."

"Name it," White said.

"Give us a ride to the Garden. We need to get there as quickly as possible."

Jamison looked at White. White nodded. "I still need to finish getting a statement from you, but it can wait till morning. Since the guys were in ski masks, there's no sense going through any mug shots."

"These guys aren't crooks — at least not in the sense that they'd be in a mug file. But you know what? They might just be stupid enough to show up at the Garden tonight in purple sweaters."

"Odds are there won't be many people in that color," Mearns added.

"If you spot anyone in purple, don't do anything heroic," White cautioned him. "Find a cop — they'll find us, and we can be there in minutes."

"Right," Kelleher said.

White put a hand on his shoulder. "Don't give me that reporter's 'Right' stuff. You told me they talked about intending to kill Vida. You don't need to be messing with these guys. Let us do our job."

"I *do* understand you. We won't do anything stupid."

"Fine, then — we'll get going. But be careful."

Kelleher nodded. He intended to be careful. He had already been careless once today, and it had almost gotten Vida killed. They didn't need anyone else beaten to within an inch of his life. But they needed to find out about that meeting — and they needed to be there. Kelleher had a feeling that the New York State high school basketball championship was not the only game that was going to be decided tonight.

FOURTEEN

BUZZER BEATER

THEY ARRIVED shortly after five-thirty. The game didn't begin until eight-thirty; the Garden was empty. Only a few people were in the press room when they walked in.

Kelleher immediately went to a phone to call Siddons. He updated him on what had happened at the hospital and asked him if he could get away from the office to help them out. They needed to keep a close eye on three people: Akley, Angellini, and Nikki. The chances were pretty good that no meeting would take place without them. It was also possible, Kelleher realized, that the meeting had already taken place. But he suspected Vida's two attackers would play some role — especially now that they had the tapes — and they weren't likely to surface before tonight.

"We need three people," he told Siddons.

"You also need a way to communicate. Why don't I bring three walkie-talkies with me."

"You guys have walkie-talkies?"

"Yeah, for political conventions."

The only time Kelleher had covered a convention for the

Herald — the '92 Democratic Convention, which had been held in this same building — the paper had used a beeper system to communicate with reporters.

"How soon can you be here?"

"Give me half an hour."

They checked the arena to make sure no one had shown up early. No one was in sight, except for one section, where ushers and security guards were being given a pregame briefing.

"They're probably telling them to make sure to be rude to everyone," Kelleher speculated. Glancing at the rafters, he was surprised to see that the curtain that blocked off the upstairs sections when they weren't used was in place. He had thought they'd sell enough tickets to the final to need the upstairs.

"I asked about that this morning," Mearns said when he pointed it out. "They're expecting just under fifteen thousand. Keeping everyone downstairs creates the feeling of a full house and makes the setting more intimate."

"It also means they can charge at least ten bucks a ticket," Kelleher remarked, remembering the sign on the box office window that morning. It didn't really matter to him one way or the other, but remembering when he had paid two dollars to sit upstairs for college doubleheaders, he thought it was a shame that that sort of price was no longer available to kids.

He suggested they grab a quick bite to eat, so they'd be ready when the building opened.

"We can't just stand out there wearing a sign that says, 'When does the meeting start?' " Mearns asked.

"No kidding. But we can be at the press table, talking to other reporters or hard at work on our computers."

Siddons showed up a little before seven, and they mapped out strategy. He would be Nikki's shadow, since she didn't know him and wouldn't be as suspicious if she noticed him walking behind her. Mearns would take Angellini; they suspected he didn't know her. Kelleher would have to take Akley, which would be difficult, since Akley would no doubt be jumping at shadows, especially if one of them looked like Kelleher.

They spread out to test the walkies and, satisfied that they worked, made their way down to press row, the walkies in their pockets so as not to be too obtrusive.

"Glad I wore pants," Mearns said.

"Me too," Siddons quipped.

Kelleher was happy to see that a number of other reporters were already downstairs. This was schmooze time for the media. Some did it upstairs over food; others liked to take in the atmosphere as the building filled up. The more people around, the less obvious they would be to their prey when they arrived.

"We're going to feel awfully silly if there's no meeting tonight," Mearns said.

"How would we feel if there were one and we didn't take a shot at it?" Kelleher asked. "My gut tells me this is it for everyone, including my two friends from this afternoon."

He scanned the seats as people came in, hoping to see two guys in purple sweaters. Mearns and Siddons also looked, making conversation as if all they cared about were the outcome of the Shelter Island–Oneonta game that would decide the state championship. Kelleher had watched Oneonta play a little on Thursday afternoon and was convinced they didn't have any one player — or any two — who could stay with Rytis Buzelis.

Shortly after the teams came out to warm up, Kelleher looked across the court and saw the Buzelis family arriving. Only it wasn't the whole family — only Arturas and Nikki. Just before they had left the press room, Mearns had called the hospital for an update on Vida. She was out of surgery and in recovery; that was all they knew. The nurse had told her Vida's mother was there.

Akley came in shortly after the Buzelises, stopping for a quick handshake with Arturas but not exchanging his usual hug with Nikki. Instead, he moved on to another section, where a number of NBA scouts were sitting — at a high school game, no less — and was joined there a few minutes later by Fred Murray. Kelleher knew Murray's team closed its regular season the next afternoon at Georgia. He was surprised to see him.

Angellini's arrival, at the height of the warmups, was like a scene out of a movie. Both bands were playing. He walked straight onto the court, shook hands with Rytis, several of the Shelter Island kids, and Joe Dierker, and then did the same with the Oneonta players and their coach. He stopped at the press table to shake hands with Bruce Beck and Jim Spanarkel, who were doing the telecast on MSG cablevision. He signed some autographs, shook a few more hands, and took a seat on the same side of the building as the Buzelises and Akley but in another section, directly behind the Oneonta bench.

"Well," Kelleher said. "Looks like the gang's all here."

"Except for the purple Vida beaters," Siddons added.

"They might be here too. The problem is, unless they're in purple, I have no way of recognizing them."

"Maybe by voice," Mearns said.

"Only if the right guy tells me to stay back in that Midwestern accent, the way he did at the apartment."

"Keep your fingers crossed," Siddons said.

"You notice these characters have spread themselves out. My guess is that's on purpose."

"They do know that we know there's a meeting," Mearns pointed out. "You told Nikki."

"Don't remind me."

It was almost 8:40 by the time they got the lineups introduced, the national anthem played, and the pregame ceremonies finished. The game started. The three reporters kept one eye on it and one eye on the stands.

The first quarter ended with Shelter Island up 24–19, Rytis having scored 20 of the 24. It was apparent to Kelleher that Rytis was going to do whatever had to be done to win this game. They had come too far now to lose.

Shortly after the second quarter began, Rytis made a steal and went in for a dunk. As the crowd erupted, Nikki, having jumped to her feet with everyone else, popped into the aisle and started toward the concourse.

"There she goes," Kelleher said to Siddons.

"Chasing her isn't the worst assignment in history, I guess," Siddons remarked.

"Be careful. Watch yourself going around corners."

Nodding, Siddons jumped out of his seat and began half-walking, half-running to the other side of the court to follow Nikki, who was moving almost languidly up the steps, undoubtedly trying not to call attention to herself.

"We'll know soon if this is a trip to the bathroom or —"

"There goes Angellini," Mearns broke in. "See ya."

She was up and gone before he could tell her to be careful too. In all probability, he needed to be reminded more than anyone. He pulled the walkie-talkie out of his pocket and waited to see what Akley would do.

Siddons's voice came crackling through. "Bobby, you hear me?"

"Loud, if not clear."

"She's going down the escalator. I think she's heading out of the building."

"Angellini just left. This must be it."

As he finished, Akley and Murray got out of their seats.

Casual as could be, they started up the aisle, stopping to talk to people on the way. Trying to be equally casual, Kelleher got up and walked to the baseline to circle the court, hoping they wouldn't look in his direction. If they did, he didn't see them do it. They reached the concourse level and turned left just as he got to the bottom of the steps at floor level.

His heart pounding, he sprinted up the steps, wanting to make sure he didn't lose them but not wanting to round a corner and come face to face with them. He reached the top of the steps, slightly out of breath, as they disappeared into a portal.

"Kelleher." It was Mearns on the walkie.

"Go," he said, walking rapidly toward the portal.

"Nick's heading upstairs someplace."

Upstairs? It made no sense. Why would Nikki go down and Nick up? Unless they were jumping at shadows. "Stay with him."

"Maybe this isn't really it." She had heard Siddons report on Nikki going downstairs.

"We'll see."

Kelleher was in the portal. Akley and Murray had just turned right to go down the hall in the direction of an escalator. Wondering which way they would go, he ran down the portal and peered around. Because Madison Square Garden is round, the halls curve. Akley and Murray were disappearing from sight up ahead. Kelleher followed, staying as close to the concession stands as possible, in the hope that they wouldn't spot him if they turned around. Even early in the game, there were lines for food.

Akley and Murray turned at the door to the escalators. He heard Mearns's voice again, whispering. "He's gone all the way upstairs. He's standing in the empty hallway, lighting a cigarette."

"Where are you?" Kelleher hissed.

"Behind section 408. He's around the curve at 406." Kelleher knew just where that was.

He reached the doors to the escalators. They had not yet been reversed to descend. Walking carefully through the door, he peeked around the corner in time to see two pairs of legs at the top of the escalator.

"They're going up too," he said into the walkie. "Larry, where the hell are you?"

"Crossing Thirty-third and Seventh."

Suddenly it clicked with Kelleher. Nikki was a decoy. "Larry, let her go."

"But — "

"Take my word for it. Get back here and find Bobby Goldwater, the PR guy. You know him, right?"

"Yeah."

"Round up some cops and head for the top level. That's where this is going down. Wait for me to call you, though, before you move."

"You sure?"

"Positive."

He had reached the top of one escalator. Convinced that the meeting was on the top level, he veered off to the steps — there was less chance of Akley and Murray turning and seeing him.

"Tamara, you still got Angellini?"

"Yup."

"Okay, stay right there. Miles and Murray should come walking down from the opposite direction in about a minute." Knowing the layout of the Garden had its advantages.

At the top of the steps he paused for breath. He walked slowly onto the concourse and just caught a glimpse of Akley and Murray disappearing around a curve.

Approaching the curve in the wall, hugging it now and walking very quietly, he turned down the walkie so it wouldn't make any sudden crackling noises. He peered around the curve in time to see Akley and Murray reach Angellini. There were no handshakes. Angellini dropped his cigarette and put it out with his foot.

"Anyone follow you?" Angellini asked.

Akley and Murray looked in Kelleher's direction. He stepped back quickly against the wall.

"Nah," Akley grunted. "They're probably chasing your girlfriend. That was a good idea."

"Hers," Angellini said.

"Listen, Angellini, let's not fuck around," Murray said. "You got this tape, let's hear it, so we can get this over with."

"Easy, boys, it's not that simple. You know we have the tape. Miles has heard it over the phone. I just wanted to let you know we've got no intention of ever using it as long as you stay out of the way."

"Hey, Nick, you got the tape or not?" Akley demanded. "The way blackmail works, you have to produce something. Otherwise, the hell with you. We'll go sign the kid tomorrow and make the father a very happy man."

"I wouldn't do that," Angellini said. "Look, Nikki has the tape."

He went into some garbled explanation about Nikki's taking the tape with her just to be safe. He was bluffing. Kelleher wanted to scream to Akley not to buy what Angellini was saying.

Akley didn't need any help. "You're full of shit, Nick. You haven't got it. Now why don't you tell me just what — "

He was interrupted by a muffled scream. Kelleher went stiff with fear. A moment later, two men appeared around the corner, one of them holding Mearns around the neck with one arm, his other hand over her mouth.

"What the hell is this?!" Murray roared.

Angellini, seeing the two men approaching with Mearns, looked as stunned as Akley and Murray. "Al — Bill — what the hell?"

The one not holding Mearns reached into his pocket and flipped something at Akley. "Here's your tape, Akley. Listen to it, then stick it up your ass and stay away from Buzelis."

Kelleher almost gasped out loud when he heard him say "Akley." What he really said was "Eakley," with the same distinctive Midwestern twang he had heard at Vida's apartment that afternoon. They weren't wearing purple sweaters, but these had to be Vida's attackers.

"Are these guys with you, Nick?" Akley asked. "And what the hell is *she* doing here?"

"We found her standing around the corner listening to every word you idiots were saying," the second one said.

"Shit!" Akley exclaimed. "If she's here, that fucking Kelleher must be somewhere close behind."

Kelleher clung to the wall, hoping they wouldn't all turn and run in his direction.

"Let's get this over with quickly," the second one said. "Here's the deal, Akley. We've got copies of the tapes. You shut up and stay clear of Buzelis, they'll never become public. Go near him, I'll personally deliver them to your buddy Kelleher."

"Wait a minute, Al," Angellini said. "Was it you two guys beat up the sister?"

"That's right, Nick. Your stupid girlfriend was dumb enough to let her get them, so we had to intervene. Just like we had to intervene when Scott Harrison found out you were connected to her."

Kelleher saw real fear in Angellini's eyes. "You? You killed Harrison?"

"So what?" Al snapped. "We told you we would do whatever

had to be done to get Bobby Taylor the hell out of Minnesota State. We did what we had to do. But none of you will say anything about it, because if you do, we'll tell the world everything *you* did. Right?"

"But what about her?" Akley indicated Mearns.

Al pulled a gun from his pocket. "That'll be taken care of shortly. If blood disturbs you, you may want to go back and watch the rest of the game."

"You'd do that right here?" Angellini faltered. "Now?"

"Good a time as any. See, Nick, you're just in this for money. You don't get it. When we say losing basketball games is life and death to us, we mean it."

"You too, Bill?" Angellini asked. "You'll never get away — "

"Shut up, Nick. We've had enough of you. Come on, Al, let's do it and get out of here before someone shows up."

Bill turned Mearns toward the wall, and Al reached into his pocket for something that looked to Kelleher like some kind of silencer. Angellini, Akley, and Murray stood frozen to the spot.

Kelleher couldn't wait any longer. He flew around the corner and dove at Al, who had turned away from him to point the gun at Mearns. Kelleher crashed into him full force. The two of them sprawled on the floor as the gun went flying. They rolled over a couple of times, each of them trying to free a hand to take a swing at the other.

Out of the corner of his eye, Kelleher saw Bill, who had let go of Mearns, hop over him and Al and reach down to pick up the gun. Just as he got it in his hands someone crashed into him, and the two of them went to the floor.

A stinging sensation just below his mouth told Kelleher that Al had nailed him with a pretty good punch. Slightly dazed, he heard a gunshot and then a scream. Al was trying to pummel him, so he put his arms up to deflect the blows. One punch grazed his right arm. Still holding the arm up, he swung a roundhouse left, dropping his right arm at the last second. Al never saw it coming. Kelleher felt the shock burning in his fist and saw Al's head arch backward. Al toppled over, losing his grip on Kelleher.

Kelleher jumped to his feet and was trying to figure out where Bill was when he heard shouting from both ends of the hall.

"*Everyone stand still!*" a voice commanded.

Kelleher froze. A second later, several policemen came around the curving wall from both directions. Kelleher exhaled a sigh of relief. He could see Siddons and Bobby Goldwater right behind the cops. Better late than never, he figured.

Glancing around to see what was going on, he saw Angellini and Murray cowering against the wall to his left. Mearns was sitting a few feet away, holding one hand to her head. She looked woozy. In front of him, Akley was on one knee, holding the gun over Bill — it had been Akley who had crashed into Bill while Kelleher struggled with Al. Bill was lying on his back, blood oozing from his pants leg. That explained the gunshot and the scream.

"Who're the good guys and who are the bad guys?" one of the cops asked.

"The guy standing there holding his hand as if it's broken is a good guy, and so is the woman sitting on the floor," Siddons answered. "The rest of 'em stink."

Kelleher, still shivering with fear, thought he heard himself laugh. Siddons had a way with words. Thank God he hadn't waited to hear back from Kelleher before getting the cops.

Akley put down the gun as the cops approached. It occurred to Kelleher that Miles Akley might well have saved his life. He was slightly sickened.

"Sergeant, what do we do with these guys?" an officer asked as he helped Akley to his feet.

"Call an ambulance for the one that's shot. Cuff the other three. We'll sort everything out at the station. He kneeled next to Mearns. "Do you need a doctor, ma'am?"

"I'm just a little dizzy," she answered. "I got smacked on the side of the head."

Kelleher looked at his hand. It was going to be sore for a while, but he didn't think he had broken anything. His jaw throbbed. "I might need a doctor to take a look at my hand and jaw."

Siddons came over. "I guess your instinct about Nikki was right. He nodded toward Bill and Al. "Those the two guys you ran into at Vida's?"

Kelleher nodded. "They're also the two guys who killed Scott."

"Who are they?"

Kelleher shook his head. "Boosters. Can you believe it? They committed murder because their goddamn school wasn't winning enough basketball games. How sick is that?"

Siddons sighed. "The sickest thing is that I *do* believe it."

FIFTEEN

-30-

THE COPS took Kelleher and Mearns to the Garden's first aid station. A doctor checked them and said they would both have headaches in the morning but nothing more. He looked at Kelleher's hand and suggested he try not to punch anyone in the near future.

The cops let them stay for the last few minutes of the game. Kelleher watched in awe as Rytis Buzelis scored the last twelve points for Shelter Island, to pull out an 81–77 victory. Seeing Rytis and his teammates hug one another and cut down the nets was bittersweet. It would not be long before Rytis learned that one of his sisters had set the other one up for a near-fatal beating and that his father had put Rytis's college eligibility in serious jeopardy by peddling him to Miles Akley and Fred Murray.

They left the Garden the same way they had arrived — in a police car. Murder and attempted murder were involved; they were taken to the homicide division way downtown. Kelleher and Mearns gave their statements while Siddons waited outside.

A lieutenant named Winston came into the room where

they were waiting to be told they could leave. Sitting down across from Kelleher and Mearns, he handed them two tapes. "Your friend outside said these were important to you. I had one of my men listen to them. They're both the same, and there's nothing on it we need, so they're yours."

"Thanks," Kelleher said, too tired to think of any other reply. He was half convinced they would be mugged leaving and lose the tapes again.

Winston lit a cigarette, smiled at Mearns, and kept on going. "You may want to know what's going on before you leave. We just checked on Vida Buzelis. She's resting comfortably at St. Vincent's and should go home in a couple of days.

"In addition to the two of you, Akley, Murray, and Angellini all gave statements saying Bill and Al confessed to the murder of Scott Harrison and were about to shoot Ms. Mearns." He smiled at Mearns. "We're going to charge them with the murder of Harrison and attempted murder on both Ms. Buzelis and Ms. Mearns."

"Did you find out anything more about them?" Kelleher asked.

Winston pulled out a notebook. "Allan R. Benjamin is president of the Purple Tide Club — the booster arm at Minnesota State. In real life he's a lawyer, bankruptcy. Wife, three kids. William J. Solomon is vice president of the Purple Tide Club. Stockbroker. Divorced, no kids. From what Angellini tells us, they came to him in early January after reading about Buzelis and told him Bobby Taylor would be fired at the end of the season, no matter what his final record was. They were going to see to that. They told him that if he could deliver Buzelis, they would guarantee him a five-year deal worth a million bucks a year."

"A million bucks?" Mearns repeated.

"Not impossible," Kelleher said. "Contract, TV, radio,

shoe deal, camp, speaking, and a bonus from the good old Purple Tide Club, they could get him to a million in no time."

"Angellini went for it," Winston continued. "That's how he got involved with the other sister — who still hasn't shown up, by the way."

"And may not anytime soon," Kelleher remarked.

"Anyway, when Harrison turned up dead, Angellini said he was terrified, but Bill and Al swore they didn't do it. They also said they would up the deal to a million five a year. So he kept at it. Decided to believe them because he wanted to, I guess."

"One more question. The two guys who came after us on the beach on Shelter Island."

Winston nodded. "Angellini hires. He says he hired them just to get the tapes from you. He told us where we could find them, in return for us not charging him with conspiracy to commit assault."

"So Angellini walks?"

Winston nodded. "So do Akley and Murray. We could have charged Akley with illegal use of a handgun, but under the circumstances, that wouldn't have been real fair."

Kelleher nodded. Other than Angellini's sending Buster and Tommy after him, none of the three men was guilty of breaking any laws.

Winston stood up. "You can go anytime."

They walked into the hallway where Siddons was waiting. "There are two cops downstairs who'll give us a ride," he said. As they started down the hall to the elevator, a door opened and Miles Akley and Fred Murray emerged. Everyone stopped; there was a momentary silence.

"I guess I owe you a thank-you for jumping Bill," Kelleher said finally.

"You may not think I'm the world's greatest guy," Akley

said. "Like I told you before, I'm not into killing." Akley paused. "Winston gave you the Shelter Island tape?"

"What about it?"

"Any way I can convince you not to use it until I explain to you what was going on that night?"

Kelleher laughed. "I don't need any explanation, Akley. I heard the whole thing."

"No you didn't."

Murray put a hand on Akley's shoulder. "Forget it, Miles. It's over. We'll live through it."

They turned and walked away. Kelleher shook his head. "Akley never gives up, does he?" He put his hand in his pocket to be certain the tapes were still there. "Let's go. We need a few hours' sleep, and then we need to write this baby."

"Finally," Mearns said.

"Yeah. Finally."

They agreed to meet at the AP office at nine the next morning. The wire had moved a short story saying that two Minnesota State booster club officers had been charged with Scott Harrison's murder. The plan was to write the whole story, detailing everything that had happened, for release for Monday morning papers. It took all day, especially since Kelleher was reduced to dictating because of his swollen hand.

The story would run in Friday's *Shelter Island Reporter*, with the *Reporter* getting credit for the story on the wire. The byline read "Tamara Mearns and Bobby Kelleher." Each had insisted the other's name go first. They had finally flipped a coin, and Kelleher had won, opting for the second spot.

Kelleher had hoped they could all go out for a celebration dinner that night, but by the time the editors and lawyers were finished doing their reading and commenting, and updates and fixes were made, it was almost ten o'clock. Kelleher made one last call to the cops before leaving. Nikki Buzelis still hadn't been found. Kelleher and Mearns thanked Siddons and agreed to meet at St. Vincent's the next morning. Vida was sitting up and feeling well enough to see visitors.

As tired as he was, Kelleher didn't sleep a wink. He knew the story would cause a huge uproar, not to mention an NCAA investigation of Louisiana, Akley, Angellini, Minnesota State, and the Buzelis family. His only concern was Rytis, who had been a pawn in the whole killer chess match. He couldn't wait for morning.

Visiting hours began at noon; Kelleher and Mearns were right on time. A nurse told them that Vida had agreed to see them. When they walked in, Vida was sitting up with a bandage on her head. Her mother was sitting next to the bed. Her father was staring out the window. He didn't even turn around.

"Vida told me what happened," Nadia Buzelis said. "Thank you."

"I'm just glad she's okay," Kelleher said. Vida gave them both weak hugs. Nikki had called the night before, to say she was in Los Angeles. Although she wasn't going to be charged with a crime, she had said she couldn't come home and face them — at least not yet.

A copy of the *New York Times*, which had carried their story on the bottom of page one, was sitting on the edge of the bed. "You saw the story?" he asked softly. Vida and Nadia both nodded.

Arturas turned from the window. "Oh yes, Mr. Kelleher, we all read your wonderful story. I suppose you are quite proud."

"All we did was tell the truth."

Arturas started to talk, but Nadia held up a hand. "Not here Arturas. Not here."

"All right then. Mr. Kelleher, would you talk to me outside?"

Kelleher had visions of a fight in the hospital corridor, but he had to give the man his say. "Fine." He followed Arturas out the door. They walked down the hall to a small lounge area that was empty.

"You have no idea what you did, do you?" Arturas demanded.

"I — we — wrote the truth."

"I know you think that, but you did not know the whole story."

Kelleher spread his hands out. "Why don't you tell me the whole story?" He was prepared to listen to Buzelis's tale of woe about raising three children in the U.S. as a poor immigrant.

"You heard all those dollar figures on your precious tape, didn't you?"

"Every one of them."

"Did you ever hear anyone say *I* was to get the money?"

Kelleher laughed. "Who was getting it, Arturas," he asked smugly, " — your favorite charity?"

Buzelis took a step toward him so he could be right in his face. "Yes. Every nickel of that money was to go to my country. Brickley was committing to millions of dollars in shoes, clothes, and equipment to Lithuania. The children there have nothing. They had also promised to build a new gymnasium in Vilnius. It would have changed life entirely for thousands of children. You ruined all that."

Kelleher felt his stomach twist into a knot. "Why should I believe you?" he asked, knowing in his gut that Buzelis wasn't lying.

"Don't. Ask Akley. Ask Rytis — he knew what was going on. I will give you phone numbers of officials in Vilnius I was working with. Call and ask them what they know about Brickley and the Buzelis family." He threw his hands up. "Millions.

Millions of dollars for children gone so you can write your stupid story. I hope you are happy."

He turned and walked away. Kelleher sat down in an empty chair and stared at a soda machine. "Why didn't someone tell me?" he said to no one. Then again, that was what Akley had been doing Saturday night. Trying to tell him. He had refused to listen.

They left the hospital a few minutes later and drove out of Manhattan through the Midtown Tunnel. Driving through Queens, Kelleher told Mearns what Arturas had said. She asked all the same questions he had, then lapsed into silence for the rest of the drive. They stopped to eat in Riverhead and reached the ferry at about four o'clock.

It was a spectacular day. Kelleher drove straight to Kissing Rock.

"What's this?" Mearns asked.

"It cheers me up to watch the sun set from here. Do you mind?"

"Not a bit."

They walked onto the beach and sat with their backs against the rock, watching the sun move west.

"Bobby, let me ask you one question," Mearns said finally. "If you had known all along that the money Akley was offering the Buzelises was for a good cause, would it have changed the story? Would you have walked away from it and said, 'It's okay to cheat and broker your kid if it's for a good cause'?"

Kelleher stared at the water and turned the question over in his head. "I guess I'd still have gone after the story. But I would have written it differently. Different tone."

"But you'd still write it?"

"Yes."

"You're sure?"

He thought again. "Absolutely. It's not our job to say it's okay to cheat sometimes but not okay to cheat other times."

She smiled, and the dimples gave him a chill. "Exactly."

They were silent for a few more minutes. Then Mearns stood up. "Let's go."

"Where to?"

"My house. We'll pick up a steak and some wine on the way."

"We? What about Mr. New York?"

She laughed. "A figment of my vivid imagination. I couldn't let you think I was *that* easy."

He stared up at her, not quite sure how to respond. She put out her hand. "Coming?"

He took her hand and stood up. As they walked off the beach, he looked back over his shoulder one last time. There was still nothing quite like sunset on Shelter Island.

Spring has returned to the mountains of northern Vermont, and Whitefork Lodge owner Max Addams is ready for another tranquil season of fly-fishing and hospitality...until a lumber company begins clear-cutting trees and Max's trout start dying by the bushel.

Soon Max discovers it isn't just the trout that are turning belly-up. With one close friend found dead in the water, his livelihood at stake and the town turning against him, Max must reel in the killer before he becomes the catch of the day.

CASTING IN DEAD WATER

 DAVID LEITZ

CASTING IN DEAD WATER
David Leitz
_____ 95779-3 $5.50 U.S./$6.50 CAN.

Build yourself a library of paperback mysteries to die for—DEAD LETTER

NINE LIVES TO MURDER by Marian Babson
When actor Winstanley Fortescue takes a nasty fall—or was he pushed?—he finds himself trapped in the body of Monty, the backstage cat.
_____ 95580-4 ($4.99 U.S.)

THE BRIDLED GROOM by J. S. Borthwick
While planning their wedding, Sarah and Alex—a Nick and Nora Charles of the 90's—must solve a mystery at the High Hope horse farm.
_____ 95505-7 ($4.99 U.S./$5.99 Can.)

THE FAMOUS DAR MURDER MYSTERY
by Graham Landrum
The search for the grave of a Revolutionary War soldier takes a bizarre turn when the ladies of the DAR stumble on a modern-day corpse.
_____ 95568-5 ($4.50 U.S./$5.50 Can.)

COYOTE WIND by Peter Bowen
Gabriel Du Pré, a French-Indian fiddle player and part-time deputy, investigates a murder in the state of mind called Montana.
_____ 95601-0 ($5.50 U.S./$6.99 Can.)

Under a wide Montana sky he plays the fiddle and dreams of the Red River. Gabriel Du Pré is a mixed-blood French-Indian cattle-brand inspector. Sometimes he doubles as a deputy. Sometimes he even uncovers murder. Like now.

A cowboy has found the wreck of a plane that had been missing for 30 years. Du Pré sees that one of the sun-bleached skulls, the one with the bullet hole, doesn't belong. He wants to avoid the matter, but a rich man's demons, another murder, and Du Pré's own past keep pulling him back—to a truth he can bury, but cannot kill.

COYOTE
W·I·N·D

PETER BOWEN